THE

HARBOR

STORMS

A novel by

MICHAEL LINDLEY

Sage River Press

Novels by
MICHAEL LINDLEY

The "Troubled Waters"
Historical *Mystery* and Suspense Thrillers *Series*
THE EMMALEE AFFAIRS
THE SUMMER TOWN
BEND TO THE TEMPEST

The "Hanna Walsh and Ben Frank Low Country"
Mystery and Suspense Series
LIES WE NEVER SEE
A FOLLOWING SEA
DEATH ON THE NEW MOON
THE SISTER TAKEN
THE HARBOR STORMS
THE FIRE TOWER
THE MARQUESAS DRIFT
LISTEN TO THE MARSH

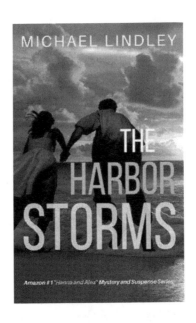

A few reader comments from over 6000 5-star
Amazon and _Goodreads_ ratings for the _"Hanna and Alex"_ series.

* * * * *

DEDICATION

A quick note of thanks to the many readers, publishing partners, book retailers and fellow authors who have been so supportive in the pursuit of these stories.

Chapter One

The call came in to Charleston County 911 Dispatch at 10:03 p.m. A resident in an affluent neighborhood near the downtown district reported sounds of what he thought were several gunshots at the house next door. Two patrol cars were alerted and arrived on the scene twelve minutes later. Detective Nathan Beatty, working late on another case, also decided to stop by on his way home when the address on the bulletin sounded familiar.

Beatty pulled to the curb along the tree-lined street of old historic homes tucked back in the shadows from the streetlamps. He saw the two patrol cars parked in the drive of the house where the possible shooting had occurred, their blue and red lights a kaleidoscope of colors flashing against the trees and houses. Neighbors from several adjoining residences were coming out on the broad verandas across the front of their homes.

The summer night was typically hot, even with the sun gone now for over an hour. He felt the wet humidity soaking his shirt and drops of sweat on his face almost immediately as he got out of the department-issued, late model Ford and walked over to the four cops just assembling behind the last patrol car. As the ranking officer on site, Beatty took charge and sent two of the uniforms to keep neighbors back.

The house in front of them was a large two-story white antebellum mansion with a surprisingly large yard surrounding it, considering the close-in downtown location in Charleston. There was a light on in two upstairs windows on the right. The black front door was slightly open, the dim light from inside illuminating the gap and two glass sidelights. The sound of classical music, violins over a full orchestra, could just be heard inside mixed with a chorus of cicadas buzzing and clicking in the trees above. Tall live oak trees draped the front yard and obscured part of the house from the street. A bare whisper of wind moved the draped Spanish moss in a slow rhythm to the music.

Beatty knew the two patrol officers from his own downtown precinct. "Ellis, go around back and take a look."

The officer pulled his service weapon and moved quickly along behind the cover of cars and then up beside the house and out of sight, a flashlight shining in front of him. Within moments, he reported back on the radio that all lights were off. The back door was locked, no sign of forced entry. A large white Mercedes sedan was parked outside the garage at the back of the property.

"Stay there," Beatty said. He turned to Officer Juan Sanchez standing beside him. "Come on."

They both pulled their weapons and Beatty led them up the walk to the front porch and the open door. As they got closer, the music grew louder. Beatty wiped the sweat from his face and tried to calm the adrenaline pulsing now. Two years past his fortieth birthday, he still worked hard to maintain his health and fitness, yet he felt his breath grow short in nervous anticipation of what lay ahead.

Slowly, he went up the few stairs of the porch first, his gun out in front. He stood to the side of the door and peered around cautiously. Light from the room upstairs fell down the large, curved stairway in the center hall illuminating an elegantly furnished foyer with several large oil paintings on the walls. A wide plank pine floor was richly polished and shined even in the low light.

Beatty yelled out over the loud music, "Charleston Police! Is anyone home?" He waited a moment for a response, but only a crescendo of violins answered back. He looked back at Sanchez. "Let's go."

Both men pulled small flashlights and held them along with their guns in a two-handed grip as they entered the big house, pushing the large door open further.

Beatty turned to Sanchez. "Check the first floor." On the radio, he ordered Ellis to stay out back. He started slowly up the winding staircase, placing the flashlight back in his pocket, keeping his gun pointed up ahead. He noticed a set of car keys laying on an ornate wood console table at the foot of the stairs next to a red leather purse. A short crystal glass, half empty with an amber liquid and no ice, rested next to the purse, condensation dripping down onto the wood surface. Beatty thought it odd there was no coaster, then pushed the notion aside.

The music seemed to be coming from the room where the light was on upstairs. He took a deep breath and felt his heart pounding hard in his chest, the loud music ringing in his ears. A drip of sweat stung his eye and he tried to wipe it away with the back of his free hand. The lighted room was off to his right at the top of the stairs at the end of a long carpeted hallway. The door there was half open. All the other doors he could see were closed.

He reached for his radio. "Anything down there?"

"Nothing out of place," Sanchez answered.

"Come on up and cover my back." Beatty waited for the uniform to join him, then started down the hall toward the open door. His steps were quiet on the plush carpet, but any noise of his approach would be masked by the blaring music.

He reached the door and cautiously peered in. The light was coming from a bathroom in what looked like the master suite of the house. A large black four poster bed stood against a far wall next to the bathroom door. The bedding was askew, and two pillows were on the floor between Beatty and the bed. He also saw several items of clothing strewn about, both men's and women's, including a red bra that was hanging from a lamp beside the bed. Small stereo speakers on each nightstand beside the bed were the source of the music.

Beatty looked back at Sanchez and motioned for him to stay in place to cover the hallway. He turned back into the room and yelled out, "Charleston Police! Come out now, hands up where I can see them!"

No response.

He stepped slowly into the room, scanning in all directions. The strobe of the lights from the patrol cars flashed through the blinds on two large windows across the front. The bedroom was spacious and had a well-appointed seating area around a fireplace off to his left.

Beatty swallowed hard, trying to calm himself, then started toward the open bathroom door. He slid a round into the chamber of his 9MM Ruger and held the gun up in front of him as he reached the wall next to the door. Carefully, he peered around the doorway, his gun now pointing up to the ceiling in both hands.

Beatty had seen a lot in his seventeen years on the job, but the scene in front of him now was among the most shocking. He recoiled at the sight of all the blood and the two bodies, one lying prone on the floor beside a large white claw-foot tub, a woman, naked. Her face stared back at him with lifeless eyes, a pool of her blood spreading across the black and white tile floor around her from gunshot wounds visible on her forehead and back.

The other body was a man in the tub. One arm lay over the side, his head back against the rim, staring up at the ceiling. The water around him in the half-filled bath was blood red. Two entry wounds were visible on his upper chest.

Beatty knew the address was familiar, as was the face of the dead man in front of him. He looked down and shook his head.

He tried to catch his breath, then reached for his radio. "Sanchez, call it in. "

Chapter Two

Hanna Walsh sipped at the white wine in the chilled glass and set it back on the arm of the weather-worn Adirondack chair in the sand around the firepit in front of her family's old house on the beach at Pawleys Island. The sun had been down over an hour and just a trace of light illuminated the sky behind her. The long expanse of beach and ocean stretched out as far as she could see in both directions. It was too hot for a fire and a breath of wind off the water helped some to cool the coming night. The air smelled of salt and scents of flowering shrubs behind them around the house.

Alex Frank sat beside her, sipping at a beer and holding her hand. Two other chairs to his side were empty. She could just see her son, Jonathan, with his girlfriend Elizabeth, in the growing darkness down at the water's edge, wading out into the low ocean swells to cool off. The two of them spending the summer here at the island, taking a break from school and time for Jonathan to continue to battle an addiction to pain meds he had revealed earlier in the year.

Her son's troubles had nearly broken her heart with worry and grief as she and Alex helped him through the difficult recovery. Alex had his own history with drug addiction to pain medications from wounds in Afghanistan and later from two different shootings in the line-of-duty with the Charleston Police Department. He had successfully navigated those dark times and had been a source of great comfort and support for Jonathan during his current ordeal.

She looked over at Alex and squeezed his hand. He looked back and she saw the thin line of his smile in the fading light.

"He seems to be doing pretty well," Alex said, looking out at the shoreline. He had returned from Washington, D.C., earlier in the afternoon from his new assignment with the FBI. Something had clearly been bothering him, but he had yet to open up to her.

"I think we're through the worst of it," Hanna said.

"You know, he'll never get this totally behind him."

"Yes..." She felt a crushing weight on her chest as the sad reality of her son's plight continued to press on her. An injury from a bike crash had left Jonathan with lingering chronic pain. The meds his doctors prescribed became stronger until they overwhelmed him with an addiction that now led to his dropping out of college, at least temporarily, she hoped.

She took another sip from her wine, feeling guilty for drinking in front of her son. His recovery required complete abstinence, including alcohol. He had reassured her that people drinking around him wasn't a problem. She knew her own consumption was bordering on excessive. It had been for the many years since her husband's death. She realized the numbing effect of a few glasses of wine on most nights helped to blur the pain and memories of past trauma but was also becoming more of an alarming trend she knew she had to face.

There had also been a few recent nights with foggy and disturbing memories she was trying to push aside. A familiar guilt flushed through her.

Hanna felt Alex squeeze her hand again and looked over at him.

"I need to talk to you about something," he said, then pulled his hand away and sat forward in his chair, turning to face her.

She could tell from the tone of his voice that something was terribly wrong. "Okay," she said tentatively, resting her glass on the chair arm beside her.

He paused for a few moments, looking out over the beach, then said, "I've been suspended from the Bureau."

"What! What on earth for?"

"There's been an internal investigation on my handling of the Lacroix takedown."

Hanna listened, suspecting this might be the issue. Xander Lacroix was a gangster who had taken over the Dellahousaye crime syndicate over the past months. She and Alex had tangled with Lacroix as he had been squeezing one of her clients with an extortion scheme that led to her death. Alex and the FBI were also closing in on the man for a possible role in the death of his rival, Remy Dellahousaye, his wife and two other men.

Lacroix's men had abducted Hanna in a last desperate attempt to close loose ends. Alex learned she was being held at Lacroix's house in Charleston and went off recklessly on his own to save her without backup. Both of them had nearly died in the episode before his colleagues and the Charleston Police arrived to take down the gangster.

She heard his voice crack as he continued.

"My little Rambo attack didn't sit well with the higher-ups. I was on probation anyway as a new agent."

"What's going to happen?"

"I'm on suspension for thirty days while the inquiry is wrapped-up. They'll be making a recommendation about my future in the next few weeks."

"They might let you go?" she said, not believing they would consider firing him.

"It's possible."

Hanna stood and moved over to sit on his lap. They both slid back into the chair. "I'm so sorry. I don't know what to say."

"Nothing to be said." He pulled her closer. "We just have to wait."

She rested her face on his shoulder and felt his arms around her.

"At least we'll have some time now to think about a wedding," he said quietly.

She looked up him, her left thumb rubbing the silver band of the ring he gave her when he had proposed a few weeks earlier on the deck above them. It was a nervous habit she carried over from her long marriage to Ben Walsh. She had continued to wear his ring for almost a year after his violent death when all the facts of his infidelity and criminal pursuits finally came to light. In the years since, she still found herself rubbing her thumb against her ring finger without thinking, though the absence of her wedding ring had always been a grim reminder of the dark ending of her marriage.

She and Alex had yet to make final plans for their wedding, his longer than anticipated assignment with the Bureau in Washington a complicating factor. He had asked her to join him there, at least until he could hopefully get reassigned back in South Carolina.

After many conversations and sleepless nights worrying about leaving all she had in Charleston and out here on Pawleys Island, her son's current health issue, and her work at the free legal clinic she ran, she had ultimately declined his invitation. She knew how disappointed he was with her decision, but he had tried to keep a positive face on the situation. He really didn't know how long his assignment in D.C. could last. He might never get a posting back in South Carolina. It was a troubling reality they both were trying to make the best of. She had seen him on two weekends since he had returned to work there after the Dellahousaye and Lacroix case was finished.

As Hanna's thoughts swirled about his suspension, she couldn't push aside the guilty thought he may be back sooner than they had anticipated, though she knew how much his work with the FBI meant to him. Getting fired would be a devastating blow for Alex, personally and professionally.

She looked up when she heard laughter and splashing out in the water. Jonathan and Elizabeth were enjoying the cool relief of the ocean. Her heart leapt to see her son happy and seemingly carefree, at least for the moment. Elizabeth had been good for him, and Hanna had grown to love her dearly.

"About that wedding," she heard Alex say.

She sat up in his lap and placed her hands on his chest. She could see the familiar lines of his face even in the darkness. "I don't want to make a big fuss," she said.

"I know, you've had the big wedding. I get it."

"Let's do it here at the beach," she said on a sudden impulse.

"Sure."

"Just a few friends and what little family there is nearby."

"I think that would be wonderful," Alex replied.

"My father and Martha are somewhere in Italy on their retirement trip. I'm sure they'll come back, whenever."

"The Skipper and Ella won't have to come far from Dugganville," he said, then laughed. "Never a party they can't make."

Alex's father, Skipper Frank, a shrimp boat captain, and his second wife, Ella, lived in the small coastal town just south of Pawleys Island. Ella was Alex's first wife's mother. The thought of the scheming Adrianne still kept Hanna up at night when she remembered the woman's attempts to win Alex back

10

a year or so ago. She was back in Florida with her son and husband now, and thankfully, they hadn't heard from her in quite some time.

"I know you're still concerned about where I'm going to end up with the Bureau... if I even still have a job."

"Let's just let this play out..." Hanna said.

"No, I've obviously been thinking about this a lot. If I do get reinstated, it's very likely I'll be posted back in D.C. where they can keep close reins on me. I know you don't want to move up there."

"Alex..."

"No, let me finish."

Hanna pushed her way up out of Alex's lap and sat again in the chair beside him.

"This may be the time..." he began, then hesitated. "This may be the time to throw in the towel on this crazy FBI gig. I know I can get a job back here in Charleston. The Department will probably take me back, or I can work in security somewhere."

Hanna leaned forward and put her hand on his arm. "I really don't want you to do that! I know how hard you've worked..."

"It's just a job. I'm much more concerned about you and me."

She squeezed his arm more tightly, a warm rush of love for this man coming over her. She tried to sort through all the emotions screaming back at her. It would mean so much to have Alex back in South Carolina permanently. They could be a real couple, build a new life together. But would he really be happy? Would all of this come between them eventually?

"I don't know what to say," she finally managed.

She heard Alex sigh in the low light of the coming night, the light from the deck above highlighting his shadowed face. "I need to let them know soon."

She wanted to jump back into his arms and hug him and say *yes, come back to me!* But was that really fair? Was that really best for both of them? Despite every reason why she wanted him to resign and come back, she knew they needed time to think this through, to not make a rushed decision. She reached for her wine and took another sip to let her emotions settle.

Finally, she said, "I don't want you to throw all of this away yet. Let's give it a little more time... to make sure it's what we both really want."

"Are you sure?"

She didn't hesitate this time. "I'm sure."

Hanna sensed someone up on the deck above them and stood to look back. A shadowed form of a woman walked up to the rail.

"Hello?" Hanna said tentatively, not expecting any company.

"Hanna, is that you?"

She knew the voice immediately and felt her face flush in anger.

"Grace, what are you doing out here?"

Grace Holloway had been her closest friend... *until she wasn't.*

Chapter Three

Detective Beatty finished what he could, working along with the crime scene investigators. Both bodies had been processed, photographed, and removed from the house just a few minutes earlier. Despite years on the job and more gruesome car wrecks and homicides than he cared to remember, he still felt queasy and a bit unsteady. He walked over and sat in an overstuffed chair he knew had already been processed. He took a deep breath and looked around the spacious bedroom.

The music had been turned off, and only the screeching sounds from the cicadas and tree frogs outside broke the quiet of the night. The three remaining investigators were wrapping up and putting their equipment away.

His captain had come by earlier, a token appearance to cover his ass, Beatty had thought. He wiped sweat from his forehead and took another deep breath. A driver's license in the deceased man's wallet confirmed what Beatty already knew. Phillip Holloway was a prominent Charleston attorney Beatty had encountered on many occasions. His close ties with the Dellahousaye crime family and a few other disreputable clients and politicians kept him high profile with the police. He also had a close, though clearly not amicable, relationship with his former partner Alex Frank's new fiancé, Hanna Walsh. Holloway had been her first husband's law partner.

Beatty wondered if Holloway had finally gotten on the wrong side of what was left of the Dellahousaye mob. This shooting definitely had their signature written all over it. Both Asa Dellahousaye and his son, Remy, were now dead. Xander Lacroix was in jail facing multiple charges of murder and racketeering. Two of Lacroix's lieutenants were keeping the enterprise going, certainly under the watchful eye of the gang leader from behind bars.

Beatty did have doubts about Lacroix's involvement in tonight's shootings. They had discovered five spent shell casings in the bathroom, all 45 caliber rounds. Professional killers would never be that careless. The front door left open also created uncertainty. A mob hitman would not call more attention to a crime scene than necessary and likely would have used a silenced weapon so neighbors wouldn't have heard and called in the shooting. And why would they take out Holloway when he was with this woman? *Much too messy*, he thought to himself.

No other obvious clues had been discovered in their early examination of the house. Fingerprints, fabric samples, and a host of other evidence had been taken, but nothing that was helpful at the moment.

The woman's purse revealed the identity of thirty-two-year-old Jennifer Falk from Sullivan's Island, just outside of town. Business cards in her wallet indicated she was also an attorney at Holloway's firm. A wedding ring led to a call to her home. The husband was there and informed of his wife's death. Two other detectives were on their way out to question the man. A jealous husband was certainly a prime suspect here.

Beatty also knew that Holloway's wife was back in town. Grace Holloway had served nearly two years in the state penitentiary following the discovery of her involvement with the man who killed Hanna Walsh's husband. Her lawyers had secured an early release for the woman when additional evidence was presented of her more limited role in the whole scheme. Beatty wasn't sure if the Holloways had re-united, though he doubted that to be the case. The master bedroom closet only had men's clothing and he hadn't come across any other signs of the woman living here.

He had officers out trying to track Holloway's wife down. She wasn't answering the cell phone they had on record, and they were uncertain of her current address. They were attempting to reach her parole officer for an update on her situation, but it was very late.

He looked at his watch and saw it was nearly midnight. He yawned reflexively, then stood as the rest of the team was getting ready to leave. He made a mental note to pay a visit to Xander Lacroix at the county jail in the morning.

Chapter Four

Hanna and Alex stood and watched as Grace Holloway cautiously made her way down the stairs in the dark to join them on the beach. Hanna tried to control the anger and contempt surging through her. There was no room in her heart to ever forgive this woman.

Grace had come by Hanna's office months earlier after her release from prison trying to make amends. Her efforts fell far short, and Hanna had quickly made it clear there was no future in their ever re-connecting. *So, what nerve to come out here now!* Hanna thought.

"Honey, I'm sorry to come by unannounced like this," Grace said as she came up to them in the sand. Hanna sensed uncertainty and even fear in her voice. She could also tell the woman had been drinking as her speech was slurred, and she balanced precariously in the sand.

"Don't call me *honey*," Hanna said quickly, doing nothing to disguise her anger.

Grace stopped with the rebuke and looked back at them, her hands at her sides. "I didn't know where else to go. I stopped by your apartment, then figured you'd be out here on the island for the weekend."

"I thought I made it clear to you..."

"Hanna, please... I need your help. I don't have anyone else to turn to."

Hanna felt Alex's arm around her waist, and he held her closer in support.

"Grace, I think you should leave," he said.

"I thought you were in D.C.?" she asked.

Alex didn't respond.

Even in the dark, Hanna could see in the porch light from above that the woman had been crying. She tried to push any thoughts of sympathy aside as memories of their formerly close relationship returned. Over the years, Grace Holloway had become like a sister, her closest friend and confidant. When it was revealed that Grace had been in a long-term affair with her husband, Ben, and had been involved in the scheme that eventually took his life, the shock had been devastating on so many levels.

She still chastised herself for being so blind to Grace's betrayal. *How could I be that close to someone and not see the true nature of the woman's intent and actions? How could I let things get so far and not see the signs of betrayal all around her?*

The whole episode continued to leave doubt in her mind in trusting anyone in her life, even Alex at times.

Her thoughts were interrupted by Grace's plea. "Can you please just give me a minute?"

"No..."

"Something terrible's happened," Grace continued.

Alex stepped forward. "Grace, please..."

"Phillip is dead!" Grace nearly shouted.

Hanna listened but was too stunned to respond.

"I went by the house tonight to talk to him," Grace said, then paused to gather herself. "I needed some money. Phillip's been helping me get back on my feet."

"What did you do?" Alex asked.

"I didn't do anything! I found him up in our bedroom. He'd been shot..."

"Shot!" Hanna broke in, reeling at what she was hearing.

"It was horrible," Grace said, crying again. "I can't describe it. There was so much blood... and another woman."

Alex stepped closer and grabbed her by her shoulders. "When did this happen?"

"Tonight... I just came from there."

"And you've called the police?" he asked.

She hesitated, starting to get hysterical, then, "No... I was too shocked, too scared. I didn't know if the killer was still around. I didn't know what the police would think."

Alex shook her to get her to focus on what he was saying. "Grace, we have to call this in. This is your house in Charleston?"

She nodded, wiping away the tears streaming down her cheeks.

Hanna stumbled back, trying to make sense of what she was hearing. Phillip Holloway had been murdered. Another woman had also been killed. While she knew Grace's husband all too well, their relationship had always been strained. Even when her husband was alive and working with Holloway, he had always been overly flirtatious with her. He had persisted in his attempts to spark something more personal, despite her repeated refusals.

Alex pulled his phone from his pocket and punched in a contact number. The call was answered on the second ring by the Charleston 911 dispatch line. After identifying himself, he was told the call had come in earlier that night, and officers were on the scene. The operator knew Alex from his time with the Charleston PD. She relayed that his old colleague, Nate Beatty, was the senior officer on site.

He stepped away up into the dunes to make his next call.

"Nate, it's Alex. What in hell's going on at the Holloway's?"

"How'd you know about this?"

"I'm standing here at the beach with Holloway's wife. She was at the house earlier and found the bodies."

"What!"

"You know she used to be friends with Hanna. She said she had nowhere else to go."

Beatty didn't respond for a moment, then, "You need to bring her back to town, now."

"She ran. She was afraid the killer might still be in the house."

"That might explain why the front door was left open," Beatty said, thinking out loud. "We need to speak to her as soon as possible, you know that."

"Right. I can make sure she gets back. You want to meet us down at the department?" Alex asked.

"It's late. I really need to get some sleep. Can we meet first thing? I'll be in early... seven?"

"We'll be there. What do you think about the shootings?"

"God awful mess," Beatty began. "The shooter nearly emptied a 45 into Holloway and the woman."

"Doesn't sound like a pro."

"Brass all over the floor, no silencer. Neighbors called it in when they heard the gunshots."

"Definitely *not* professional," Alex said.

"I think we've got a real good chance of a jealous spouse. We need to talk to the Holloway woman. We've got the husband of the other DOA coming in, too. The mistress was another lawyer at Holloway's firm."

"Why am I not surprised," Alex said. "The man is... was a total creep. He's been coming on to Hanna for years."

19

"Let's meet at seven," Beatty said. "I gotta get home for a few hours."

"We'll be there." He ended the call and came back around to the fire pit. Hanna was standing there with her son and girlfriend.

"Where's Grace?"

"She went up to the house to the bathroom," Hanna said, looking behind her.

"Oh no...!" he said, running quickly toward the steps to the house. He ran across the porch and into the house. He walked quickly to the first-floor bathroom and found it empty. He listened for a moment and heard no movement upstairs.

He ran to the street-side of the house and looked out one of the windows to the long driveway. The taillights to Grace's car braked and then the car sped away toward the bridge to the mainland.

He dialed Beatty again.

"What?"

"She split while I was on the phone with you. Must have gotten spooked when I said I was calling it in."

"Who's our local sheriff up there, Stokes?"

"Right, Pepper Stokes. I'll call the department."

Chapter Five

Grace Holloway watched the beam of her headlights on the dark empty highway back to Charleston. Her vision was blurred by tears and the latest pull from the pint of whiskey on the seat beside her. The front windows were down in the Mercedes sedan her husband had allowed her to use after her release from prison.

Her husband! Phillip is dead!

Images from her bedroom flashed in her mind and she moaned as she remembered the blood and carnage.

She knew it was a desperate attempt coming out to the island to try to get Hanna back on her side. She needed someone to help. She had nowhere else to go. Hanna's rebuke caused her to grimace and reach for the whisky pint again. The alcohol burned in her throat as she emptied the bottle. She threw it out the open window and put both hands back on the steering wheel, trying to focus on the road and put memories of the past evening aside.

All the blood!

Without warning, a shape rushed toward her lane from the dense woods along the highway. She slammed on the brakes instinctively as the deer came into view in her headlights and stopped suddenly and looked back at her. The impact was a thunderous explosion of crunching metal and shattering glass as the deer flew into the windshield and up over the top of the car.

Grace screamed as her face smashed into the airbag deployed from the steering wheel. Her hands fell helpless to her side as the car began a slow spin to the right and then a jarring halt as it veered down into a water-filled ditch.

She lay back against the seat, her breath short and labored. Then the pain drifted into her consciousness, first across her face, the bridge of her nose, then her chest against the seat belt strap.

With the windows still down, the sounds of night birds in the trees filtered in. She opened her eyes and saw the smashed glass across the front of the car, the airbag hanging limp now from the steering wheel. She touched her bruised face and saw blood as she pulled her hand away.

"Holy shit!" she whispered to herself, reaching now for the seat belt release. Her entire body ached from the impact. The car settled precariously on an angle to the passenger side. She managed to push her door open and then she fell into the warm and brackish water in the ditch when her feet found no purchase.

She lay there for a moment, trying to catch her breath, her face just above the surface of the water. Then thoughts of alligators and snakes gave her a sudden burst of panicked energy, and she began crawling out of the shallow water and up onto the grassy bank.

There was a piercing sound of a siren, then flashing blue lights in the trees coming up behind her. She looked back and saw a patrol car pulling to a stop, then a police officer getting quickly out and rushing up.

She heard his voice but was too stunned to respond.

"Ma'am! Ma'am! Are you okay?"

Am I okay?

Her mind was a blur of images and sounds from the past night and the sudden impact of the deer on a lonely country road.

No, I am not frigging okay!

Chapter Six

Alex had called the Sheriff's dispatch off the island to alert them to Grace's sudden departure, describing the car and the situation, explaining the woman was a material witness in a Charleston murder. He also gave them Nate Beatty's number with the Charleston PD to call if they found her.

He hadn't expected to get Sheriff Pepper Stokes this late at night but planned to call him in the morning for an update.

He lay now next to Hanna in the big bed with windows looking out into the darkness and the ocean beyond. A warm breeze lifted the gauzy curtains in a slow rhythm. She had fallen asleep almost instantly, and her breathing was slow with soft gasps. Her light brown hair fell across her face lying sideways on the pillow, just visible in the light coming in from a half-moon. She was wearing her familiar gray *Duke* t-shirt and her bare legs had pushed the sheets down to the end of the bed.

Grace's visit had clearly shaken her, and one more glass of wine before they went to bed had probably been one too many, he thought.

So, Holloway is dead.

He remembered a few random encounters with the slick attorney and the disreputable clients he chose to do business with, including the Dellahousaye crime family. Too many people who ran in those circles seemed to find themselves dead, he mused as he rolled on his back and looked up at the ceiling fan turning slowly above him.

He closed his eyes and cringed in the dark as he remembered his last run-in with Xander Lacroix, the aggressive young gangster who was still trying to wrest control of the illicit Dellahousaye business network, even from behind bars. He realized he was lucky to be alive himself as his reckless attempt to save Hanna from Lacroix and his goons had almost cost both of them their lives.

He reached out and found Hanna's hand beside her pillow and turned to face her again. He had never felt a stronger love for anyone before he met Hanna. His relationship with her had grown stronger over these past few years despite incredible challenges and dangers they had both faced. At times, he felt guilty about the risks he had brought upon her, and his selfish ambitions to build a career with the Bureau presented new challenges that would continue to come between them.

That may all be over now anyway, he thought, closing his eyes and willing himself to sleep as thoughts of his current suspension took over again. He thought back on their earlier conversation on the beach about him quitting and moving back to Charleston. He knew it was best for their future together, but he was also conflicted with walking away from a career that had been his ultimate job. He couldn't bring himself to accept that he had failed, that the Lacroix incident was real proof he wasn't up to the challenge.

He felt the slightest press from Hanna's hand in his own. He reached over and brushed the hair away from her face and leaned in to kiss her on the forehead. As he lay back, a rush of dread pushed through his sleepy consciousness, and he closed his eyes tight, hoping the coming days would see them both through to a wedding and long life together. His work and his career might be another matter.

I love you, Hanna Walsh!

Alex squinted in the early morning light coming in off the beach as the buzz of his phone beside the bed woke him. Hanna stirred as he reached over and grabbed the cellphone before walking quietly out into the hall.

"This is Frank," he said softly, heading down the steps now toward the kitchen.

"Alex, it's Pepper."

"Morning, Sheriff."

"We've got your girl."

"My girl?" Alex repeated, as he quickly recounted the past night's encounter with Grace Holloway in his mind. In the kitchen now, he pushed the "On" button on the coffee pot.

"Damn fool nearly killed herself," Alex heard Stokes say.

"What?"

"One of my men was out on the road looking for her after your call last night. He found her car in a ditch. She was trying to crawl out of the water when he came up. She hit a deer but was drunk as a damn skunk."

"Is she okay?"

"A few cuts and bruises. Nothing serious. We've got a watch on her down at the hospital. The doc told me they'll release her later this morning. We'll bring her down to the office."

"Did you call Beatty in Charleston?" Alex asked, pouring the early drip from the coffee pot into his favorite mug.

"Yeah, he's coming up."

Alex thought about the murder of Phillip Holloway and his latest "girlfriend" and Grace's possible involvement. "You mind if I come over?"

"This is not the Bureau's concern, Alex," Stokes said firmly. "We appreciate you calling us in on this, but we'll take it from here with the Charleston PD."

"This is personal, Pepper," he replied.

There was a pause with no answer from his friend, the County Sheriff.

"I'm on suspension anyway," he continued.

"What?"

"Long story."

"Let me guess," Stokes answered, "that Lacroix dust-up."

"You heard."

"Yeah… sounds like you're damn lucky to be on the right side of the dirt."

Alex couldn't help but chuckle, even as a chill swept through him. He took a long sip from his coffee. "I'd really like to be there, Pepper."

"Unofficially, then?"

"Yes, I told you I'm on the sidelines."

"Right." A pause again. "Okay. I think Beatty will be up here around ten. We'll see you then."

Alex ended the call as Hanna came down the stairs and shuffled slowly into the kitchen. The previous night's excesses with the wine bottle were evident in her flushed face and swollen eyes.

"Don't look at me!" she scolded, as she held her hands up to cover her face. Her hair was a wild tangle. She'd put a white silk robe on over her t-shirt.

He pulled her into her arms and felt her hair against his cheek as she fell into him. He loved the smell of her shampoo. He handed her his cup, and she took a sip before handing it back.

"God, why did you let me open another bottle of wine?" she moaned.

He didn't reply, but held her closer, rubbing her bare neck.

She pulled back. "Who called?"

"It was Pepper." He relayed the conversation about her former friend and the accident on the road.

"And she's okay?"

"Sounds like nothing serious."

Hanna walked to the cupboard with the coffee mugs, pulling one down and filling her own cup. "Do you think Grace was really involved in this shooting?"

He thought for a moment, then, "We'll learn more this morning. Stokes agreed to let me come in with Beatty from CPD."

"But you're on suspension."

"He knows that. It's not a Bureau issue anyway."

"You sure you want to get in the middle of this?" she asked.

"Just curious."

"I can't believe she thinks I would help her," Hanna went on. "After all she's done, she has the nerve to come out here!" she continued, her hand shaking in anger as she tried to sip the coffee.

"I'll try to find out what's going on," he said, and then his phone buzzed again. He looked down and saw his father's name on the caller ID.

"Hey, Pop, you're up early."

"Makin' a run on the *Maggie Mae* this morning" he heard the graveling voice of his old man say. "You wanna join us? Shrimp are runnin' strong these past few weeks."

"Can't today, Pop." He expected a fiery response but instead a pause, then...

"Son, just so ya know, your ex is back in town. Got in to Dugganville late last night. Found me and Ella down at *Gilly's*."

"Adrienne?" Alex asked in surprise, noticing Hanna turn with a concerned look, placing her coffee cup down on the counter.

"Guess her husband tossed her out down in Lauderdale. Not sure what happened yet," Skipper Frank said.

Alex's gut churned as he thought about the chaos that always accompanied his ex-wife.

"Dropped her off at Ella's old place last night before we came home," Skipper went on. "Sure, we'll find out more later this morning. I'll keep you posted."

"Don't bother," Alex replied quickly. "Nothing I need to know or care about."

"Okay," his father replied tentatively. "Just thought you should know."

"Yeah, thanks." Alex hesitated and looked over at Hanna again. She had her arms crossed with a concerned scowl that was to be expected. She'd had her own bad experiences with the crazy Adrienne. "Have a good day out on the salt, Pop."

"Thanks, kid!" Skipper Frank growled back. "Get your ass down here soon. Me and Ella want to catch-up and bring Hanna with you! Love that girl!"

His father had married Adrienne's mother, Ella, a few months back, many years after Alex's mother had been killed in a car accident. Skipper's and Ella's feisty relationship had somehow continued to survive. Alex had come to know the new Mrs. Skipper Frank far better than when he was married to her daughter. He had actually come to really like the woman and the usually positive force she had been in his father's life. They both still drank too much and fought like crazed dogs at times, but he knew they truly loved each other.

"I'll be down soon, Pop. I promise."

"Best to Hanna," he heard his father say, then the line clicked off.

"That horrible woman is back in South Carolina?" he heard Hanna say, looking up.

Alex sighed heavily. "Afraid so." He walked over and poured more coffee and pulled her close again. "Nothing to worry about. We'll keep our distance."

Hanna tensed. "I'm not worried about you."

"I know." He thought for a moment about his former wife and then the son she'd had with her next husband. His father hadn't mentioned the boy, Scotty. He wondered if he'd come north as well. He took a deep breath. *Not my problem!*

Chapter Seven

Former Senator Jordan Hayes sat in the living room of a fashionable suite on the top floor of the Mayflower Hotel in Washington, DC, waiting impatiently for the arrival of his client, a wealthy Saudi trying to make further inroads with the family's business interests in the States.

At seventy-two years of age, the defrocked legislator still cut a handsome figure of wealth and power. His silver-gray hair was neatly trimmed and framed a face tanned by many days on the golf course both here in Washington and at his palatial home along the Atlantic coast in South Carolina. He was dressed smartly in an expensive blue blazer over a starched white shirt with cufflinks showing the official seal of the Senate of the United States.

It had been two years since he was forced to step down from his elected position and powerful seats on both the Intelligence and Judiciary Committees of the Senate following disclosure of his ties to the Dellahousaye crime family in his home state of South Carolina.

He had recovered quickly to establish a highly sought-after and extremely lucrative consulting practice that provided access and influence among the most powerful political and business leaders in the world. Washington seemed to have a very short memory when it came to balancing past corruption and the future promise of new connections and new deals.

Hayes looked at his watch again and was about to stand to leave when he saw his client come through the door to the sleeping quarters in the suite accompanied by two bodyguards, all Saudis dressed in traditional robes and Keffiyeh headwear. The larger man on the right, Hayes knew was his client's personal bodyguard, a man named Ahmad that he had met on previous occasions. He was certain the men were heavily armed beneath their robes.

The highly placed and obscenely wealthy Bassam Al Zahrani was the 45-year-old son of one of his country's most prominent families. *Baz*, as he was known to close friends and associates including the Senator, had lived mostly in the United States since coming to the country to attend school at Dartmouth, then business school at Harvard. He had remained there overseeing his family's ever-expanding business interests in banking, real estate, and technology, as well as numerous pursuits that were never disclosed.

Hayes rose to greet his friend and client. "Baz! So good to see you!" He offered his hand and both men shook and then embraced before sitting across the small table from each other in plush upholstered chairs. The bodyguards stationed themselves strategically nearby.

"My friend,' Al Zahrani began, "please forgive my tardiness..."

"No need to explain," Hayes cut in, masking his irritation with practiced ease. "How is your father?"

"I'm afraid his health declines, but he refuses to cut back." The man's speech had an accent shaped more by his time in New England than from the origin of his birth. The sharp features of his dark face were edged with a closely trimmed black beard.

A servant who had let Hayes into the suite stepped forward to pour coffee for both men.

Hayes said, "You called this meeting. What can I help you with?"

Baz sipped from his coffee, then said, "I wanted to personally thank you for the introductions in Charleston."

"It was nothing," Hayes replied, holding a hand up in mock sincerity.

"Well, it has led to a very profitable relationship that cannot be understated. Your firm will be receiving a significant show of our appreciation."

"Thank you."

Baz smiled back for a moment to let the impact of his promised generosity sink in. "There is one other thing..."

"Of course," Hayes said, leaning into the conversation.

"There are some troublesome questions being asked."

"And what would that be?"

The Saudi looked out the expanse of windows for a moment, then uncrossed his legs and leaned forward. "There is an environmental group who have issues with our continued development efforts in the South."

The former Senator nodded, "Okay... "

"You may have heard of their exploits.... quite aggressive in efforts to stall oil and gas expansion as well as real estate projects."

"You mean the *Green* organization, I assume?"

"Yes, then you know what I'm concerned about?"

"Baz, we have a team assigned to following this group very closely. They're raising concerns with several of our clients," Hayes continued.

"They're becoming quite persistent."

"And what sort of assistance do you need with these people?"

"They somehow seem to fly beneath the radar. The media continue to praise and glorify their work in the name of saving the planet from climate demise."

"Their leader has become quite the media darling," the ex-Senator agreed.

"Yes, and what they fail to report on is he's totally corrupt, taking in millions of dollars from big donors and corporations around the world, lining his pockets considerably along the way."

"Yes, I'm aware," Hayes said. "So, you think a bit more exposure may help to put some pressure on their future exploits?"

"Yes, I do." The Saudi shook his head in disgust.

"Of course, you're concerned about your new development project down in Florida, the environmental issues that are surfacing?"

"Exactly."

Hayes nodded, then said, "I think I know how we can help."

"Let me stress the urgency of this matter, Senator."

Hayes was not immune to the rush he continued to feel when people addressed him by his former exalted title. "I understand completely, Baz. Is there anything else?"

The Saudi smiled and relaxed back into his chair. "I'm planning a small get-together next week down at the beach house in Charleston for a few of my friends. I hope you can join us with the young Miss..." Al Zahrani hesitated on the name of Haye's latest girlfriend, a thirty-something rising news anchor at one of the prominent cable news channels, a rare slip of etiquette on the Saudi's part.

"Jenna... Jenna Hawthorne," Hayes replied.

"Yes, of course. I hope you and the lovely Ms. Hawthorne can join us. Invitations are going out later this morning."

"Thank you for including us," Hayes said. "And I will be back in touch soon with a point of view on *Green*."

"I knew we could count on you," Al Zahrani said, standing and reaching his hand out to end the meeting.

As Hayes closed the door behind him and turned down the elegantly appointed hotel hallway, he smiled and thought about the amazing good fortune he had enjoyed these past months and the easy money that continued to flow in. Clients like Al Zahrani were providing a lucrative supplement to his already sizable fortune amassed over his years in powerful and influential roles in state and federal government positions.

When his association with the Dellahousaye crime family had forced his resignation from the Senate, he spent several anxious months expecting the Feds to continue digging into his past associations and *business* dealings. Surprisingly, they had quickly lost interest for reasons he was still trying to uncover. Other scandals and crimes seemed to have become more important.

As he reached the elevator, his cell rang, and he pulled it from his jacket pocket. The caller ID indicated it was his executive assistant housed in his South Carolina offices. He took the call.

"What is it?"

The man's familiar voice seemed strained and hesitant. "Sir, I thought you should know right away."

"Yes?" Hayes answered impatiently.

"Phillip Holloway was found murdered in his home last night."

Hayes didn't respond right away.

"Sir?"

The defrocked Senator looked in both directions down the hall before walking into the elevator. Finally, he responded. "Holloway?"

"Yes sir."

"Murdered?"

"He was found shot in his bathroom with a married woman from his law firm. Apparently, they were having an affair."

Hayes was well aware of the lawyer's latest conquest. "How did you hear?"

"It's all over the local news this morning."

Sure it is, Hayes thought. "Send me some of the clips." He ended the call abruptly and stepped out into the lobby of the plush hotel. As he walked out into the heat and bright sunshine of the coming day, a smile came across his face. *Holloway was such an idiot!"*

Chapter Eight

Hanna drove up in front of the old and elegant two-story home that housed the law firm she worked part-time at on Pawleys Island. The free legal clinic she ran in Charleston raised barely enough money from donors and grants to cover expenses and keep the doors open. Her dead husband had left her nearly broke. She had been forced to sell their heavily mortgaged home on the Battery in Charleston.

While she had managed to hold on to the Pawleys Island home her family had owned for generations going back to before the Civil War, the taxes and expenses were staggering, and she was just making enough money on the side here at the local law firm to keep her head above water.

As she got out of the car and walked toward the front door to the offices, she couldn't get thoughts of the Holloways out of her mind. Phillip Holloway was dead, found murdered with another woman in his house in Charleston. His ex-wife and Hanna's former best friend, Grace, had shown up unexpectedly at the beach house the previous night drunk and nearly hysterical about finding Phillip dead. Now, she was in custody here with the local Sheriff and a possible suspect in the murders.

Hanna shook her head in bewilderment at the continued chaos and calamity that seemed to follow the

Holloways. She was greeted by the law firm's receptionist and paralegal, Barbara.

"Morning, Hanna!" The sixty-something woman always had a bright smile and welcome for all who came in. "Your nine o'clock is waiting in the conference room."

Hanna cringed as she thought about the latest distasteful divorce she was immersed in here on the island and the unfortunate woman she was now representing in the case against a philandering husband. *And why did I become a lawyer?*

She stopped into her office first to check messages and gather files for her appointment. Her small office was cluttered with old furniture and filing cabinets. One window looked out over the marshes next to the house. She sat down and sifted through a short stack of pink message slips. One caught her eye immediately, a name she had never expected to see again.

Christy Griffith was a former client she had represented in an extortion case and murder of the woman's father by Xander Lacroix and the Dellahousaye crime family. As the young Ms. Griffith threatened to expose the gangsters to the authorities, she was the victim of a deadly attack as an assailant pushed her in front of a city bus in downtown Charleston in front of Hanna's horrified eyes.

What very few people knew was that the woman survived the attack, despite news reports to the contrary. After a long recuperation from near-fatal injuries, she was placed in the Witness Protection program by the Feds for her ongoing cooperation in providing evidence against Lacroix.

Hanna had one conversation with Christy Griffith before she was moved and relocated to an unknown new town to hopefully live out the rest of her life beyond the vengeful eye of Xander Lacroix. She had never expected to hear from her again but felt compelled to return the call.

Griffith answered on the second ring. "Oh Hanna, I'm so glad I was able to reach you!"

"Christy, are you okay?"

"I'm fine, but I really needed to speak with you. I wasn't sure who else I could call."

"It's so good to hear your voice," Hanna said. "After we last spoke and they whisked you away, I wasn't sure we would ever talk again."

"Well, I'm fairly well-settled now in this little town in the middle of nowhere I can never tell anyone about."

"I'm glad to hear that," Hanna replied, looking at the clock on the wall. "Christy, I apologize, but I'm running really late, and a client is waiting."

"Sure, and I'm sorry for bothering you with this, but I have a friend who may have a problem."

"You've been in touch with her?" Hanna asked in surprise.

"A few months ago, I was going crazy. I don't know anyone here. I'm not supposed to talk with anyone about my past. I needed someone I could confide in. She's been my best friend since we were kids."

"I'm not sure the Feds are going to be very happy about this."

"I don't care," Christy said defiantly. "I'm calling to ask a favor."

"Of course."

"Would you please meet with her?"

"What's going on?"

"Her name is Penny Hampton. She lives in Charleston."

"And what does she need help with?" Hanna asked, glancing at the clock on the wall.

"She has a new boyfriend that may be getting into some trouble."

"What kind of trouble?"

"I'll let her give you the details," Christy replied, "but he's Syrian and my friend thinks he may be involved in some terrorist group."

"Terrorist!"

"Your boyfriend, Alex, works for the FBI, right?" the girl asked.

"Yes, but..."

"Can you please just see her?" Christy pleaded. "I'm worried about her."

Hanna thought about Alex's suspension from the Bureau and answered tentatively, "I'm not sure what Alex can do. Let me check with him." She looked up at the clock again. "I really need to run, Christy."

Hanna knew she would do anything to help this woman who she had almost gotten killed as they tangled with the Dellahousaye clan. "Have your friend call the office to make an appointment. I'll talk to Alex tonight."

"Hanna, thank you so much!"

"You try to be safe out there... wherever *there* is," Hanna said as she left the office and walked down the hall, phone to her ear and her other arm loaded with files and notes. "I'll be back in touch as soon as I can." She ended the call as she walked into the conference room.

An hour later, Hanna was trying her best to stay awake as her client droned on about her mistreatment at the hands of her third husband, a wealthy doctor who was leaving her for one of his nurses. Her head was throbbing from the lingering effects of too much wine on the beach the previous night. She squeezed her eyes tight to try to push away the pain and gather her thoughts for the sake of the woman across from her.

She jumped in and interrupted. "Okay, I understand. Let me reach out to Joseph's attorney and register our concerns. Another round of mediation is probably the best course." As she said it, she was already dreading sitting in the same room with this disaster of a couple. She hated herself for thinking this way and knew she should be more sympathetic, but the woman had also been cheating on the husband, and both sides in this situation were clearly at fault. *Ah, the life of an attorney!*

After she had seen her client to the door, Hanna returned to her office and pulled out her phone to call Alex. The call went to voicemail, and she hung-up without leaving a message. They were supposed to meet for lunch later after he finished with Grace Holloway at the Sheriff's office. She was anxious to hear the latest update on the death of her old and former friend's husband.

As she sat behind her desk to make a few notes about the meeting she had just concluded, Hanna thought again about her discussion with Alex about quitting his job. She brushed her hair back behind her ears and looked around the clutter on her desk as her thoughts wandered. She knew there was no clear answer to this situation. Obviously, she wanted Alex back full-time, but how could she live with herself if he sacrificed his career and a job she knew he loved? *The Bureau may make our decision for us,* she thought as Alex's suspension and possible firing loomed

She remembered that Alex's ex was back in town again, and Hanna was certain there would be trouble ahead. *Why can't this woman leave us alone!*

Chapter Nine

Alex listened as Grace Holloway continued to describe the crime scene she had supposedly come upon unexpectedly last night to find her former husband lying in a tub full of blood with his naked mistress lying dead on the floor beside him.

"I told you before," Grace protested, "I tried to call Phillip earlier to tell him I was coming over to the house. You can check my cell phone."

The old sheriff, Pepper Stokes, rubbed his temples as he looked out the window at the palm fronds hanging down. "And you were going there to ask for money?"

Charleston detective Nate Beatty jumped in. "Miss Holloway, we've been through all that and we are already checking your phone calls. What I want to know again is why you didn't call the police or Emergency when you found them lying there. One or both of them might have still been alive."

Alex watched as Grace grimaced and shook her head. She looked a mess after a long night in a jail cell and all she had been through the previous night. They had been interrogating the woman for close to an hour, and she was clearly being evasive about what had actually happened at the Holloway home.

"I must have gone into shock or something... I've never seen anything more gruesome. There was so much blood. And then I thought, what if this killer is still in the house? I ran out the front door and my first thought was to go to my old friend, Hanna Walsh. There's no one else I can turn to. That's how I ended up down there on Pawleys Island."

"So, you thought you needed a lawyer, not an emergency team for the two victims?" Beatty pressed.

She started to cry, and Beatty stood in frustration. "We're not getting anywhere here. Let's get her transferred down to Charleston, where we can continue this."

"Are you arresting me?" Grace cried out in desperation.

Stokes said, "Ma'am, you're facing charges here for drunk driving. Your blood alcohol level was off the charts when we brought you in. We won't hold you, but we will be following up."

Beatty said, "We need to continue this down in Charleston. There are a lot of unanswered questions. Before we go, let me ask again, did you know your former husband was having this affair with this woman?"

Grace pulled another tissue from the box on the table and wiped at her dripping nose. "I've told you, Phillip always had someone on the side. I've known about it for years, but I didn't know about this woman specifically. I've never met her either."

Alex watched as Beatty shook his head impatiently.

"You really don't think I killed them!" Grace pleaded. "God, I would never do that! I'm not a killer! I don't even own a gun."

"Your husband *did* own guns, though. Isn't that correct?" Stokes asked.

Grace nodded and continued to try to hold back her sobbing.

"We will find out if one of those guns was a 45 caliber," Stokes continued.

"Alright, we're done here," Beatty said, heading for the door. "I need to get back to Charleston. Sheriff, you're making arrangements to have her transferred?"

"We'll have her down there later this afternoon, as soon as I can get one of my deputies freed up."

"Thank you, I'd take her myself, but I have a couple of other stops." Beatty said, turning to Alex. "Anything else?"

Alex had been thinking since this interrogation began that from what he knew previously from his interactions with Grace Holloway, there was no way she was capable of such wanton violence, even if she did find her former husband with another woman. Clearly, she hadn't been particularly concerned about his affairs in the past. Hanna had even told him that Grace had confessed to her about knowing about Holloway's dalliances but laughing it off and telling her at least it kept him away from coming after her for sex. She had dangled the keys to her big Mercedes in front of Hanna. *Hazard pay*, she had called it.

Alex looked up at Beatty. "One more thing," he said before returning his gaze to Grace Holloway. "Why did you think Hanna would even consider helping you after all you've done to her?"

Grace frowned and looked away, then said, "As you can imagine, I don't have many friends left and I certainly don't have money anymore."

"Hanna is not a friend!" Alex said curtly.

"I thought..." she began, then hesitated. "I have some information that I think Hanna would want to know about her husband, about Ben."

Alex looked back in surprise. "So.... you were going to bribe her with whatever this *information* is to get her to help you?"

It wasn't going to be a bribe," Grace pleaded.

Alex shook his head, then said very directly, "Leave Hanna out of this!"

Chapter Ten

Bassam Al Zahrani sat in the back of the long Maybach sedan, his two bodyguards in the front as they drove across the Potomac River on the Key Bridge in Washington on their way to the airport and his private plane for a trip back to South Carolina. He watched the murky brown current slip beneath them as he thought about the meeting with the former *esteemed* Senator, Jordan Hayes. The man was as corrupt as they come in D.C., but Zahrani was used to dealing with corrupt politicians. It was the easiest way to get difficult things done quickly. The money was certainly not an issue. Lining the pockets of a few greedy *public servants* put hardly a dent in his family's vast fortunes.

Hayes would again be useful in providing information and prompting action that couldn't be traced directly back to him or his family. Al Zahrani's father was near death back in Riyadh. He hadn't been lucid for years as dementia had rotted his brain. Bassam had been running much of the family's empire, and more recently, taking the enterprise in new directions.

The bounty of Saudi oil had made his entire family enormously wealthy, but of course, there was never enough. The Al Zahranis had padded their wealth with the proceeds from real estate, banking, technology, and numerous other legal businesses and investments. Bassam had also moved them down darker paths to profits in illegal weapons trading, stolen art and antiquities, and his latest ventures in the global drug trade.

The risks were considerable, particularly since he had access to more money than he could ever hope to spend on even more lavish homes, airplanes and yachts. He had grown bored with all of that long ago. It wasn't about greed or extravagance. It was about power. It was about ideology. It was about ambitions that went far beyond his current life of privilege and excess.

His only brother, Khalid, had taken a different path. Both shared a common zeal for the worship of Mohammed and a deep faith in the Muslim religion and cause. Both had dreams of a world again dominated by the teachings of their faith leader, a world returned to order and proper values that the West had long ignored and even scorned.

There would be retribution of the most severe kind and Bassam and his brother would take their rightful place of power as the Muslim faith again controlled the world order. Or at least he had thought so, until a year ago, when a U.S. Air Force drone and a Hellfire missile had found his brother deep within the ISIS territory he controlled in Syria and blown him to early martyrdom in Paradise with Allah.

The feared ISIS leader, known only as Salaam, had not been traced back to the Al Zahrani family. Khalid had abandoned the comforts of wealth to join the brotherhood in the dessert, amassing a vast army and network of fighters around the world, eventually taking a leadership role as the Caliphate continued to grow.

Bassam had learned of his brother's murder at the hands of the Americans as he was crossing high above the Atlantic on a return trip from Paris. His rage had been overwhelming, and he had been tempted to have his pilot guide their Falcon jet into the White House as they approached the American coast.

Clearer thinking had prevailed as he quickly realized much more work was needed to continue to support his now-deceased brother's efforts. He had focused his rage on energies that grew his wealth and ability to support the true destiny of Muslim supremacy across the world.

We are so close, he thought, as Reagan Airport approached out his side window.

Al Zahrani reached for his untraceable satellite phone and placed another call.

"Yes sir," came the curt and determined reply.

"Tell me we are ready to move forward."

There was a pause, then, "Only a few loose ends."

"Loose ends!"

"Nothing to worry about."

"All I do is worry about your incompetency!" Al Zahrani barked back.

He heard a tone of irritation in the man's reply.

"I've told you this will come together as we've planned. There are just a few more details..."

"Are we on schedule or not?" Al Zahrani barked.

There was a hesitation in the man's voice, "We will not let Allah down."

"There will be no delays! Am I clear!"

"No delays!"

"Praise be to Allah," Al Zahrani hissed before ending the call.

Chapter Eleven

Glenn Pyke was far from an imposing man, but his slight build and sallow face belied a determined will and inner strength that had allowed him to build a powerful organization. Standing only a few inches over five feet tall and pressing the scales to barely register 150 pounds, Pyke used his fierce determination and typically caustic yet highly effective gift of oration and influence to attract and lead a vast network of devoted followers. He had also been able to garner financial support from many well-intended donors who shared a common fear.

Fear was the lifeblood of Glenn Pyke's success. He used it like a weapon with allies and enemies alike as he built his once small group of disciples into a serious force in the global climate change movement. The organization known simply as *Green* now had offices in twelve countries around the world with a staff count nearing 1000 and growing rapidly.

Green was embraced not only by many wealthy donors and corporate benefactors but also tens of thousands of individuals who parted with smaller sums each month in support of work to bring attention to the impending demise of the global environment as man continues to pollute and destroy the planet at an alarming rate, or so Glenn Pyke and his followers continued to press the narrative.

As he sat at his desk in a plush office overlooking downtown New Orleans, Pyke had sandaled bare feet up on his broad mahogany desk, rumpled khaki shorts exposing spindly white legs and a t-shirt with the *Green* logo and a message that warned, *"Go Green or Die!"* With a phone to his ear, he was shouting at an associate in Paris who had failed to deliver on securing a new donor that would have greatly helped to fund the organization's expanding operations in Europe.

He ended the call abruptly with a blistering and profane tirade. He was in a foul mood from his earlier call with his leading benefactor. The man was a constant irritant. His demands were continuing to grow more difficult and dangerous, yet the funding he provided was enabling far beyond the stated mission of Pyke's organization. The diminutive leader of *Green* was skimming a sizable portion of the organization's fundraising through multiple accounts and phony companies and accumulating a considerable fortune hidden away in Caribbean and Swiss banks.

Despite the Saudi oil magnate's staggering contributions, the more recent demands for extreme action were putting all that Pyke had acquired at significant risk. It wasn't as if *Green* had not mobilized a more secretive initiative to raise the levels of climate fear on their own. More fear meant more zealot followers, cowering at the threat of global Armageddon and more than willing to open their pocketbooks to save the world.

The stealth efforts had begun small at first, a few fires in the West, an occasional chemical spill, doctored research findings elevating threats of warming, melting, flooding, air contamination and more.

But his donor clearly wanted to raise the stakes. This new operation would make headlines around the world and build a populous clamoring for retribution and extreme response. Pyke and a small team of his closest confidants had

49

been working tirelessly in planning a series of calamitous events that would shake the world. *Green's* role in any of this would be buried so deep in layers of obscurity that Pyke felt confident the end result would be only to their advantage in growing desperation and support for *Green* and other climate fighters.

And yet, many sleepless nights and haunting dreams had plagued Pyke as he feared two things. The first was the slim chance that his role would be exposed and all he had worked for would come crashing down around him. He had an escape plan to flee the country in the rare event this occurred. More troubling were his concerns about the Arab's endless power and influence. Pyke continued to doubt the benefactor's motives and feared he would not hesitate to sacrifice anyone who posed a threat to his own personal and business interests.

As Pyke stood and walked to the wall of windows across the back of his office, a chill swept through him as he envisioned masked killers silently entering his home on Lake Pontchartrain and slitting his throat.

Chapter Twelve

Alex stopped in front of his father's house on the tree-shaded road along the river in Dugganville, the small fishing and shrimper town he had grown up in. His father's shrimp trawler, the *Maggie Mae*, was resting at its dock across the street from the house. Wind off the water pushed the Spanish Moss in a slow dance hanging from the live oaks and brought the musty smells of marsh and Low Country flora and fauna up across the land. The tall abandoned fire observation tower loomed high above the tree line just down the street. Alex and his friends had jumped the fence on numerous occasions in their youth to climb to the top and drink beer or make-out with girls.

He knew his father, Skipper Frank, would be heading out soon for an afternoon and evening chasing schools of shrimp on the *Maggie Mae* off the coastal waters of South Carolina, but he wanted to check in on the crotchety old bastard before he headed back to Charleston.

The Skipper's memory and mental acuity had been deteriorating noticeably the past couple of years, and Alex was continually monitoring his father's current state, knowing that soon he would have to put an end to the Frank family's shrimping heritage. It was not a day he was looking forward to, knowing his father would fight fiercely to continue his life on the water. With his brother gone, lost to the fighting in

51

Afghanistan, and his own interests in continuing his law enforcement career, he knew that time was running out for the Franks in the shrimp business.

Alex closed his car door and felt the summer heat and humidity wash over him. He started up toward the low house with a screen porch across the front nearly obscured with high shrubs rarely trimmed back. He looked up when the old screen door squeaked open and his father's recent bride, Ella Moore Frank, burst out onto the porch.

"Alex! Damn, it's good to see you, boy!" she gushed as she rushed down the steps and pulled him into a tight embrace and gave him a wet kiss on the cheek. It was midday and he could already smell the alcohol on her breath. It wasn't unusual for Ella to have a Bloody Mary, or two, for lunch to *"take the edge off,"* as she described it. His father was usually a ready and eager participant.

Alex had actually come to love Ella, and despite her poor influence over his father's already excessive drinking and carousing, she had been a somewhat stabilizing force in the Skipper's life. Though they were often out late together down at *Gilly's*, the local watering hole on the river, Ella somehow managed to get his father home before his typical inclinations to get into fights or lose excessive money in poker games.

He had known Ella far too well when he was married to the woman's daughter, Adrienne. The thought of it made him pause as it always did when visions of his scheming and cheating ex-wife managed their way back into his brain. He remembered his father's earlier call warning him that Adrienne was back in Dugganville, estranged from her second husband down in Florida and now residing a couple of blocks over in Ella's house. He would take great care in avoiding a run-in with the former Mrs. Alex Frank.

He managed to free himself from Ella's boozy hug. "How are you doing, Ella?"

"Never better!"

"You look great," he said, trying to sound sincere. Actually, she looked a total mess, her dyed red hair pushing out in all directions, her old flowered dress a crumpled mess. Her feet were bare and dirty from working out back in the vegetable garden she had convinced her husband to help her plant.

"Skipper told you my girl is back," she said hesitantly.

Alex just nodded.

"Nothin' to worry about," Ella continued. "She's got her son, Scotty, with her and he's all she can handle now. I'm sure in a few more days she'll get over this latest dust-up with *what's his name* down in Ft. Lauderdale and take her pretty butt back down there."

Alex certainly hoped so but knew in his heart that with Adrienne back in South Carolina, there would certainly be more drama ahead. "Where's the Skipper?" he asked, trying to quickly change the subject.

"Had to run down to the hardware to pick up a couple things for the boat. Should be back any time. How about some iced tea? Just brewing up another pitcher in the sun out back."

"Sure."

They made their way through the house and out the back door to a small wood deck looking out at the dense foliage across the back of the lot. Ella grabbed a couple of glasses of ice on the way, leaving the open bottle of vodka on the counter. She grabbed the pitcher catching the sun on a low step and poured them both full glasses. They sat at a wrought iron table and let their tea chill.

"How's the old man doing, Ella?"

"His memory, you mean?"

"Yeah. Any more episodes out on the water?"

"He's got a new kid workin' crew who's pretty sharp. I don't have no worries with the Skipper out there. The kid has good experience and he's keepin' the old coot out of trouble."

Alex nodded but wasn't as confident as his new stepmother. The Atlantic Ocean is a dangerous environment and can turn deadly very fast. He looked over when he heard voices coming through the trees. There was a path at the back of the lot to another house hidden behind them. He watched as his ex-wife's son, Scotty, came out into the lawn, followed by his mother.

The boy spotted Alex and yelled out, "Mom, look who's here!" Adrienne followed next, coming out of the woods and smiling when she saw her ex-husband.

Alex cringed and thought quickly about running back into the house, out the front door and away, but knew he had to stay and endure the coming nonsense. Scotty ran up onto the deck. Not a year ago, Adrienne had tried to trick Alex into believing the boy was his own son to get him back. She had finally confessed her treachery when her current husband returned to make amends and take her back to Florida.

"Hey Alex, we're back!" Scotty yelled out.

"How you doin', kid?"

"Super!" The boy had grown considerably since Alex had last seen him. "You wearing your gun today?" he asked.

"No... no, I'm off duty."

"Can we go shoot sometime?"

"Scotty, that's enough!" Adrienne scolded as she came up the deck and over to Alex. She leaned in and kissed him, catching him on the cheek as he turned his lips to the side. "How are you, hon?" she gushed, the cleavage from her tight white t-shirt amply exposed.

Alex pushed his chair back and stood to leave. "Scotty, it's good to see you, but I need to go find my father. You take care now."

"The Skipper took me out for a ride on the *Maggie Mae* and we caught a ton of shrimp!" the boy said, gushing with excitement.

"Alex, don't rush away," Ella said.

"Really, Alex," Adrienne said. "I won't bite."

"Not so sure of that," Alex said under his breath.

"I was going to call you," Adrienne continued.

Alex felt a cold rush of dread. This woman had provoked so much chaos and calamity in his life.

"I'm thowin' an anniversary party for Ma and the Skipper. You and your girlfriend... what's her name?"

"Hanna," he replied, shaking his head.

"Right! You and Hanna just have to come. It's this Friday night."

He thought quickly and knew there was no way Hanna would come near this woman deliberately again.

"Alex, you'll break my heart if you don't come," Ella said.

He took a deep breath, then, "We'll see. I'll need to check."

"You do that, Hon," Adrienne cooed.

"Enough with the *Hon* nonsense, okay," he said, turning to Ella. "If I miss the Skipper down at the hardware, you tell him I stopped by and have him call me when he can."

"Sure will, son," Ella replied, standing and taking a long drink from the tea. "You take care."

Adrienne reached for his hand as he stepped away from the table, but he avoided her grasp. "See you Friday, then?"

He looked back at the face that had once been his first love and a sight he longed for when he was away from her. How quickly that had all changed. Without answering, he turned and walked back into the house and out the front, driving away with the hope of finding his father in town.

With no sign of the Skipper at the hardware, Alex headed to the next location his father would most likely be found, *Gilly's Bar*. It wasn't unusual for him to have a couple beers with his friends before heading out on the water. Not the safest habit, but one that the old man had continued for decades.

Sure enough, he was planted in his usual seat at the bar, Gilly delivering another cold Bud Light, and two friends listening intently to another tale from the legendary shrimper, Skipper Frank. Alex came up and touched him on the shoulder. The old man turned, and a huge toothy grin spread across his tanned and wrinkled face.

"Damn! What a nice surprise!" the Skipper gushed. "Pull a stool over for him, boys."

"Hey Pop, can't stay for a drink, but need a quick word."

The Skipper looked at his buddies. "Be back in a bit."

Father and son walked down the steps to the parking lot, and both stood at the rail of the walkway along the river. One of the town's fishing guide boats was coming back in from an early trip on the backwater.

Alex looked over at his father's weathered face, still staring at the approaching boat. "Just stopped by the house and spoke with Ella."

Skipper Frank looked back and scowled. "The woman's pissed at me again for working too much. Wants to do some traveling. Thinks I'm made a money or something."

"Maybe you should cut back some."

"Not you, too!" his father flared.

"Hear you got a new deckhand."

The old man snarled, "Damn snitch! Tells Ella every damn thing! Should have fired his ass a long time ago."

"Good crew are tough to find around here."

"Look, son, I got nowhere else to go. This is my home. This is my job. You take me off the water, you're gonna kill me!"

Alex hesitated, looking back at his father's concerned face. Finally, he said, "There's gonna come a time when you need to step away. Why not now when you can do it on your own terms?"

"You want me to sell the *Maggie Mae*?"

Alex just stared back.

"Might as well cut off my right arm!"

"Do me a favor," Alex offered. "Do yourself a favor. Think about making this your last season."

"Hell...!"

Alex jumped in. "Listen to me! Take these next few months. Enjoy your time out there... and start thinking about shutting it down."

The old shrimper didn't respond, staring back with glazed eyes from his midday beers.

"You're killin' me, son."

"Just think about it... for me and for Ella, and for your own damn sake."

The old man pushed by him to head back up to the bar. "Gotta settle my tab," he growled as he walked away.

"Love you, Pop!" Alex yelled as he watched his father storm away. *This is not gonna be easy!*

Chapter Thirteen

Hanna pulled into the sand and gravel driveway leading back to her beach house. Heavy scrub and low palms on both sides obscured the house from view until she came around a final bend. The old white two-story with green roof shingles dated back to before the Civil War when her distant great grandparents, the Paltierres, had owned the place. It had endured nearly two centuries of wind and weather yet remained strong and sturdy against even the more recent heavy storms that had battered the Carolina coastlines.

She drove her late model Honda sedan up to the back of the house and reached for her leather bag, heavy with files from work. The scents of gardenias and magnolia blossoms greeted her as she stepped out into the humid heat of the day. The sky was a shimmering deep blue with wisps of clouds drifting above.

Her son Jonathan's car was pulled off to the side under the shade of a sprawling live oak tree. As she climbed the steps to the back door into the kitchen, she wondered why Alex hadn't called yet about meeting for lunch. She had a sudden vision of Alex's ex-wife back in South Carolina again but quickly pushed the thought aside as Jonathan's girlfriend, Elizabeth, rushed out the door, nearly knocking Hanna down the stairs. The sight of the girl's face was immediately alarming. She was obviously frantic, and tears streamed down her flushed face.

"Oh, Hanna! I was just trying to call you!"

Hanna grabbed her by the shoulders to keep them both from falling. "What in the world is going on?"

"I don't know... I don't know," she started.

Hanna shook her gently to get her to focus. "Elizabeth?"

"It's Jonathan..."

Hanna had an instant rush of fear surge through her. "Where is he?"

"I can't wake him up!"

"What?" Hanna was already rushing into the house. "Where is he?"

"In our room..." Elizabeth was following close behind. "I just found these."

She turned and saw the girl was holding a prescription pill bottle and immediately went into full panic mode. She raced toward the stairs to the upper floor.

From behind, she heard, "Hanna, I'm so sorry, I didn't know."

She came through the door to her son's room and stopped abruptly, staring at her son lying face down on the bed, his arms splayed wide and face buried in a pillow.

"Jonathan!" she cried and hurried to the bed and sat beside his motionless body. She reached out and touched his bare shoulders, gently shaking him. "Jonathan, please! Please wake-up!"

She turned him on his side, and he continued to lay limp beside her, his eyes closed and face seemingly lifeless. She felt at his neck and was relieved to find at least a weak pulse. "Elizabeth, call 911!"

Hanna paced in the waiting room of the hospital, the doctors and nurses refusing to allow her into the Emergency room where they had taken Jonathan from the ambulance. She and Elizabeth had ridden in the back with one of the paramedics. Jonathan had yet to regain consciousness or show any signs of recovery, though a faint pulse was giving her some hope they had found him in time.

His struggle with pain meds this past year after his bicycle accident had never reached this severity, at least as far as she knew. His latest rehab stint had been so promising. *How can this be happening?* she thought in desperation.

She reached Alex on his cell as they raced to the hospital. He had just left his father in Dugganville and would be here any moment. She looked over and saw Elizabeth sitting in a chair against the wall, her face buried in her hands and gentle sobs racking her body.

With all her will, she tried to press down the waves of panic. *This can't be happening!*

She heard the outside door slide open and turned to see Alex run into the waiting room. He rushed to her and took her in his arms. She lay her face on his shoulder and felt her tears soaking into his shirt. "Oh, Alex..."

"How is he?"

"I don't know yet! They won't let me back there."

"Let me find someone," she heard him say as he pulled away. She watched as he went over to the reception desk, pulling his wallet out. He spoke with the young man there for a few moments, showing him what she assumed to be his FBI credentials. The attendant nodded and stood to go back into the suite of Emergency rooms.

Alex came back over and took her hand, leading her to a row of chairs beside Elizabeth. The girl looked up with a tear-streaked face and gave Alex a nod of recognition.

Hanna sat beside Alex. "What did he say?"

"He's going to find someone we can talk to."

A young female doctor came through the swinging doors a minute or so later, a chart in her hand. Hanna stood immediately and rushed over to the woman, Alex close behind.

"How is he?" she pleaded.

The doctor had a look of grim determination as she glanced up from the charts. "You're his mother, right?"

"Yes, dammit!" Hanna shouted. "What's happening?"

Alex stepped up. "Please, what's going on?"

The doctor took a deep breath. "I'm sorry..."

Hanna felt her heart nearly explode in her chest. "No...!" Alex reached around her shoulders to steady her.

The doctor said, "Your son is very weak. I'm not sure..."

"But, he's alive?" Hanna demanded.

"Barely."

Even this bleak hopeful news gave Hanna little comfort.

"We have a full overdose team working on your son," the doctor continued. "The pills he took are very dangerous." She turned to Elizabeth, still sitting against the wall. "Do you have any idea how many he's taken?"

"No... no, I'm sorry!" the girl sobbed back.

The doctor's stern face grew suddenly sympathetic as she turned back to Hanna and reached out to touch her shoulder. "Please, give us some more time. We're doing everything possible." She turned and walked back into the ward.

Hanna felt Alex pulling her into his arms and heard him whisper, "If he's made it this long... he's a strong kid." He held her even tighter.

Hanna felt a surge of anger and turned to Elizabeth. "How could you let this happen?" Immediately she felt sorry for the outburst, but said, "Why didn't you tell me about this?"

"I swear I didn't know!" Elizabeth said, shaking her head and wiping at the tears in her eyes. "He's been doing so well."

Hanna walked over and sat beside her. "I'm sorry, dear. It's just..."

"I know, I know..." the girl whimpered.

61

Chapter Fourteen

Grace Holloway sat alone in the rear seat of a sheriff's cruiser on her way back to Charleston. Her head still pounded from the excess of drink the previous night, and her body ached in more places than she could count from her car crashing into the ditch. A wave of nausea pushed up into her throat again as her body and brain struggled to recover.

She forced the queasiness back and asked the deputy driving, "And what happens when we get to Charleston?" She saw his eyes glance back in the rearview mirror.

"I'm dropping you at the downtown Charleston PD precinct. Detective Beatty will be meeting us."

"And will I be arrested?" she asked."

"That's up to them, ma'am."

The thought of spending even another minute behind bars sent a shiver of fear through her. She had served over two years in the state penitentiary for her complicit role in the death of Hanna Walsh's husband. Early release was a blessing she still couldn't believe as her attorney found additional evidence that convinced the court the original sentence was too severe. *I didn't pull the damn trigger, for Pete's sake!*

She still woke most nights in fearful sweats as memories of the horrors of her time in prison kept after her. *I will never go back to that place*, she thought, shaking her head and closing her eyes against the glare of the bright

Carolina sky. She noticed her hands shaking in her lap and clenched them together in a cold and clammy grip.

A frightening vision flashed in her mind of the grisly scene at her former home the past night, the body of her husband and his new lover lying in so much blood!

Phillip is dead!

She shook her head to chase away the images and looked out over the countryside passing by... a farmer on a tractor working a dusty field, black cows in a fenced pasture with a distant white house barely visible through the thick cover of trees, a hawk sitting motionless on a fence post surveying the ground for his next meal.

Phillip is dead, she thought again. They had been married for over twenty years, and for the most part, it had been a what... how would she describe it? A p*roductive marriage...* certainly not a loving one. She had been well aware of her philandering husband's many affairs. She had enjoyed her own occasional dalliance. But it was a *productive* partnership. He was a very successful attorney making obscene money that she only too gladly spent. She had been the dutiful law partner's wife, attending all the right events, sucking up to the big clients, *all the bullshit,* she thought.

And now he's gone... and good riddance!

Her thoughts turned to the money... so much money. His money... their money! She had talked to Phillip recently about her financial problems. She could never get a job. *I won't get a damn job!* He had been helping her with a small allowance since her release from prison and was paying for the tiny apartment she was currently living in downtown. She barely had enough to buy groceries every week, she thought in disgust.

At their last discussion, he brought up the "D" word. *He wants a damn divorce!* He wanted to move on. There was someone else in his life now that she had been away. *Someone else! That bitch in the bathroom last night!*

She clenched her fists even tighter. *God, there was so much blood!*

Chapter Fifteen

Ex-Senator Jordan Hayes sat on the comfortable couch in the living room of his latest girlfriend, Jenna Hawthorne, the television news anchor, home for lunch and perhaps some additional fun before her shift began down at the network later in the afternoon. The majestic skyline of Washington, D.C. spread across the expanse of windows of her condo just off Pennsylvania Avenue.

With a cell phone to his ear, he watched as she fussed in the kitchen preparing a salad. He would have preferred a big deli sandwich, but the woman was a vegan, and all meat was banned. *A small price to pay*, he thought as he gazed at her impressive bare legs and backside barely covered with lime green panties just peeking out beneath a sleeveless t-shirt.

He knew she was only with him for his influence and ability to pull the right strings for her career, but it was easy for him to get beyond all that. He'd been doing it for years with numerous young women, even before his wife died. *One of the perks of DC power*, he had always rationalized.

The person he was waiting for came on the line and he stood and walked down the hall, closing a door in the spare bedroom. The editor of New York's leading newspaper would always take his call. They actually had a tee time at his club in DC this Saturday.

"Billy, sorry for the interruption," Hayes said. "I know you're a busy man."

"Never a problem, *Senator*," came the expected reply. "What can I help you with?"

"Can I be frank?"

"When are you not?" the man replied with a chuckle.

"You and everyone else in the damn *mainstream* media continue to kiss these environmentalist asses..."

"Jordan..."

"No, let me finish. I know it fits the narrative and makes the White House look like the evil, uncaring Conservative bastards they really are, but I suggest you need to be a bit more balanced, particularly with people like this Pyke guy with this *Green* organization."

"What about him?"

"You know as well as I do, he's as crooked as they come. He hides behind this climate crusader façade while his bank accounts continue to skyrocket. We even hear he's manufacturing events and calamities to up the fear factor."

"Really, Jordan..."

"Billy, listen to me!" Hayes demanded, walking to the window and watching the traffic pass below. "What's even more troublesome is the negative impact he's having on real commerce around the world, not just against the oil companies and serial polluters, but real development and growth that drives our economy. This *Green* bullshit is going to run our country down the pisshole!"

"What are you suggesting?" the newsman asked.

"You know what's really going on with this guy. Put a little heat on him. Let the public know he's not the saint he's been made out to be."

"And tell me why I would want to do that?" came the reply, irritation clear in the man's voice.

"My friend," Hayes said, trying to soften the tone of the conversation. "You know I wouldn't come to you with this if it wasn't important to mutual friends. And it will be great for your *investigative journalism* cred!"

There was silence on the other end for a few moments, then, "I'll take care of it."

"I knew you'd understand, Billy," Hayes said, a broad smile spreading across his face. "See you Saturday for breakfast at Congressional before golf."

There was no response as the line clicked off. Hayes smiled again and made one other call before going back out to the kitchen. Jenna was putting two bowls of salad down on the table for lunch. Her auburn hair was piled on top of her head. She turned and smiled as he came up and took her in his arms.

"You know what I'm really hungry for," he whispered in her ear as his hands drifted lower. She turned and kissed him on the neck before pulling one of his hands away and leading him back over to the couch.

Chapter Sixteen

"Let's go for a walk," Alex said, standing to take Hanna's arm.

"I need to be here when the doctor comes out," she protested.

"They have our numbers. We won't go far. You need some air."

Hanna reluctantly rose and looked down at Elizabeth. "Are you going to be okay?"

The girl nodded back, her face still traced with tears.

Alex led Hanna toward the door to the steamy heat outside the hospital. The glare was blinding. He had his sunglasses tucked in the neck of his shirt and he put them on. He watched as Hanna shielded her eyes to let them adjust. There was a sidewalk leading to the right that curved into some nearby woods and welcome shade.

When they got under the shade of a large live oak, he put his arm around her waist and pulled her close, turning to face her. He could see the strain and worry in her expression as she looked up to him.

"I'm so afraid I'm going to lose him!" she said, leaning the side of her face against his chest.

"They have him stabilized. That's got to be a good sign."

"I should have seen this coming, Alex," she said with a sad note of desperation.

"Even Elizabeth didn't seem to know. I don't need to tell you, this addiction is a dangerous thing. I know only too well. Your body feels pain and your brain says you need something to take the edge off... and then a little more. These drugs are so strong, it doesn't take much to go too far."

"Where does he get this stuff?"

"It's out of control. It's everywhere."

They both turned to keep walking deeper into the woods. To get Hanna's mind off the drama inside, even for just a moment, he said, "We sat down with Grace this morning. Would you like to hear about it?"

She didn't answer for a few moments, obviously lost in thought about the danger her son was in. Finally, she said, "Do you really think she killed Phillip?"

He thought about the interrogation and the questionable responses they'd heard back. "I think she is certainly a suspect. She finds her husband with another woman in her old bedroom. They both end up dead."

Hanna said, "I still can't believe Phillip is gone."

"You've told me in the past Grace was never really concerned about his cheating, but who knows, she's been through a lot. She's financially on the brink, and he may have been threatening to cut her off."

"Where would she get a gun?"

"No weapon has been found yet, only the shell casings. It's possible she knew where Phillip may have kept a gun. Do you remember her ever saying anything about it?"

He watched her shaking her head as she replied, "No, I don't think it ever came up."

"What's most concerning to me," Alex said, "if she really did find them already shot and obviously horribly wounded, why didn't she call 911 for help?"

"She said she was afraid the killer was still in the house."

"But even after she left and was on her way down here to the island, she still didn't call for any medical help to get to the house, let alone the police."

"And she ran when you called Beatty back in Charleston," Hanna continued.

"Exactly. None of it really adds up to support her innocence. She's down at the Department now with Beatty for further questioning. They're also bringing in the husband of the other victim."

Hanna said, "Knowing Grace, she probably recruited him to commit the murders."

Alex thought about that possibility for a while as they turned to head back to the Emergency Room. He would call Beatty later for an update.

As they walked back into the cool air of the hospital and the waiting room where Elizabeth was still sitting against the wall with her head in her hands. Alex looked over when the double doors pushed open and a new doctor they hadn't spoken with yet came in. He watched Hanna hurry over to the man.

"How is he?" she pleaded.

The older doctor pushed his glasses up on his shaved head, then said, "We have him completely stabilized now. His vitals are close to being back to normal."

"Thank goodness!" Hanna said. "Can I see him?"

"He's still very groggy and we want him to rest as much as possible," the doctor replied.

"I want to see my son!" she demanded.

The doctor hesitated, then said, "Five minutes."

"Can they come with me?" Hanna asked, nodding toward Alex and Elizabeth.

He reluctantly nodded yes. "Please don't do anything to excite or agitate him, am I clear?"

Alex watched as Hanna was on her way toward the doors before the doctor had even finished. He let Elizabeth go ahead and followed both women back into the exam rooms.

Hanna felt like her heart was going to burst out of her chest and she couldn't calm her breathing as she walked through the curtains where the nurse indicated Jonathan had been treated. When she saw him, she stopped immediately in total shock. There were tubes in his nose and mouth, wires connected all over his body. But even worse, his face was deathly pale, more than when she found him back at the house.

As she approached the bed, she sensed Alex and Elizabeth coming up behind her. Jonathan was lying on his back, his face up to the ceiling and his eyes closed as if he was in a deep slumber. She reached out for his right hand and grimaced at the cold, lifeless grip.

"Honey, I'm here," she said softly. "We're all here. You're going to be okay."

She paused for a moment, her emotions welling up as she looked at her always vital and strong young son now laying there so helpless and weak.

Jonathan's eyes fluttered, then opened slowly. He looked confused and even a bit frightened, and she squeezed his hand more tightly.

Slowly, a sense of recognition came across his face. He looked directly at his mother and said, "I'm so sorry... I'm so sorry."

She gently leaned down over him and placed her head beside his on the pillow, then whispered, "I love you so much. We all love you so much." She stopped for a moment as the tears came and she struggled to continue, then said, "We will get through this."

She felt his arms come around her, pulling her close. In a teary voice, he said, "I just don't know how I could have let this happen again. I'm so sorry."

Hanna sensed Alex's hand on her back, and she lifted to see his concerned face behind her.

Alex said, "Jonathan, you know I've been right where you are today. We will all help you through this. You *will* get through this."

Hanna felt her love for Alex Frank wash over her again and knew she was so blessed to have him in her life. *We will all get through this!*

Chapter Seventeen

Skipper Frank was a proud man, though not overly concerned about appearances or *niceties*, as he would call manners and social graces. His old jeans and work shirts always looked like he'd had them on for a week and the ball caps he wore to cover his thinning gray hair were sweat-stained and smelled of shrimp. Shaving more than once a week was rare, and today's stubble was nearing two week's growth.

He stood in the pilot house of his shrimp boat, the *Maggie Mae*, as he steered the old trawler out through the navigation markers in the river toward the vast Atlantic ahead for the afternoon and evening shrimp run. As usual, he had Rod Stewart's popular hit and his boat's namesake playing loudly on the ship's old CD player as he always did at the start of a new run.

His deckhand was up on the front deck, securing lines and preparing the rigging of the big booms that held the shrimp nets. The three beers Skipper had slugged down at *Gilly's* over lunch with his pals barely phased him and his senses were on full alert and his excitement high for a successful day on the water.

His buoyant mood soured when he remembered his encounter with his son earlier in the day. *The damn kid thinks I can just give all this up*, he thought to himself as he watched the gulls fly around the boat, hoping for an easy meal. "Sooner cut off my left nut!" he shouted out over the roar of the twin diesels, though no one could hear him.

Deep down, though, he knew his mind and his senses were slipping. He was having more trouble remembering things and just seemed to get confused too often.

His new wife, Ella, as damned ornery as she could be at times, had been a true blessing. She was always there for him and, without much fuss, had been helping him through some more recent bouts with his memory failing.

Just this morning, she had to remind him that her daughter and Alex's ex-wife, Adrienne, was back in town and staying over at Ella's house. As soon as she mentioned it, he, of course, recalled talking to Alex about it.

The crazy woman is back in Dugganville, he thought. *Nothin' good ever seems to come of having her around again.*

He and Ella had argued before he left about the anniversary party Adrienne wanted to throw for them. He never turned down a good party but didn't like a big production with him the center of attention. He'd much rather just gather down at *Gilly's* with all his and Ella's friends and have a good drunk, but of course, that was pretty much every night's activity.

He couldn't help thinking Adrienne was only trying to come up with another reason to get close to Alex again. There was a time when Skipper thought his son had found the perfect wife. She was beautiful and smart and the two of them were inseparable. Then Alex went away to the war and Adrienne started to stray. By the time he got back and found out what was going on, there was no saving the marriage. But not so you'd know with Adrienne. She was apparently up to her old tricks again, and it wasn't beyond her to pull anything to try to lure Alex back.

Skipper had come to really love his son's new girlfriend, Hanna. She and Alex had been through so much yet seemed

74

destined to be together. They were good for each other, he thought as his concern for Adrienne's latest plot continued to eat at him.

He steered the *Maggie Mae* past the last channel marker. The Atlantic was glass calm with only a whisper of wind from onshore. The deep blue sky was patterned with a wisp of high cirrus clouds. Two dolphins came up alongside and played in the wake pushing out from the old boat. The air in the cockpit was heavy with the scents of salt and fish. He pressed the throttle forward to speed up as he turned south along the shore about a half-mile out.

The sound of another boat powering up out of the channel caught his attention. He turned to see a big white center cockpit fishing boat with three high-powered outboard motors surging up to speed. They turned south as well and were only a few hundred yards behind the *Maggie Mae's* stern before they veered left over the shrimp trawler's wake and then came up close to pass on the port side.

Skipper Frank cursed to himself as the boat approached. *Damn idiots! Got a whole damn ocean out here!*

As the boat sped alongside then past, not more than a stone's throw away, Skipper saw three men sitting on the bench seat of the boat's cockpit. They all had ball caps with brims turned backwards to keep them from flying off as the boat continued to gain speed. One of the men looked over and made eye contact with the old fisherman looking out from the pilot house. The man appeared to be of Middle Eastern descent with a heavy black beard. As Skipper looked closer, all three men had a similar appearance.

He gave them a middle finger salute out the open window as they passed, and the one man returned the gesture.

"Damn idiots!" he cursed aloud this time.

His foul mood was broken by the sound of his cell ringing in his pocket. He pulled out the phone and saw his wife's caller ID.

"Hey!" he answered in his gruff, gravelly voice.

"What time you think you'll be back in tonight?" Ella asked.

"Late, why?"

"How late?"

"I don't know, woman! When the damn hold is fulla shrimp!"

"Adrienne and Scotty are comin' over for dinner. Thought it would be nice if you could get back to join us."

He resisted the temptation to say what he was really thinking. He wanted no part of his former daughter-in-law's schemes. Instead, he said, "I'll call you later this afternoon. Let you know."

"You be careful out there today, Hon," she warned.

"Water and wind are perfect. We're gonna have a great day!"

He ended the call and looked out ahead. The three men in the big skiff were now almost a half-mile ahead and racing away toward Charleston Harbor. A big oil tanker about a mile out moved slowly on a similar course.

A beautiful day on the salt! he thought, as he yelled out to his mate to get the nets ready for the first pass.

Chapter Eighteen

Detective Nathan Beatty took a deep breath to calm himself as he sat across the interrogation table from the woman whose husband and his mistress had been found murdered the previous night. Grace Holloway had admitted to being at the grisly crime scene but continued to insist she found them both presumably dead from multiple gun shots and then ran without calling the police or paramedics because she was afraid the killer was still in the house. When repeatedly asked about why she didn't call for help after leaving the house, her best response was *total shock* from discovering the blood-soaked bodies and fear of being implicated in the murders after her recent release from prison where she had served time for murder-related charges.

None of this was adding up and Beatty was quickly losing his patience with this woman and her highly questionable story. His frustration was magnified from his earlier session with the dead mistress's husband.

Trevor Falk had voluntarily come in for questioning earlier in the morning after being informed of his wife's murder the previous night and answering preliminary questions from the two cops who had gone out to his house. Beatty really hadn't known what to expect but was completely surprised by the man's lack of emotion or grief over his wife's untimely and violent death. If anything, he seemed most upset that his wife had been found in another man's bedroom. The fact that she had several bullet holes in her didn't seem to be nearly as upsetting. He had a questionable alibi for his whereabouts during the approximate time of death that was currently being checked out.

Beatty had developed an uncanny sixth sense for guilty perps in his many years on the force. Both Grace Holloway and the victim's husband were setting off *guilty* alarms in his brain, but he knew there was much work to be done to build a solid case against either of them.

The other theory being discussed was Phillip Holloway's penchant for doing business with unsavory characters who were known to make people *disappear* when they became threats. It was well-known that Holloway was connected to the Dellahousaye crime family now being run by Xander Lacroix. Beatty's next step was to arrange for a meeting with Lacroix in the state penitentiary as soon as possible.

His thoughts were disrupted by the irritating and buttery drawl of the woman across from him.

"Are you done, or can I get home now?" the new widow whined.

Beatty looked across at her tired face, disheveled hair and bandages, and bruises from her car crash up near Pawleys Island last night. Another member of the investigation team sat beside him, and he looked over at the young woman who had joined the detective squad just a few months earlier. She returned his determined stare with an expressionless gaze, apparently not wanting to share an opinion.

Beatty turned back to Grace. "We are not going to hold you at this time, but we consider you a prime suspect in this case and require that you not leave town for any reason."

He watched her face redden. "How can you think I could possibly shoot two people like this, my God!"

78

"Please calm down, Ms. Holloway," Beatty replied evenly. "We have to pursue all possibilities at this point. I hope you understand. Also, Sheriff Stokes in Dugganville may want you back on the drunk driving charges. I will touch base with him before we let you go."

He nodded to his associate beside him to go out and make the call to Stokes. When she had left the room, Beatty said, "Just one more thing. We're going to have our forensics team take some samples from your hands and arms."

"What on earth for?" Grace complained.

"Trace elements of gunshot residue, ma'am."

"Oh, for Pete's sake!" Grace protested again.

The forensics team was completing their work, and Beatty stood as his young associate came back into the room. She came up beside him and said, "The sheriff doesn't need her back in Dugganville. They're pursuing the drunk driving charge and a trial date will be set."

Beatty heard Grace mutter something under her breath. "Ms. Holloway, you're free to go. Do not leave town. We may need you back for additional questioning at any time. Is that clear?"

"Very clear, Detective!"

Beatty returned to his desk and made the call to set up the meeting to see Xander Lacroix over in the pen. His next call was to his old colleague, Alex Frank.

He heard Alex say, "Nate, what's the latest?" obviously seeing his name come up on his cellphone caller ID.

He filled Alex in on what little he'd learned from the Holloway woman and the deceased mistress's husband.

Alex said, "Except for the brass left behind at the murder site, this all screams professional hit to me."

"I agree," Beatty replied. "I have a time set to see Lacroix later this afternoon. You want to sit in?"

There was a pause before Alex answered, "Hanna and I have an issue up here we need to deal with. Thanks for the offer, but I have to pass."

"Okay, just thought I'd check," Beatty said. "Wondered if you might want to have a little *talk* with the asshole that almost turned out your lights.

Again, a pause on the line. Finally, Alex said, "The next time I see Xander Lacroix, it will be just the two of us and in a place where we can do more than chat."

Beatty could hear the angry resolve in his old colleague's voice. "Don't blame you a bit, man. I'll let you know how it goes."

Alex asked, "What's next with Grace Holloway?"

Beatty explained what they had agreed upon.

"I don't want her bothering Hanna, Nate."

"She's to stay put here in Charleston. I'm going to have a watch put on her. You let me know if Hanna has any trouble with her."

"Will do."

Chapter Nineteen

Alex ended the call with Beatty and walked back into the hospital waiting room where Hanna and Elizabeth were sitting together and speaking softly. Hanna got up and came over to meet him.

"The doctor said they're going to hold him for observation tonight."

"Okay," Alex replied, "They're sure he's out of danger now?"

She nodded. "He wants us to get him into rehab again immediately."

"I think that's best."

Elizabeth came up to them, her face ashen and drawn. "Thank you so much, both of you. I thought I ..." She couldn't finish.

Hanna took the girl in her arms and held her close.

After a few moments, Alex said, "Why don't we all get back to the house, maybe pick up a pizza or something for dinner on the way."

He watched as Hanna hesitated. He said, "There's not much more you can do here now. He needs to rest."

On the way back to the island, Alex filled Hanna in on the latest in the Holloway murder investigation.

"And they let Grace go?" Hanna said incredulously.

"They're watching her."

"God, I hope so!"

"We'll see what Beatty can get out of Lacroix."

Hanna blanched at the mention of the gangster's name. "I guess we shouldn't be surprised this monster can get people killed sitting in a prison cell. What do you think Phillip could have possibly done to get on the wrong side of Lacroix?"

"Hard to say, and he may not be involved in this."

Alex turned into the drive through the heavy tree cover back to Hanna's house at the beach. The late afternoon sun was streaming through the palms leaving soft shadows along the sand. A covey of pigeons feeding along the side flushed and flew up into the branches of a big live oak.

Walking into the kitchen at the back of the house, Elizabeth excused herself to go try to take a nap. They had ordered food to be delivered while driving home, and Hanna had also called the rehab facility Jonathan had previously gone to. Arrangements were made for him to be taken up there in the next day or so, as soon as he was released from the hospital.

Alex went to the refrigerator and pulled out a pitcher of iced tea, pouring two glasses over ice for them, then a splash of lemonade on top. He sat beside Hanna at the long dining table in the next room.

"I thought he was past all this," she said, a note of sad desperation in her voice.

"We don't ever get totally free from the hold these pills have... I'm sorry."

"I know, but..."

"This clinic is very good..."

"See how much good they did this last time!"

He fought the urge to keep pressing the issue, knowing he wasn't going to be able to reassure her.

Hanna sipped at her tea, then said, "I thought Elizabeth had been such a good influence. They seemed to be doing so well."

"These drugs are a ticking time bomb," he replied, trying to push back thoughts of his own dark days lost in the fog of dangerous pain narcotics.

The pizza came, but neither of them could find an appetite.

Alex walked to the front of the house and looked out over the beach to the calm blue Atlantic. "How about a swim?" he yelled back. "It's so damn hot."

He felt Hanna's arm around his waist as she came up to join him. She laid her head on his shoulder and he pulled her closer.

"Come on, let's go," he said.

Even in the heat of summer, the bracing first chill of the ocean can give you second thoughts about the wisdom of seeking comfort in the depths of the Atlantic. Hanna felt the initial cold shock as she dove out into the face of the next rising swell. The wave swept over her as it broke, pushing her down and back toward shore. She opened her eyes and, through blurred watery vision, saw the sand below and the sun's bright light above cutting through the green and blue currents in shafts of yellow. She let herself sink down further and reached for the sand, cool to her touch.

Random thoughts and images from the day's horrifying events raced through her brain. She squeezed her eyes shut, trying to chase away the memories, then jolted when she felt a hand on her back.

Turning, she saw Alex lying now on the ocean floor beside her. Another wave swept over and pulled them apart as the swell broke directly above them. She pushed to the surface and gasped for her first breath, pushing her hair back from her face. Alex came up next to her, then dipped quickly beneath the surface again before coming up a few feet away.

Hanna was immediately struck by how fortunate she was to have this man come into her life. Dealing with her son's challenges alone would be so much more difficult. Her time together with Alex these past few years had been filled with unthinkable tragedy and danger yet balanced with a growing love and affection that had helped them through.

And now a marriage! she thought.

She remembered her earlier phone conversation with her client in Witness Protection. She hadn't had time to brief Alex on the woman's concern that a friend may have found herself in a relationship with someone who could be a threat.

Alex came to her and pulled her close, the water lifting them on each successive wave. She told him quickly about Christy's concerns.

"And you have an appointment with this woman tomorrow?"

"Yes, first thing, unless something happens with Jonathan, and I need to reschedule."

"Do you want me there?" he asked.

She thought about his offer for a moment as another wave swept over them and pulled them apart. They both started swimming back toward shore. When they were waist-deep, Hanna turned to him and said, "Let me meet with her first. Her name is Penny Hampton. If there's a credible risk, I'll let you know right away."

Later, hunger finally caught up with them and Hanna warmed the pizza, and both managed to eat. They sat at the kitchen counter with glasses of iced tea sweating on the counter next to their plates. There was no sound from upstairs, where Elizabeth must have still been napping. The early evening sun behind the house illuminated the room in a soft orange glow.

She watched Alex reach for his tea, taking a long drink before saying, "Not to darken the mood any further, but there's a little more drama building up in Dugganville."

Hanna felt her senses go on full alert as her skin felt a prickly rush.

"Skipper and Ella have an anniversary coming up. Adrienne's throwing a party."

"And she wants you to come," Hanna said quickly, her anger rising.

"She wants us *both* to come."

"And when is this?"

"Friday night."

"Great..."

"You really don't need to go," Alex said.

She thought about it for a moment. Skipper and Ella had become like family to her, and she wanted to help them celebrate their special occasion, but the thought of Alex's ex being there made her stomach churn sour.

"Let me think about it," she finally said. "I need to see how Jonathan's doing by then."

"Of course."

"I need to call the hospital and check in with the nurse."

Alex nodded as she reached for her phone. She was finally connected to the nurse's desk on Jonathan's floor and was reassured to hear he was sleeping and all his vitals were recovering. She ended the call.

"He's doing fine."

"Great," Alex said, standing to take the plates to the sink.

The sound of footsteps on the back deck surprised her, and she turned to see the familiar yet unwelcome face of Grace Holloway. Alex had also seen her and rushed over to open the door.

"You need to leave, now!" he said.

Hanna watched as Grace backed up a couple of steps in surprise.

"I just need a minute," she pleaded softly.

Hanna walked over to the open door and peered out at her former friend. Her face was battered and bandaged from her accident. Her clothes were a mess. She would never have allowed herself out in public looking like this in her previous life with Phillip, she thought as she tried to calm her anger.

Alex said, "You're not supposed to leave Charleston. I'm calling Beatty." He reached in his pocket for his cell.

"No, please! Just give me a minute," Grace pleaded.

Hanna stepped forward. "I have no time for this, you need to leave."

"Hanna, please, just a minute."

Alex stepped back into the kitchen, and she could hear him talking to his old colleague. She stared at Grace for a few moments, then said, "A minute..."

"Can I come in?"

Hanna moved aside and let the women come past. She followed Grace into the dining room and sat across the old oak table from her. Grace placed both hands down in front of her, almost in a confessional way. She took a deep breath then said, "I came up the other night to tell you about something. I got spooked when Alex called the police and then I smashed my car..."

Hanna jumped in, "Grace, what in the hell do you want?"

"I need to share something with you... about your husband, about Ben."

Hanna grimaced as she thought back to the treachery of this woman, the affair she'd had with Ben, the role she had ultimately played in his murder. She stood up in anger. "That's enough! We're done here!"

Grace didn't react, continuing to sit and stare back.

"Grace, I want you to leave now!"

Alex came into the room, ending his call. "Charleston PD wants you back in the city immediately. I thought they were watching you."

"They were sending a car by my apartment once every hour or so, but I needed to get out, to get up here to see you and Hanna."

"You could have called," he said.

Grace continued, "Hanna, you obviously know there was a lot of money that came up missing with Ben and the project he was working on."

Hanna didn't respond.

"The Feds think they've wrapped all that up, but there's more."

"More what?" Hanna said, her patience about gone.

"More money."

"What are you talking about?" Alex asked.

"When Thomas was killed..." Grace began, then stopped.

Thomas Dillon was another former friend of Hanna and Ben Walsh who had conspired with Grace to steal money from her husband's land deal with the crime syndicate that ultimately led to both Thomas's and Ben's murder by the Dellahousayes.

"What about Thomas?" Hanna asked.

"All the money wasn't recovered. There's more down in an island bank."

"I don't care about any of that, and I want nothing to do with that money!" Hanna said.

"We're talking about at least a million dollars, dear..."

"I don't' care how much money!" Hanna blurted out. "It's blood money!"

Grace turned to Alex for support. "Don't you think Hanna should share in what's rightfully hers? She lost her house, her savings..."

"Grace! That's enough!" Hanna shouted.

Alex said, "If this is true, I'll get the Charleston FBI involved and they'll talk to you about this."

"I'm not going to work with the Feds," Grace protested. "All they've done is screw me over in the past..."

Hanna interrupted, "Because you were guilty! Because you could have prevented Ben's death!"

"Hanna, please," Grace protested. "You have a right to this money."

"And what's in this for you?" Alex asked.

Grace hesitated, looking back and forth between the two of them, then said, "I would expect a cut, of course."

"A cut?" Alex repeated.

"I need the money!" Grace said. "Phillip practically cut me off, and now he's gone, and I have no idea what's to become of the estate. I'm sure he's taken me out of everything."

Hanna's was nearing an explosion. "And now you've killed him!"

Grace stood. "No! No, how could you think that? You have to believe me."

Alex said, "Alright, enough now. Beatty wants you back in Charleston, now. I'll have Will Foster from the Charleston Bureau office come and see you tomorrow."

"I won't talk to them!" Grace insisted. "Alex, I thought you and Hanna would work with me..."

"You don't have any choice," Alex answered. "You need to head back."

Grace looked down and sighed, then turned to Hanna. "Please, this is the right thing to do. This money was yours and Ben's."

Hanna had finally had enough. "I don't want to hear about this again, and I don't want to see your face again! Am I clear?" She watched as Grace shook her head and grimaced. She started toward the back door.

"Just think about it," Grace pleaded.

Hanna and Alex stood on the back porch of the beach house and watched as Grace Holloway pulled away and disappeared through the trees to leave.

Alex said, "Beatty may put her in custody after this little stunt."

"Good," Hanna said, turning to go back inside. She went to a small wine refrigerator under the kitchen counter and pulled out a chilled bottle of white wine. Her hands trembled as she struggled to open the bottle. Pulling down two glasses, she poured a full portion for both of them.

She walked out to the front deck of the house, the ocean calmer now as the day moved toward another end. The glow of the sunset from behind the dunes reflected out over the water. A lone couple walked by on the beach, holding hands. She took a long drink and as Alex came up next to her, said, "I thought we were past all this."

"Let Foster and the Bureau deal with her."

She turned to face him. "I don't care how much money there is. I want nothing to do with any of that. It's cost me so much already..."

"I know," Alex replied, putting an arm around her waist and pulling her closer.

She suddenly remembered the phone call when the Charleston Police informed her that Ben had been found shot in an alley downtown. It was the first in a series of nightmare moments that were to come.

And now it's all back again!

Chapter Twenty

Baz Al Zahrani sat back on the comfortable leather seat on the aft deck of his 120-foot motor yacht anchored off the beaches just south of Charleston. This was only one of his many grand ships in the family fleet. The "crown jewel" was a 320-foot massive ship, appropriately named *Unfathomable*, that was berthed much of the year in Monte Carlo. This current boat had been brought up from Miami earlier in the week as he anticipated spending more time in Charleston, at least for the next few days until the *operation* was completed.

The wind was blowing in a steady push from the southeast, white-capped swells sweeping by the big boat and barely causing it to move with the sophisticated gyros onboard keeping it nearly motionless on the rough surface of the ocean. They were just outside the shipping lane and several large tankers had been passing nearby. The sun was down almost below the skyline of the city, far to the north and west.

His chief steward came up from below deck in a smart black and white uniform with a tray full of appetizers and a pot of strong tea. The servant placed the tray on a table beside his boss, then bowed before backing away. Baz didn't acknowledge the intrusion as he was fixed on a message on his secure phone from the man in L.A. spearheading the West Coast attack. The fact the man would be dead in a few days was not even on the

Saudi's mind at this moment. He was only focused on the intricate plot that was finally beginning to unfold.

He placed the phone down and poured some of the steaming tea. *It will be a long night,* he thought, as final preparations would require considerable focus. His core team was below, following up on numerous details.

As he thought through the current state of preparedness, he was beginning to get comfortable with the likelihood of success in nine of the ten cities being targeted. The attack teams there had been carefully recruited and screened. The chain of command was an entangled web of contacts that would never be traced back to him. The leaders he spoke with had no idea of his real identity, only that he was the supreme commander of the operation. All would soon be dead and disposed of, including the men below deck. There could be no trace of his involvement. He was confident in his plans to let others take the fall for the calamity that would soon unfold.

Only the city of Charleston, just across the stretch of water out beyond the rail of his ship, was still a question mark for him now. Baz was growing more worried about the soldier selected to lead the operation in South Carolina. The more he learned of the man, the more uncertain he became. He knew there wasn't time now to make any changes in personnel. His only hope was to put pressure on the three men assigned to this nearest target and make it abundantly clear that failure was not an option. The safety of each of their families relied totally on their ability to successfully complete the mission.

He reached for the phone and dialed one of the many numbers he had committed to memory. The voice that answered was tentative and guarded.

"Yes sir..." the voice said.

"Listen to me and listen very carefully," Baz growled. "You have failed on multiple occasions now to meet the deadlines set."

"Sir, let me..."

"I said listen!" Baz shouted. "We will tolerate no further delays. You will report back by 8 a.m. tomorrow and there will be no excuses. Am I clear?"

"Yes sir!"

"I do not need to remind you that your holy mission will be rewarded by Allah," Baz continued. "Your failure will be met just as quickly by the most painful and severe retribution against your families."

"We understand, sir," came the shaky reply.

"8 a.m.!" Baz shouted, then ended the call.

Tariq Sendaya heard the line go silent. He swallowed hard and wiped at the sweat streaming from his brow. He looked across the small apartment at the two men who had been working with him on the assault. Both returned his gaze with frightened stares. He placed the smartphone down and began shouting orders to the men in Arabic. They cowered under his intense commands, nodding profusely.

When Tariq finished his admonishments, the two men rose quickly and went to their small tables in different corners of the apartment to continue with preparations.

He was startled when his regular cell began buzzing on the table beside him. He looked at the screen. It was the woman. He considered ignoring the call, but knew he was supposed to meet her later in the evening and thought he should confirm plans.

It had been a mistake, he knew, to begin a relationship with a woman during the lead-up to this operation, but he had been unable to resist during a chance meeting a few weeks ago at the coffee shop down the street. Knowing full well his days on this earth were numbered, he was unable to resist the temptations of a woman's companionship in these last days of his life.

His wife and family were far away in New York. He knew he would never see them again, but his recruiters had assured him that they would be more than well cared for in the future... if he was able to successfully complete his orders. They would be far better cared for than he would have ever been able to provide with his meager earnings from a security job at a small company across the Hudson River from New York City.

He loved his wife and two sons but knew he could never provide for them in the fashion they deserved. His sacrifices in the name of Allah would not only send him off to Paradise, but also give his family a safe and secure life ahead.

He answered the call and heard the American woman's voice. "When are you coming over tonight?"

Thoughts of another evening in this woman's bed crept into his mind. It had been a welcome diversion from the stress of the coming mission. He looked at his watch, then answered, "One hour."

Penny Hampton ended the call with the handsome Syrian she had recently met and found herself involved with in a purely physical relationship that had seemed to be the right escape for both of them. It had been months since she'd had a boyfriend, and her job down at the insurance agency offered little hope of meeting anyone interesting.

She knew Tariq was probably married and may even have children. It did bother her to be helping him in violating those vows and commitments. She had simply been tired of being alone and Tariq had come along at the right time. Her hand shook as she placed the phone back down.

Just a few days ago she had begun to sense alarming revelations about her new lover. Guarded phone calls, angry conversations, hurried departures and late arrivals had all begun to build her suspicions. Then, two days ago, she had overheard him speaking on the phone and the gist of the conversation had sent chills through her.

There was some sort of attack planned. Tariq and others were planning an attack. His Middle Eastern heritage only heightened her suspicions.

I'm sleeping with a terrorist!

Her first reaction was to end the affair immediately and distance herself as quickly as possible from Tariq. He would only ever share his first name. But, as she continued to stress about the situation, she knew she couldn't just walk away from what might be a dangerous threat right here in her own city of Charleston. She had decided to see him one more time and learn as much as she could about whatever plot he was engaged in.

In desperation, she had shared her concerns with her friend, Christy Griffith, who was currently hidden away in some remote town in Witness Protection. She spoke with her by phone several times each week. Christy had advised her to meet with a local attorney who was connected to a man in the FBI who might be able to help head off whatever plans Tariq was involved in. She had scheduled a meeting for the next morning with the attorney's office downtown.

One hour! he had said.

Tariq Sendaya pushed the button for the woman's apartment on the fifth floor of the downtown building he had been spending too many nights these past weeks. As the elevator rose, his mind was clouded with the details of his mission, just two days away, along with thoughts of the amorous Penny and the pleasures that lie ahead.

The earlier call from his handler and top commander of the mission still sent fear coursing through him. If he knew of these liaisons, there would certainly be swift retaliation for both he and his family.

Only two more days and he would strike at the enemy in the most severe way, bringing calamity to the region that would take decades to recover from. Then he would be honored for all time in Paradise... and his family would be secure.

He knocked gently on the door at the end of the hall and heard the woman approaching. When she opened the door, he could tell at once something was different about her expression, her demeanor. Normally, she would greet him with a massive smile and hurry him inside for an evening of forbidden fun. Tonight, she was clearly concerned about something, though she quickly tried to recover with a thin smile.

"Come in, how are you?" She stood to the side to let him pass.

He looked around the apartment but saw nothing amiss. His senses were on full alert as he turned to her. He stared at her for a few moments, and she looked away nervously, walking away into the kitchen.

"Would you like something to drink?" she yelled back.

He didn't answer and followed her into the next room. He walked up behind her as she stood in front of the open refrigerator. Normally, she would have been pulling him to the bedroom.

What is going on?

He reached for her arm and turned her to face him.

"Patience!" she said, trying to manage an easy and expected response, but it was clear she was nervous and concerned about something.

"Tell me what's the matter," he demanded, and she looked back in surprise, maybe even fear.

Fear! What does she know?

"Nothing!" she replied too quickly.

Tariq grabbed both of her arms and shook her angrily. "Tell me what's going on!"

He saw tears forming in her eyes and then he knew. He was certain. Somehow, she knew. She must know something. Thoughts of the warnings from his handler rushed back to him and he knew he was in a desperate situation.

He gripped her arms more tightly and she cried out in pain.

"Tariq, please!"

He slapped her hard across the cheek. "Tell me! Tell me now!"

Her tears were flowing now, and she tried to pull away. "Let me go!"

The more she struggled, the more he knew this whole affair had gone terribly wrong. *If anyone finds out...*

He felt her make another attempt to pull away and he hit her hard, this time with a closed fist. It obviously stunned her, and she fell back against the counter as blood began leaking from her nose. He felt a rage burning within that this woman, this infidel, this whore could ruin his plans, could endanger his family.

His hands went to her throat, and he watched her surprised and terrified expression as he pushed her back against the stove, his grip tightening.

It was over quickly, and he stood back as she sank lifelessly to the tile floor. He looked down for a moment, feeling a wave of nausea. He had never killed, and the shock of it was overwhelming.

He left her there, walking quickly through the apartment for any signs of his past visits. Reassuring himself that he could not be linked to the woman, he went to the door and looked down the hall.

How many people have seen me here? he thought as he moved quickly down the hall to the elevator.

And then he saw the security camera up in the corner. He quickly reasoned it was much too late to deal with any past visits that may have been recorded.

No one knows who I am, and in a few days...

Chapter Twenty-One

Hanna reached for the cup of juice and handed it to her son, who was sitting up with pillows propped against the wall of the small hospital room. She had come by early to see him before having to return to Charleston for meetings with clients.

Jonathan had been alert and feeling much better but was terribly upset about the concern he had caused. He was more worried about everyone else having to deal with his problems than he was about his own health. He had tried to explain the pain he had been dealing with the past couple of weeks from his bike accident and how the pills weren't helping. He knew he shouldn't be taking more, but the pain was becoming unbearable. He had never had such a severe overdose reaction, and he had no memory of how he had let it get so far out of control.

"The doctor agrees you need to go back into rehab as soon as possible," she said gently, trying to upset his fragile mood.

He looked back at her, frowning.

"This won't take care of itself, honey."

"I know," he said, the sadness in his voice nearly breaking her heart.

"We don't have any other choice."

"I know, Mom. I know."

Hanna was driving back to Charleston. The morning traffic was heavy as usual on Highway 17 back to the city.

Reluctantly, Jonathan had agreed to another session of rehab, and she left him to rest a few more hours before she would come back to pick him up when the doctors said he could be released this afternoon.

Her son's overdose had frightened her more than anything she had ever experienced. Even the shock of her husband having been found murdered three years ago paled in comparison. It was a visceral fear that she might have lost a son she loved more than anything.

She braked quickly as a car pulled out in front of her. Her thoughts shifted to the coming morning and the demands of another day of trying to help so many at her free legal clinic, many who had nowhere else to turn. She remembered that Christy Griffith's friend, Penny, had made an appointment to meet with her first thing. She was still surprised her friend and former client had been so reckless to reach out to a past acquaintance when all guidance from her handlers demanded she never do such a thing. *Loneliness can be a terrible burden.*

She walked into the back entrance to her clinic in the old house in the Historic District of Charleston. The familiar noises and commotion greeted her as she walked to the front to let her assistant, Molly, know she was back from the island.

"Is my first appointment here?" Hanna asked, looking down at her watch, a gift from Alex on her last birthday. She was running late as traffic snarled closer to the city. She scanned the small waiting room and saw several people waiting to see lawyers, but no one she recognized.

Molly said, "No, she was supposed to be here at 9. I have her cell. I'll try to reach her."

"Thank you."

"How was your weekend?"

Hanna wasn't in the mood to share at the moment. "One to remember... one to remember," she repeated as she started back down the hall.

At 10 am, Molly knocked on her open office door and stepped in. Hanna was deep into a case file for a client facing eviction. She looked up at her long-time employee and now close friend.

"I'm starting to get a little worried about your nine o'clock," Molly said. The woman was so insistent on seeing you this morning, and I switched around another appointment so we could get her in. And then she just stiffs us."

"You can't get hold of her?"

"Won't answer her cell or my texts."

Hanna tried to switch gears and focus her thoughts for a moment. She began getting more concerned when she recalled Christy Griffith's worry about her friend and this person she had met who seemed to be a dangerous character. She tried not to let her mind overreact. *But what if this guy was truly bad news?*

"You probably didn't get her address?" Hanna asked. She watched as Molly shook her head, no.

"Find out where she lives and let me know as soon as you can."

Molly's eyes opened wide in worry. "You think something's happened to her?"

"Let's hope not." As Molly walked out, Hanna picked up her phone and scrolled through to click on Alex's number.

He picked up right away. "Did you get down there, okay?"

"A lot of traffic, as usual."

"Typical."

"I think there may be a problem," Hanna said tentatively.

"Is Jonathan okay?"

"Yes, I saw him before I left the beach. He's doing much better, just really down about how much he scared us."

"Is he going to be okay with rehab again?"

Hanna thought back to their discussion. "Not real happy about it."

"Sure... so what's this problem?"

She stood and walked to the window, looking out over the heavy green tree line and shrubs filled with bright flowers at the back of the property. "You remember I told you last night about my former client who's now off in Witness Protection."

"The Griffith girl."

"Right," Hanna said, an empty feeling growing in her gut. "The woman she referred to me didn't show up this morning."

She waited a moment for Alex to respond, but he must have been thinking through the situation.

"Alex, I'm afraid something's happened to her. Christy was really worried about this guy she's been seeing."

"You can't reach her?" she heard him ask.

Molly walked back into the office. "I have her address. It's actually just a few blocks from here."

"Did you hear that?" Hanna asked Alex.

"Yeah... I want you to stay away. I'm calling Foster over at the Bureau office. Let them check this out this morning. Call me if you learn anything else. Text me that address."

Hanna said, "I have a really bad feeling about this."

"Let's see what Foster finds out. I was getting ready to leave for the city, too. I'll try to catch up with the Bureau team after they've checked out the woman's address. I need to go by the office there anyway to do some paperwork and fill them in on this nonsense Grace is trying to get you involved in."

"I thought you were on suspension. What paperwork?"

"It's related to that."

"What's happening?" Hanna asked, worried now he hadn't told her everything.

"Just the normal bureaucratic crap."

She wasn't reassured. "Okay... please call when you hear anything from the FBI team."

"I will. Love you!"

"Love you, too..." She heard him click off.

Molly came over and gave her the address to Penny Hampton's apartment.

Chapter Twenty-two

FBI Special Agent Will Foster stood on the fifth floor of the woman's apartment with one other agent and the building supervisor who was unlocking the door for him. He had tried earlier to get someone to answer, but there had been no response. The super pushed open the door and stood aside.

Foster yelled out, "Federal Bureau of Investigation, Ms. Hampton! Hello!"

No answer.

He walked into a narrow hallway and could see windows and the skyline of Charleston beyond. Out of extreme precaution, he pulled out his Glock 9mm semiautomatic. He clicked the safety off and held it at his side, pointing to the floor.

"Ms. Hampton!" he yelled again. The only sound was the muted traffic noise from outside the windows. He came into the main living area and turned to see the kitchen on the right. There was a low bar counter with two chairs. A bedroom door was to the left.

He stopped suddenly as he came around the counter.

The young woman lay on the floor, arms and legs splayed out at unnatural angles. The side of her face pressed against the white tile. Her eyes were open but clearly lifeless. There were ugly purple and blue bruises visible on her bare neck.

Foster took a deep breath, then turned back to his colleague, who was peering into the bedroom. "Call the locals, we've got a DOA."

Alex was making coffee in the kitchen of the FBI offices in downtown Charleston. He'd been laboring over forms the Bureau needed him to complete and needed a break. He felt his phone vibrate and looked at the screen. It was Nate Beatty from the Charleston PD.

"Nate, what's the latest?"

"Why the hell didn't you call me with this?" came the angry response.

"What're you talking about?"

"I'm here with your pal, Foster, from the Bureau."

Alex had a bad feeling sweep through him. He reached for the cup of steaming coffee and started back to his cubicle.

Beatty continued. "Foster's boys call me and tell us we've got a homicide down here. You remember I work in Homicide, right?"

"Nate, what happened?" Alex asked, sitting back down behind his laptop and papers.

"Seems your tip this woman might be running with a bad dude was correct. Somebody strangled her to death last night."

Alex felt his stomach churn. "Hanna got the call from an old client. A friend was worried about her new boyfriend maybe being involved in some bad stuff, maybe even terrorism."

"Right, and why didn't you call us in first on this?"

"Counter-terrorism is Bureau work, Nate. You know that."

"Well, for now it's a homicide, and it's on my plate."

"You got anything on the boyfriend yet?"

"Forensics team isn't finished yet," Beatty said. "Haven't found anything obvious. The security cameras in the lobby and hall outside may give us something. Still waiting."

"What do we know about the girl?"

"Office assistant at a little insurance agency out on the west side. Sent a couple uniforms over. No one there knows about a boyfriend."

Alex said, "Would you mind keeping me posted? Hanna will want to get back with her client."

"Sure, man."

"What's the latest on the Holloway investigation?"

Beatty replied with an angry tone, "We're bringing the wife, Grace, back in. I'm really pissed she skipped town not hours after we told her to sit tight."

Alex closed the laptop and put all the papers in the top drawer of the desk. *Enough already*, he thought.

"What did the Holloway woman want from Hanna?" Beatty asked.

Alex stood to leave and headed toward the hall elevator. "She claims there's some cash that Hanna's husband supposedly stashed away somewhere down in the islands. She wants us to help her recover the money in exchange for a healthy cut."

"You're kidding, right?"

"No, I wish I was," Alex said, pushing the elevator button for the first floor, then stepping in when the doors opened. "Hanna is really upset about this, as you can imagine. She thought this was all behind her."

"You got the Feds involved?" asked.

"Yeah, I'm just leaving there now," Alex said. "Is Foster still there with you?

"Let me look."

Alex walked out into the heat of the morning, the sun bright and the streets almost steaming. Beatty came back on the line. "Foster is still here. He wants you to call."

"Will do." He ended the call and went to get his car in the garage parking lot down the street. He needed to get over to Hanna's office and let her know her friend's concern about Penny Hampton was very real.

When he got to his car, he turned the air conditioning on Max and waited for the air to cool some as he called his fellow agent, Will Foster. His suspension from the Bureau gnawed at his gut, and after all the time and effort to finally secure his position, a reckless decision to go after Xander Lacroix alone may have cost him his career.

"Will, it's Alex."

"Beatty filled you in?" Foster asked.

"Yeah. You got anything else yet on the killer?"

"Just took a look at some of the security footage. We've got a thirty-something Middle Eastern male coming and going from the woman's apartment on several occasions. I've got it sent over to the facial recognition team. We'll see if they can get a hit on this guy."

"No one in the building could help?" Alex asked, backing the car out to start over to Hanna's office.

"Not so far. Thanks for calling us in on this. Wish we'd gotten there earlier."

Alex said, "CCTV cameras in the area might pick this guy up."

"Exactly," Foster said. "I'm gonna want to talk with Hanna's source on this. You said she's in the WP program. Did Hanna get a phone number?"

"I'll find out. Headed over there now. Probably has it in her cell from Recents."

"The Hampton woman may have told her more about the boyfriend that can help. If this asshole has a terrorist connection, I want him put away fast," Foster said.

"I'll get back to you after I see Hanna," Alex said, ending the call and placing the phone down on the console. The traffic was still heavy, and he probably could have walked to Hanna's office faster. He was not looking forward to telling her about the death of her client's friend. *She has enough to worry about.*

Chapter Twenty-three

Hanna felt her heart sink, and she leaned back in her desk chair as Alex shared the devastating news about Christy Griffth's friend. "Oh please, no!"

"I'm sorry," Alex responded, sitting on the desk next to her. "I wish we knew about this earlier."

Hanna pressed her palm into her forehead, trying to make sense of the situation. "What in the world happened?"

"Will Foster and an FBI team went to her apartment this morning. They found her strangled."

"Strangled!" She pushed her chair back and began pacing around the office.

Alex said, "There is video footage of a Middle Eastern man coming to her apartment several times. Will has the tech team trying to ID him."

"Christy is going to be devastated. She was afraid something like this might happen."

Alex came over beside her as she looked out the window. "I assume you have her number in your *Recents* caller ID?" he asked.

She hesitated, still thinking about having to break this news to her friend. "I suppose."

"Will wants to speak with her."

"I need to tell her about this first," Hanna protested. "She trusted me to try to help her friend, and now she's dead!"

"Let me call Will," Alex said. "We'll work something out."

An hour later, Will Foster sat down in Hanna's office with both her and Alex and a conference phone in the middle of the table.

Foster said, "Hanna, I'm sorry we didn't get to her sooner. You didn't know Penny Hampton?"

"No, I've never met her. The call from my friend Christy was the first I had even heard of her."

Foster pulled several photo prints from his bag and laid them on the table. Hanna looked through them and saw pictures of a young man with dark hair and Arabic features, coming down a hallway apartment.

"And I assume you've never met this person before?" Foster asked.

Hanna shook her head slowly, looking closely at the pictures. "And you think this man's a terrorist? Here in Charleston?"

"That's what we need to find out, quickly."

Alex leaned in. "Will tells me there is suspicious chatter being picked up by National Intelligence in several cities around the country, but apparently nothing here in South Carolina... yet."

"Hanna, this is all highly confidential, but it is critical we close all loose ends as soon as possible," Foster said. "I would like you to call Ms. Griffith. I apologize in advance for putting you in this position, but I'd like you to explain how you brought us in at her request and then let me take it from there. Okay?"

"Fine," Hanna said, the pit in her stomach like a dark hole in space. Her hands trembled as she reached to dial the number on the conference phone. Christy Griffith answered on the second ring.

"Hanna! Is that you?"

"Yes..." she replied hesitantly.

"I was about to call you," Christy said. "I've tried to reach Penny several times. She's not picking up and her mailbox is full."

"Christy, I'm so sorry..." Hanna began.

"What?" came the tentative reply.

"I'm here with Will Foster and Alex Frank from the FBI."

"What's happened?" Christy asked, her voice rising.

"Ms. Griffith, this is Special Agent Will Foster with the Charleston regional office of the FBI. I'm sorry to inform you we found your friend deceased in her apartment earlier this morning."

All three in Hanna's office sat staring at the conference phone for a moment, but there was no reply.

"Ms. Griffith, I'm sorry we weren't able to intervene in time," Foster continued. "It appears your friend was the victim of a homicide."

"Oh God, no!" came the defeated sigh over the phone.

Alex said, "Christy, we have several photos of a man we believe is Penny's boyfriend you were concerned about. We would like to text these photos over to you."

Foster said, "We're assuming you've never met the man, considering your current remote location."

"That's correct," came the sad reply. Hanna could hear low sobs coming now.

"I'm sending them right now," Foster said. "Please check your phone."

As they waited for her to find the pictures, Hanna looked over at Alex. He returned her gaze with a reassuring nod, as if to remind her they were doing all they could at the moment.

Finally, Christy said, "I have them. I'm looking at the first photo. I don't know this man. Penny met him long after I left Charleston."

"So, you never met him while you were still here in town?" Foster asked.

"No! I told you Penny met him just a few weeks ago."

"I understand," Foster said. "Did Penny tell you anything else about this man?"

"They met at a coffee shop near her apartment."

"Do you know which coffee shop?" Alex asked.

"Probably the Starbucks just around the corner. That's where she always went."

Hanna watched Foster reach for his phone and place a call. He turned away for a few moments talking with someone, then returned to the conference call. "Ms. Griffith, we're sending someone over to talk to the crew at the coffee shop. Did Penny mention any other meetings or locations?"

"Only her apartment," Christy responded, her voice cracking. "Have you spoken with the building manager there?"

"Yes," Foster replied. "He helped us with the video footage and still photos you're looking at, but he never saw the man in person."

"Penny was getting a bad feeling about this guy. He called himself Tariq and was involved in something dangerous."

"No last name?" Alex asked.

"No, just Tariq is all she told me."

"And she never mentioned anything specific?" Foster asked.

Christy hesitated on the other end of the call, then said, "No, that's all I can remember."

"Okay, thank you, Ms. Griffith," Foster said, standing and placing his hands down on the table. "Again, we're very sorry about your friend's passing. We're doing everything we can to track down this individual. Of course, you will let us know if you think of anything else?"

"I will, sir, thank you," Christy replied.

Hanna said, "Christy, I'm so sorry. I called in Alex and his associates at the Bureau as soon as I could," knowing though that she should have moved more quickly. The guilt was tearing at her. "I know you're not supposed to reach out, but don't hesitate to call if I can do anything for you."

"Thank you, Hanna," came the reply. "Just help them find this guy!"

Foster had left earlier, and Alex convinced Hanna to leave her office to get a quick lunch. They walked together now down the shaded walk toward a diner they frequented just two blocks away.

The midday sun filtered through the tall live oak and palm fronds looming above. The tall old historic homes along the walk were like majestic beacons from an earlier age. Many had ornate stone and iron gates leading up the drives or front walks. On any other day, Hanna would marvel at the beauty of this street and all the grand sites of the city she had chosen to call home. Today, all she could think about was how much she was letting the people in her life down.

Her son was recovering from a near deadly drug overdose. A friend who had confided in her and trusted her to help a woman in trouble had now been found murdered. She knew in her soul she had so much to be thankful for in a life of early abundance and love as a child, a wonderful education, and now a career she found tremendously challenging and rewarding.

Then, she thought again of her immediate family. Her now-deceased husband had proven to be both unfaithful and a crook on the wrong side of some very dangerous people. Her son had always been her ray of hope and joy. His challenges were terrifying, but she was confident that with Alex's help, they could all get beyond the current danger.

And yes, there was Alex Frank. He had come into her life during the darkest of times and helped her through some frightening challenges. They had grown closer over time as their relationship developed to a point where she knew they were both truly in love with a wedding on the horizon, despite having to overcome continuing threats from ex-wives, dangerous gangsters, and Alex's own past demons.

But here we are, walking down one of the most beautiful streets in America, together, safe, a new life ahead, she thought as they approached the restaurant.

Alex watched as Hanna Walsh sat across from him in the tiny storefront diner, the bustle of the lunch crowd all around. He could see the drain of the past two days in her tired and drawn face. He reached across the space between them and stroked her cheek. She met his gaze and managed a thin smile. Leaning back, she pulled her short brown hair back behind her ears, took a deep breath, and sighed.

"You can't blame yourself for what happened," he said.

Hanna shook her head and frowned again. "I didn't take Christy's call seriously enough. I should have called you and the Bureau immediately and insisted you find this girl..."

"Please, don't..." Alex broke in. "We will find this guy. I don't know what he's involved in, but we will find him."

"I'm sorry, too little, too late."

"Hanna..."

"Why is Will letting you work on this?" she asked. "You're supposed to be on suspension."

Alex felt the bite of reality in the situation he found himself in. "I asked Will if I could help unofficially. His boss in DC would have his ass, but he's short-staffed and he needs some extra arms and legs."

His cell buzzed and he pulled it out. There was a text from Foster. "He read it and then looked up at Hanna. "No luck with workers down at the Starbucks. Two people remember seeing the guy but nothing more."

"I'm sorry."

"There's another shift coming in this afternoon. I'm going down there."

"Are there any other leads?"

"Will has people checking with leaders at local mosques, Arab organizations. Hopefully, we'll get something back soon on the facial recognition check. They also have the CCTV cameras programmed to ID this guy if they pick him up on the street."

"They can do that?"

Alex nodded, thinking about what other possible leads could be followed up on. He needed to call Beatty and see what the Homicide forensics teams had come up with.

The server came up and took their orders of deli sandwiches and iced tea. As he walked away, Hanna said, "I don't know why I'm thinking about this now, when the world seems to be crashing down around us, but what's this nonsense about your ex throwing a party for Skipper and Ella?"

Alex blew out a long breath. He had been trying, unsuccessfully, to put the event out of his mind. Adrienne was planning the party for Friday night. It was the last place he wanted to be. Another evening with Adrienne was not something he needed to deal with, and certainly, he didn't expect Hanna to go.

"I'll deal with it," he finally said.

"You think I'm sending you up there alone with that woman?" Hanna said, a forced smile spreading across her face.

"You really want to go?"

"I don't ever want to see your ex-wife again, but there's no way I'm leaving you alone with her."

Alex started to protest.

"You know I trust *you*," Hanna continued.

"Nothing will happen... I won't let anything happen."

"I'm going!" Hanna said.

Alex had to smile and look back at the woman who had become his new partner in life. *What a blessing!*

Chapter Twenty-four

Detective Ned Beatty sat in the windowless interrogation room, the dull gray walls closing in and the air dank and stale. The heavy door opened, and he watched as Xander Lacroix was led in by a prison guard. The young gangster had grown a beard since Beatty had last seen him at trial months ago, but other than the drab prison uniform, he seemed to be faring well in the state penitentiary. He had been convicted on charges of murder, kidnapping, and extortion and sentenced to forty years.

Beatty had little doubt that Lacroix had an army of lawyers working to overturn the convictions or at least reduce his time behind bars.

"Detective, it's been too long," Lacroix began as he sat across the table.

Beatty nodded to the guard and said it was okay for him to leave the room.

When alone, Beatty said, "You look well, Xander. Food must be good here."

Lacroix smiled back, his face lined with street tough hardness. His hair was cut short and graying. He leaned in, "Okay, what the hell you need?"

"You heard about the attorney, Holloway? I know the two of you have done some business in the past."

"What about him?"

Beatty studied the man's face for a few moments for any sign of recognition of Holloway's murder. "We found him and his mistress with several bullet holes in them over at his house a couple nights ago."

Lacroix remained expressionless. "Sorry to hear about that. He was a nice guy... an idiot, but a nice guy."

"Any idea who he got sideways with?" Beatty continued.

Lacroix rubbed his chin, considering the question. "You know he ran with a bad bunch."

"Like you?" Beatty replied.

The gangster just smiled again.

"Don't tell me you don't know about this?"

"Yeah, I heard."

"What'd you hear?"

Lacroix didn't respond and looked around. "We get some coffee in here?"

"This isn't a social call," Beatty said firmly. "What do you know about Holloway's murder?"

"You're smart, Beatty. You need to follow the money."

"What're you talking about?"

"Holloway had a lot of clients with big bucks and big bets on the table. Follow the money. Look at the risks."

"You think somebody needed to shut him up?"

Lacroix paused in reflection, his head tilting to the side. "Could be a jealous wife. I remember his old lady got taken down in that old Dellahousaye land deal."

"We're looking at that."

"Who's the broad?"

"The other DOA?" Beatty asked and then continued. "Another lawyer from the same firm. She and Holloway had apparently been an item. We're checking on the husband, too."

"Heard it was pretty messy," Lacroix said. "Jealousy is a powerful motivator."

"Tell me where you heard that?"

"I got sources, man."

"Yeah, I'm sure you do." Beatty stared back hard. "Shooter left brass all over the floor. Probably heard that, too."

"Like I said, messy," Lacroix said. "Not professional. And why take out the broad? I'd be looking at the spouses, Detective."

"Was Holloway still doing legal work for your businesses, Xander?"

"I'm out, man! I'm stuck in here 24/7."

"We know you're still pulling the strings. What did Holloway do to get on the wrong side with you guys?" Beatty pressed. "He was pushing Dellahousaye hard before they all went down."

Lacroix smiled and stood up to leave. "You got this all wrong, Beatty." He knocked on the door for the guard.

Chapter Twenty-five

Glenn Pyke slammed the phone down in its cradle and cursed so loudly his assistant in the next room came in to check on him. When she peeked her head in, he yelled again for her to get out. He got up from behind his massive desk in the New Orleans headquarters office of *Green* and paced around on the plush carpeting in his bare feet.

The final question from the reporter at the New York paper had caught him completely off guard and sent him over the edge.

Now, could you please tell me about the financial improprieties surfacing about Green? *Is it true you've been enriching yourself from the donations coming into your organization?*

The discussion had been going fairly well up until that point. The woman had set up the interview under the guise of interest in profiling the recent good work *Green* had been doing to bring attention to worsening air quality in China and India that far dwarfed any gains being made in other locations around the world.

She had seemed genuinely interested in his narrative about the pressure that *Green* was bringing to governments all around the world on air and water quality which was, indeed, quite true. And then, out of nowhere, she went for his throat with the money question. He had been so stunned and surprised, he couldn't even respond.

When he finally managed to start in with a flimsy and halted response, she came at him again with an allegation, which was actually true, that he and *Green* had been behind a recent environmental accident that severely polluted a popular trout stream in Wyoming. He finally lost control and simply slammed the phone down. *What an idiot! I need to call her back.*

The more he thought about it, the angrier he got. He also knew there was no explanation for the money trail that led to numerous offshore accounts with only his name on them. *And the Wyoming chemical spill! How did she find out?*

In desperation, he hurried back over behind his desk and found his cell under a pile of papers. He found the number for his lead attorney in New York and placed the call.

After a couple of minutes, he was connected to Charles Wainwright, senior partner of one of the more prominent law firms in the city. The firm of Ellis Wainwright had represented *Green* for years and had also been instrumental in helping Glenn Pyke set up what he thought was an airtight financial structure that would continue to line his own pockets while maintaining the illusion that the massive donations coming into the organization were being appropriately allocated to good work around the world.

"Hello Glenn," came the calm and distinguished response. "How have you been?"

Pyke tried to keep his hands from shaking as he placed the call on *Speaker* and set the cell down on his desk. "I was fine until about five minutes ago when a bitch reporter from this New York paper set me up with a hit piece on *Green!*"

"Glenn, please calm down and tell me what happened," Wainwright said. "Who is the reporter?"

"A woman name Allende or Allendale... I don't remember!"

"And what did she want?"

"She knows about the money!"

There was no response from the attorney, so Pyke yelled out again, "She knows about the damn money, Charles!"

"We shouldn't be discussing this on the phone, Glenn," came the curt response.

"I don't give a damn about where we talk about this! I pay you too much money for shit like this to happen."

"Glenn, please..."

"No, you listen!" Pyke demanded. "You need to put a stop to this. We cannot let this story get out!"

"How did you leave it with her?" Wainwright asked.

Pyke didn't answer, knowing his panicked termination of the call was a huge mistake.

"Glenn?"

"Just take care of this! Am I clear?"

"Okay, let me look into it. I'll be back in touch."

Pyke ended the call and turned to the credenza behind him. He pulled aside a cabinet door of rich Mahogany and reached for a bottle of the latest bourbon he favored. Drinking straight from the bottle, he let the whiskey burn down into his gut, then took another long drink.

Senator Jordan Hayes was about to tee off on the tenth hole of Congressional Country Club when he heard his cell buzzing in the golf cart. He walked over and looked at the caller ID screen. It was the newspaper editor. His two playing partners protested as he took the call, walking away out of earshot.

He heard the editor say, "We've got Glenn Pyke on the rack right now, but we really don't have enough to run with yet."

"Well, get it then!" Hayes demanded.

"These Cayman banks are airtight, and Pyke hung up when we brought up the money issues."

"We need someone else on the inside," Hayes said. "There has to be someone. If it takes a little cash to get someone talking, you let me know."

"Well, I just got off the phone with Pyke's attorney here in the city. Big ass firm with a lot of clout. He threatened everyone, including my grandchildren, if we try to run with this story."

"That's bullshit!" Hayes spat. "Keep digging!"

"Jordan, you're putting us in a very difficult position... "

"This is your job, dammit! You're supposed to ferret out this kind of corruption and bring it to your reader's attention. You said he hung up on the reporter?"

"Right..."

"Well, run the piece and say that the head of *Green* refuses to discuss financial misdealings in his organization. The fact he won't even discuss the situation is damning enough, right?"

"Let me get back to you, Jordan," the editor replied and then ended the call.

As Hayes walked back to his guests on the tee, he thought about whether he needed to call his client, Baz Al Zahrani, with an update. *Not yet!*

The crew finished securing lines to the big yacht at the pier in Charleston Harbor. Al Zahrani sat in a deeply cushioned lounge chair on the foredeck of the massive ship, his satellite phone to his ear as he listened to final preparations for the assault in San Francisco.

"Excellent!" he replied when the man finished the update. "And you're sure the timing for Thursday morning will still work?" He nodded, looking out over the busy Charleston seaport as the man replied in the affirmative. "Very good!"

He signed off and turned as the steward came up on deck.

"Sir, please excuse me," the uniformed attendant began. "Your car is ready to take you out to the beach estate."

"Thank you," Baz replied. "And how are plans for the reception at the house for tomorrow night?"

"Everything is confirmed, sir," came the crisp reply.

"Very well. I'll be ready to leave in a few minutes." The servant backed away, bowing as he left. Baz began running through the guest list in his mind for the party he was throwing for his third wife, who was still sleeping off the excesses the two of them had enjoyed the previous night.

It should be quite a gathering, he thought, *and excellent cover for my whereabouts the night before the calamity that was about to descend on the United States of America.*

Chapter Twenty-six

Tariq Sendaya looked over the charts for the shipping lanes surrounding Charleston Harbor for the hundredth time. The papers were laid out on the small desk in the apartment he shared with his two team members for the assault. As he looked at the red mark indicating the specific location of Thursday's assault, a sick nausea swept through him, as he tried to block the visions of his final moments in the physical world when their mission came to its ultimate conclusion is a fiery inferno.

One of his men came over and whispered an update. He nodded and sent the man away.

His thoughts suddenly turned to the woman... his lover, who now lay dead in an apartment just a few blocks away. He wondered if the police had found the body yet.

Her death had come suddenly when he realized she might be a threat to his mission. Failure would put his family in extreme danger. He could not let that happen. The final moments of Penny Hampton's life flashed through his mind, and he suddenly felt light-headed and sickened as the memory of her terrified eyes looked back as he strangled the last breaths from her lungs.

It was time for prayer, and he pushed all other thoughts aside.

Alex sat in the back of a Starbucks coffee shop, sipping at the strong dark roast coffee he had ordered. He had been watching the shift change behind the counter. Even though he was officially on suspension from the Bureau, Will Foster had *"unofficially"* given him the go-ahead to follow-up on any leads that might help track down the potential terror threat the now deceased Penny Hampton had warned of.

Earlier interviews with the staff here at the coffee shop had not turned up any usable intel on the man in the pictures who appeared to be the boyfriend. Some acknowledged they had seen him but knew nothing more about him.

There was a lull in the line waiting to order coffee, so he got up and walked up to the register. He introduced himself and showed his FBI credentials. Two other employees came over to join the woman in front of him when they heard *FBI*. He pulled a photo of the suspect from his bag and showed it to the staff, asking if anyone had seen the man or knew anything about him.

A slight young man at the back pressed forward, leaning in to take a closer look. Alex watched as his head nodded in the affirmative.

"Sure, I remember him. Comes in most nights after dinner hour. Never leaves a tip!"

Alex felt a rush of excitement. "Any specific time?"

The boy thought for a moment. "Not sure... maybe after seven."

Alex looked at his watch. It was a little past six o'clock.

"Do you have a name, maybe a credit card receipt you could pull up?" he asked.

The crew conferred and didn't seem to think there was any way to locate an earlier receipt like that.

"I think he pays with cash," the boy said.

Alex nodded and said, "Thank you, everyone. If you see this man, please act as you normally would and as soon as possible, contact me at this number. He slid one of his Bureau cards across the counter.

Alex went out and sat in his car to call Foster. His colleague picked up right away.

"What have you got?" he asked.

"Just spent time with the next shift here at the coffee shop. One guy recognized the man in the photo. Thinks he comes in usually after seven. They don't have a name or anything else. I think we need to get a snatch team down here right away."

"Agree," Foster said. "Keep an eye on the place until I call you back."

He moved his car further down the street to be less noticeable. With a clear view of the entrance to the Starbucks, he sat back, his senses on full alert.

He jolted when the ring of his cellphone caught him by surprise. He checked and it was Hanna on the caller ID. "Hey."

"What's the matter?" she asked. "You sound nervous."

"We may have something on the Hampton girl's killer."

"That's terrific!"

"I really can't talk right now," he said. "Is everything okay?"

"I need to work late to try to get caught up," she replied. "Didn't know what time you were coming back to the apartment. Just wanted to let you know."

"This could take some time. Hopefully we can grab this guy tonight. Not sure if Will can let me in if there's an interrogation..."

"Please let me know if you find him."

"Sure." He paused, thinking about their earlier conversation. "You sure you're good with the anniversary party Adrienne's pulling together up in Dugganville?"

"No, I'm not good with anything about that woman!" she protested. "But there's not much I can do about it, and there's no way I'm sending you up there alone with her!"

He could tell she was teasing him by the tone of her voice. "Should be exciting."

"No doubt," Hanna replied. "Call when you can."

Thirty minutes later, a full contingent of FBI team members was in place in and around the downtown coffee shop. Alex had been told to stay where he was in his car and be available as back-up if needed.

Will Foster was in another car down the street in the opposite direction. Their long-time colleague, Sharron Fairfield, was inside sipping coffee with her laptop open, along with several other customers. They also had a man posted in sight of the back alley. An agent back at the office was monitoring CCTV camera feeds in the area to provide an early alert if the man was seen approaching. All were wearing concealed earpieces and microphones and on the same radio frequency.

Alex thought back to the time Agent Fairfield had expressed her interest in starting a personal relationship with him which he quickly squelched, much to Hanna's satisfaction. *Another chapter in my totally messed-up love life,* he thought.

He looked at the clock on his dash... 7:14 p.m. *This guy better show up!*

He heard a scratch on his radio feed, then, *"This is Porter downtown. We have a man approaching from the south, two blocks from the shop. He's wearing jeans and a white t-shirt... no hat. Gotta be the guy."*

Alex looked in his rear-view mirror down the block behind him. At first, he didn't see anyone, then the man came into view. He was too far back to see the face clearly, but he certainly matched the description Porter had just provided.

The suspect would walk right by Alex's car, so he was immediately concerned he would be made. He reached for his cell, holding it up and pretending to talk into it as if he was a motorist pulled over to take a call. He used his free hand to pull his service weapon out and place it on the seat beside his leg nearest the door where the man wouldn't be able to see it.

"I've got him, too," Alex said, loud enough for his radio mic to pick him up. "Coming up behind me."

Foster said," I'll take him at the front door. Jimmy, come around from the alley on my signal in case I have any trouble."

Alex could see Foster get out of his car down the street just as the suspect walked by on the sidewalk to his right. Alex kept his eyes forward, continuing to talk into his phone. Out of his peripheral vision he could tell the man had gone by unsuspecting.

Suddenly he veered between two parked cars and jogged across the street to avoid an oncoming car, the coffee shop just another block up on that side.

Alex put his phone down and checked his gun again. Foster was approaching the front door to the Starbucks from the other direction.

"Everyone stay where you are," Foster whispered on the radio feed.

Alex could feel his tension rising as the suspected terrorist and Agent Foster approached each other. Foster walked by the coffee shop and passed directly by the suspect before turning quickly, coming up behind the man, pinning his right arm up high behind him and shoving him violently into the brick wall of the building.

"Jimmy, now!" Foster yelled.

Alex stayed in the car as ordered and watched as Foster threw the man to the sidewalk face down, then kneeled on his back and placed a gun to the back of his head.

"Do not move!" Foster screamed. "FBI! You are under arrest!"

Agent Jimmy Delgado came quickly out of the alley and rushed over to assist, pulling the suspect's arms together behind him and securing them with a zip-tie. Foster pulled the man to his feet and immediately began pushing him down the street towards his car, Delgado behind, scanning the scene for any other potential threats.

Foster said, "Sharron, we've got him. Let's all get back to the office. Alex, I want you there. Good job, everyone!"

Tariq Sendaya felt the rough brick scratch painfully at the side of his face as his unseen assailant threw him up against the wall. His arm was bent to the point of breaking behind him. Before he could protest, he was thrown to the ground. He was stunned for a moment as his head hit the pavement.

When he heard the words *FBI*, he felt a sick wave of fear rush through him. Images of his wife and two young sons back in New York came to him.

I have failed! Allah, please have mercy!

Chapter Twenty-seven

Hanna glanced up at the clock on her office wall and sighed when she saw it was after eight. She had been going since early this morning when she left the island to get back up here to the city. The stress of her son's overdose and the death of Christy Griffith's friend in Charleston were draining her concentration.

Alex had called thirty minutes earlier to tell her they had arrested the suspect in Penny Hampton's murder and a possible terror threat. It had done little to ease her guilt in the young woman's death and not responding more quickly. Alex thought he would be quite late down at the Bureau office as Will Foster had asked him to join in the interrogation.

The rest of her office building was dark and quiet. Everyone else had left hours ago. It was normally so hectic and loud. She sipped at the coffee cup beside her on the desk and spat the cold liquid back, sighing and shaking her head.

She had five more case files in front of her she knew she had to review before morning. She thought about the bottle of wine chilling in her refrigerator in the apartment upstairs but immediately pushed the thought aside.

That will not help!

For some reason she couldn't fathom, Grace Holloway came to mind. Remembering the confrontation with Alex and Grace up at the beach house and the woman's insistence she help recover money supposedly hidden by her deceased husband, Ben, down in the Caribbean.

Hanna squeezed her eyes tight and tried to get her mind focused on her work, but the thought of Grace and her latest scheme would not go away. It still gnawed at her every day that she had been duped by this woman on so many occasions. If they hadn't seemed to be the closest of friends for such a long time, the hurt and embarrassment of the whole situation wouldn't sting as badly, she thought.

Hanna suddenly remembered the night she was home at their old house on the Battery when she got the call from Charleston PD that Ben had been killed. After finding her son and having him come home to tell him of his father's death, Grace was the next person she had called. Through a long night with the police and a thoroughly numbing experience the next day with notifying family, funeral details, constant media inquiries for an interview, the crushing weight of grief, Grace Holloway had been at her side and a tremendous source of comfort.

Only later would Hanna learn of the woman's deceit, her affair with Ben, and ultimately her role in his death.

And now she's back!

Hanna tried to think back on any possible indication Ben would have given about even more money secreted away to offshore banks. She had been through this so often with the FBI when they were investigating his murder and the failed land development scheme with the mob. She had been told by the authorities that all remaining proceeds and hidden investments had been recovered.

She knew Grace was desperate and in an irrational state. Her husband, Phillip, had also been found murdered, the victim of a gruesome attack that had also taken the life of his latest mistress. She had also been cut off financially.

And now Grace is considered a suspect in the deaths!

Hanna knew in her heart she wanted nothing to do with any money or property related to her husband's past dealings. In her mind it was all *blood money.*

She was startled when her cell buzzed in her purse on the floor beside her desk. She reached down and saw her son's name on the screen. An instant bolt of fear rushed through her. *Oh God, please...*

"Jonathan?"

His weak voice frightened her even more when he said, "Mom, I don't want you to worry..."

"Worry about what?" she jumped in, leaning back in her desk chair with a hand over her eyes, hoping with all her will he was safe.

"Me and Elizabeth..." he began and then hesitated.

"What?" she demanded. "What about Elizabeth?"

"We've decided to take some time..."

"Time for what?"

"We need to get away and get this all behind us."

"Get away! What are you talking about?"

"Mom, I don't want you to worry."

Jonathan!"

"We just need a little time away..."

"Jonathan, you need to get help. We're going to get you some help for this."

"I just can't do that right now," she heard her son protest with the saddest tone. "I really can't do it."

Where are you going?" she said, trying to hold down the panic that was surging through her.

"Just away. Just for a while."

"Jonathan, please. We need to talk about this," she pleaded.

"Elizabeth agrees. She's coming with me. We'll be okay. We have each other. I just need some time to get better."

"Jonathan, you need professional help to deal with these drugs," Hanna said more sternly. "This won't just magically go away."

There was no response.

"Jonathan!"

"I'll call you soon, Mom. Please don't worry. I love you."

And the phone went dead.

Hanna sat back, staring helplessly at the ceiling, her heart beating hard against her chest.

This can't be happening!

Her next thought was to call Alex, but she knew he was busy downtown with the FBI interrogation team. She thought of leaving quickly to drive up to Pawleys Island.

Maybe I can still catch him.

She knew he would be long gone before she could get there. Calling the police didn't seem like a viable option.

I don't want him arrested, for Pete's sake!

Chapter Twenty-eight

Grace Holloway parked two houses down from her old home, pulling up along the curb as the light faded through the heavy cover of trees. Streetlights were coming on and lights through the windows of the big houses cast shadows out across the broad verandahs. She got out and locked the car, the night sounds of tree frogs and lingering songbirds filtering down the street.

She looked both ways to see if any neighbors were out. The street was deserted, at least for the moment. She moved quickly down the walk and up the drive to the big brick colonial. Moving to the back in the fading light, she could still make out the elegant patio area and pool deck where she had previously hosted so many events and gatherings. It all seemed a distant memory now.

She still had a key to the back door and let herself in quickly, again looking in both directions to see if anyone was watching. Inside, she pulled a small flashlight from her purse, not wanting to turn on any lights and raise suspicion. The flow and smell of the house was warm and familiar, and a pang of regret overwhelmed her as she thought of how far she had fallen from her old affluent and comfortable lifestyle.

Keeping the light low to the floor, she made her way through the opulent kitchen, then through the long dining room and across the front of the house to her now-deceased husband's den. She pushed open the heavy oak double doors and slipped in, closing them behind her. Turning, even in the low light, she could see the familiar furniture and décor of the room. It smelled of old leather and cigar smoke, a nasty habit she had constantly argued with Phillip about.

Over the past months since her release from prison, she had tried on multiple occasions to find time alone in this room. The night Phillip met his unfortunate yet well-deserved end, she thought, there was no time. She had needed to get away as quickly as possible. Now, there was nothing but time. Phillip was gone. The police investigation was continuing, but they had found all they thought they needed here.

But they didn't know about the secrets and treasures Phillip had hidden away in this room.

She moved across the plush carpet to the desk and then around to a bookshelf across the back wall filled with law books, a vast fiction library, and memorabilia and photos that Phillip had treasured most.

Grace had always hated this room. It represented everything she despised about her worthless and corrupt husband, his arrogant excesses, ruthless alliances, heartless dalliances. And on top of all that, he was an atrocious lover, she thought.

How did I put up with this for so long?

She forced herself to focus on the true purpose of her visit. Moving over to the far right side of the bookshelf wall, she moved aside several books, exposing a small button against the back. When she touched it, as expected, the deep brown mahogany panel behind the books lifted to reveal a wall safe.

Hopefully, he hasn't changed the combination since I've been gone.

She shined the light and turned the numbers she had kept in her memory for years. Phillip had never shared them with her, but she found a note tucked away in his briefcase one night when he was passed out from too much bourbon after dinner.

She turned to the last number and then reached for the handle. It wouldn't move and her first thought was the bastard had changed the combination. She tried again, and this time, there was a satisfying click and the heavy metal door swung open.

Her heart started beating faster and she realized she was breathing hard as she pulled the safe door fully open and then shone the light inside.

Her first reaction was a surprised, "Holy crap!"

She reached in and pulled out four stacks of U.S. currency. Placing them on the desk, she moved closer with the light and saw the bills were wrapped with a paper strap and the outside bills were all 50's. In her mind, she quickly did the math... stacks of 50s, probably 50 to a stack... a nice find of $10,000.

Returning to the safe, her light revealed ten more stacks of bills, another $25,000. She placed all the money in the large bag she'd brought in.

Behind the money, she found three file folders stuffed with documents. All went into the bag. At the back of the safe, she reached in to bring out a bright silver revolver with a wood grip. The gun was heavy and fully loaded.

This must be the .45 he always bragged to his buddies about.

The gun also went into her bag along with a box of shells, then she took one more look in the safe. She almost didn't see it in the low light but reached back to find a notecard. Examining it in the wash of the flashlight, she saw ten numbers typed out and nothing else.

An account number? A password?

Satisfied she had emptied all the contents of the safe, she closed it and pushed the button to close the cabinet wall. The panel quietly slipped back into place. She reset the books and then turned to her husband's desk. Sitting in the deeply cushioned leather chair, she reached for the center drawer. It was locked, as were all four other drawers on each side. She remembered watching Phillip hide a key when he didn't see her come into the den.

On the back credenza, there was an ornate wooden box. She opened it and smelled the rich aroma of the cigars he kept. Pushing some of them aside, she found the small key. One lock on the upper left corner of the desk opened all the drawers. In the center drawer, she didn't find anything of interest, a few pens and paperclips, a handful of documents that appeared to have no value to her.

The other side drawers held many file folders, each labeled and in alphabetical order. She began browsing through them, not entirely sure what she was looking for. There were tax files, documents for homes, cars, a boat, some client files. None of it caught her attention until a single file near the back of the last drawer caused her to pause. She pulled it out and opened it in front of her on the desk. There was no label on the file. The single page document inside was a ledger of balances.

At the top of the first column was an initial balance of $2,500,000.

What!

Beneath the initial balance were a series of withdrawals in various increments, typically around $10,000. At the bottom, a current tally showed $2,150,000.

She scanned the rest of the sheet and saw a telephone number with an area code she didn't recognize, probably international, she thought. She placed the ledger sheet in her bag with the other items.

Closing all the drawers and re-locking the desk, she returned the key to the cigar box. Her mind was swimming with the possibilities of all she had found. Suddenly, she felt lightheaded and reached for the desk to steady herself. Taking a moment and several deep breaths, she gathered herself and started for the door.

One other item caught her attention. On a wall with many framed photos, most of Phillip with various celebrities and politicians, there was also a photo she remembered well. She walked over softly and shined the light at a small color photo, framed in black like all the others. It was a picture of her and Phillip with Ben and Hanna Walsh at a company event. The men were in tuxedos, she and Hanna in smart evening dresses. It had probably been taken ten years earlier, she thought, trying to remember the night.

She had always been drawn to the picture. The handsome face of Hanna's husband stared back at her again, and she allowed herself to remember some of their more intimate times together. She shook her head as sadness washed over her.

How did everything go so wrong?

Chapter Twenty-nine

Alex stood outside the interrogation room at the Bureau offices, looking through a one-way mirror at the man they had just brought in. He was sitting at a small table, his hands shackled to a D-ring at the center. A black hood covered his face.

The man had come quietly with no protest or struggle but offered no response to any of their early questions. The wallet in his pants revealed a New York driver's license with the name Tariq Sendaya and an address in Brooklyn. The New York office had already sent a team there to investigate. They found a wife and two young sons. The wife was undergoing additional questioning and the house was being searched thoroughly.

Will Foster came up behind Alex. "Nothing more from New York, yet and D.C. just called with a preliminary background check. Our Tariq here is a security guard. No priors. No known terror connections but born and raised in Syria until coming over to the states five years ago. Still staying under a work visa."

"Apparently, not a very loyal husband, either," Alex added, still staring at the hooded man.

"Jimmy and I are going to start on this guy," Foster said. "Text me if you have any line of questioning you think we should go down."

"Will do."

Alex watched as Agents Foster and Delgado entered the room and sat across from Tariq Sendaya. They left the hood on as a device to continue to intimidate the suspect.

"Mr. Sendaya," Foster began, and the man jolted back in his chair, the shackles holding his hands to the table. "You're in a good bit of trouble here. We know you were in the apartment of Penny Hampton the night she was strangled to death. I'm sure we'll have DNA and fingerprints soon to confirm you are the killer." He paused for a response.

Alex continued to watch as the man just shook his head back and forth slowly, apparently in denial of the charges. "You have certain rights under the laws of this country." Foster read him his Miranda rights.

"Now again, about the death of Penny Hampton. You have nothing to say?" Foster pressed.

"I don't know what you're talking about," came the muffled reply through the hood, the voice with a distinctive Middle Eastern accent.

"Let's cut the bullshit, Tariq," Delgado said. "We have you on video in the woman's building, going into her apartment on multiple occasions, including the night of the murder."

"I don't know this woman," Sendaya replied.

"Of course, you do," Foster cut in. "The woman told a friend all about you."

With a nod from Foster, Delgado got up and went around the table, pulling the hood off. Alex watched as the man squinted in the harsh light, holding his head to the side.

Foster continued. "We've been to see your wife and sons in New York."

The man looked up in surprise. "They have nothing to do with this."

"To do with what, Tariq?"

He didn't answer.

"We will very likely deport them back to Syria while you're doing time for the murder."

"I didn't kill anyone!"

"Why are you here in Charleston?" Foster continued as Delgado came around to sit beside him again. "You live in New York. What are you doing down here?"

Sendaya just stared back, his lower lip trembling slightly.

"I'm sure your wife will be very interested to hear about your affair with Ms. Hampton."

"I don't know this woman!" Sendaya protested.

Delgado reached for a remote control on the table and pointed it at the television screen on the wall beside them. The still image from the security camera came up of Tariq Sendaya standing at the door of Penny Hampton's apartment. There was a date and time indicated in the lower corner of the screen.

Foster said, "This is you the night of Ms. Hampton's murder."

Delgado pressed *Play*. The video began and they all watched as Penny came to the door, letting him in with a hug before closing the door. Delgado fast-forwarded just a few minutes later and started the video again. The door opened and Sendaya hurried out, this time with no sign of the woman.

Foster looked back at the suspect who met his gaze.

"I would like a lawyer," Sendaya said.

"Of course," Foster replied. "Do you have a lawyer?"

Sendaya shook his head no.

He nodded for Delgado to leave and make arrangements.

Alex watched as Delgado left the room and walked past to check on a court-appointed attorney. He had an idea, and he sent a quick text to Foster, who read the message when his cell buzzed.

He turned back to Sendaya. "We know you often purchase multiple cups of coffee from the shop downtown. Who else are you down here with?"

No response.

"Mr. Sendaya, I have the authority to look more favorably on this murder charge, perhaps involuntary manslaughter, something that would keep you from a life sentence, maybe even a death sentence."

Again, no response.

"We could also look at a more favorable outcome for your family."

This brought a slight nod of recognition.

"But you need to be straight with me about why you're here in Charleston."

"I want to speak with my attorney!"

Foster nodded back, then said, "We have information that you're involved in a planned attack on our city."

Sendaya tried to mask his reaction, but Alex could see the panic in his eyes.

"Let me guess," Foster continued, "whoever is behind this will likely take out your failure to complete this mission on your family in New York. Am I correct?"

"No..." Sendaya started to protest.

"If we let the media know a potential terror suspect has been captured and ID you for all the world to see, what will your associates do to your family, Tariq?"

"You can't do that!"

"Of course we can, and we will, immediately, if you don't start filling in the blanks."

Alex watched as Sendaya lowered his head to the table.

"Tariq!" Foster shouted. "We're losing time!"

The man looked up, panic and fear now written across his face. "You won't be able to protect my family!"

"We will put them in custody until this is all resolved. I can promise you they will be safe."

"If I betray them, they will kill my wife and children," he said weakly. "I can't tell you!"

Chapter Thirty

Hanna reached for the wine bottle on her kitchen table and filled the glass nearly to the brim, some of it spilling red drops on the light blue tablecloth, but she paid no attention. She took a long drink then stared at her phone on the table again. She had been holding off on calling Alex about Jonathan. She knew he was busy with the man they had captured in the Penny Hampton murder.

She had called Jonathan's cell at least five times, but he wasn't picking up. She was so furious with him for running from this problem. She had a terrible feeling about him and Elizabeth trying to deal with this on their own.

Finally, she couldn't wait any longer. She pressed the number for Alex's cell. He picked up almost immediately. "Hey..."

"Alex, I've got..."

She was interrupted when Alex jumped in with an excited voice. "We've got this guy confessing to the murder, and there does appear to be something coming down."

"What?'

"I can't talk about it, but I may not be back until very late."

"Alex, it's Jonathan."

"No, what?"

"He's gone!"

"Gone?"

She reached for her wine glass and walked into the living room, collapsing down on the couch. "He called earlier to tell me that he and Elizabeth are going away."

"Going away?" she heard him respond, clearly with as much concern as she was feeling. "He can't do that!"

"I know, I tried to tell him, but he just wouldn't listen."

"Where are they going?"

"He wouldn't tell me. I've been trying to reach him. He said he'll tell us as soon as they get settled."

"Hanna, I'm so sorry," Alex said, then paused. "I don't know what to tell you."

"I thought about driving back up to the island, but I'm sure they're gone by now."

"You sound like you've had a little to drink. Maybe it's best you stay put," he said. "I'll try to get back as soon as I can tonight, but there's some serious stuff coming down we have to deal with."

"I know," she said, reaching over to place the wine glass on the side table. "Is there anything I can do? Do you need anything?"

She waited while he considered her offer.

"Could you call Christy back?" he finally asked. "I'm sure she'll be pleased to hear we've got this guy."

"Of course."

"Ask her if she can recall any other bits of information Penny might have shared about him. Anything could help."

"I'll call her right now," Hanna said, relieved to have something else to focus on.

"I'm so sorry about Jonathan," Alex said. "We'll figure out how to track him down. I promise."

"Thank you!"

Christy Griffith's phone rang six times and Hanna was about to end the call when she heard her friend's voice. "Hanna!"

"Hi, I'm so glad I caught you."

"My phone was in the other room."

"I have some news," Hanna said. "They have a man in custody they think killed your friend." As she said it, the guilt she was carrying returned and she winced, trying to push the thought aside.

"Oh, thank God!"

"He may also be involved with some sort of plan, but Alex and the FBI are still trying to track that down."

"Who is he?" Christy asked.

"I don't have the details yet," Hanna replied. "But, Alex asked me to check with you again to see if you can remember anything else Penny may have told you about this guy."

She waited for Christy to respond, thinking again about how Penny Hampton might still be alive if she hadn't been so slow to respond to her friend's call for help.

"I don't know, Hanna. I think I've shared everything with you and Alex." Another pause, then, "You know, she did tell me the man was from New York. I think I already told you that. And he said he had some friends who had come down with him to do some work."

"To do some work?" Hanna pressed.

"Yes, but I don't recall anything specific."

Hanna thought for a moment, then, "Do you know of any other friends Penny has here in Charleston."

"Well... I don't know if they're still hanging out, but she used to be close to this woman she worked with. I'm trying to remember her name... Sophia, maybe."

"Okay, that may help, thank you," Hanna said, thinking about this new lead. "If you think of anything else..."

146

"Of course, I'll call you right away," Christy said. "Please keep me posted on what's coming down."

"I will. Please be safe!" Hanna said, ending the call.

She looked at the time on her phone. It was far too late to try to track down Penny's friend tonight. *First thing in the morning*, she thought. She composed a quick text to Alex to alert him to this potential new thread and that she would check it out in the morning.

She turned to look at the half-full glass of wine on the table, then held herself. *Enough, already!*

She went into the kitchen and put on water to boil for a cup of decaf tea before bed. Her thoughts returned to her son, on the road to *who knows where* with his girlfriend. The cold shock of fear returned as she thought about how dangerous Jonathan's addiction had become.

She said a silent prayer as the water began to boil and she reached for the tea bags in the cupboard.

Chapter Thirty-one

Bassam Al Zahari put the secure satellite phone down in disgust on his desk in the richly appointed den of his beach house on Isle of Palms, an exclusive enclave along the barrier islands east of Charleston. His team leader in Charleston was not answering his repeated calls. He had sent a man to the apartment to check on the situation and was expecting a call back at any time. He had his doubts about this man from the beginning.

We are too close now to have this mission fall apart, he thought, standing and walking out the door to a massive deck across the front of the house. The Atlantic lay calm and passive, a slate gray in the fading light of the day. A school of dolphins flowed by just offshore, surfacing one after the other in a steady procession. Further out, the lights of commercial ships sparkled on the horizon.

Imagine the chaos in two days, he thought.

His phone buzzed, and he listened as his man explained he was at the apartment of Tariq Sendaya. His two accomplices were there but had not seen Tariq for several hours.

"They say he often goes out for a long walk."

"How long has he been gone?" Baz demanded.

He listened to the buzz of conversation on the other end.

148

"Over five hours," came the reply.

"Five hours!" Baz was furious and fought to control his emotions. He had to remain strong. "Does he have his phone with him?"

Another conversation, then, "Yes, sir!"

Something's gone wrong, Baz thought, his thoughts racing to decide on the right course of action. "Stay there, make sure everything is set for Thursday morning. Report back as soon as you can." He ended the call and walked back into his den.

As he sat behind his desk, there was a knock at the door. "Come in."

His lead house servant came through the door and bowed. "Sir, arrangements are set for the reception tomorrow evening. We're expecting approximately one hundred guests. Do you have any questions?"

Baz managed to focus his attention away from the attack to respond. "No, I assume you have everything in order."

"Yes, sir!"

"Have you briefed the wives?"

"Of course, sir. They have been fully informed."

"Thank you," Baz replied. "That will be all."

The servant bowed as he backed out of the door.

Baz thought about the gathering planned for the next night, the eve of the ten assaults across the country. Politicians, business leaders, sports and entertainment celebrities would all be in attendance and totally unaware of the disasters that would come to ten major cities across the U.S. the next morning, and no idea their host was the mastermind.

Total fools, he thought. *Useful idiots!*

Glenn Pyke rode alone at 18,000 feet in his Gulfstream G550 jet, a last-minute trip to New York to meet with the editor of the newspaper that was trying to take him down. He was desperate to get the situation under control after he had lost his composure with the reporter.

They had agreed to delay their story on *Green* and his supposed financial misdealings, which of course, were very real. His attorney had strongly encouraged him to meet with the newspaper exec personally and put out this fire, or at least limit the damage. They had a meeting planned for 8 a.m. in the morning over coffee at their offices.

He looked out the window of the airplane, the smell of the rich leather seats permeating the cabin. He sipped from the bourbon on ice in front of him. *Where in hell did they get their information?*

The sun was just about to fall below the far horizon to the west, the sky a deep purple with stars just beginning to show. The lights of several cities sparkled below through wispy clouds.

He was on the verge of full panic mode since the disastrous call with the newspaper. All he had worked for was at stake now. He could see it all crashing down around him. *I might even be indicted!*

And what terrible timing with whatever plot the Saudi was about to launch. Pyke knew he was a minor player in some operation that he had been assured would lend massive support for his cause... and his pocketbook. He had only provided some briefings from past intelligence prepared on various oil companies. He was surprised by Al Zahrani's insistence that *Green* cooperate, but the Saudi's enormous financial incentive on top of threats of catastrophic disclosures of *Green's* true character more than convinced him to take part.

And what if this damned paper has sniffed this out, too!

Senator Jordan Hayes watched the D.C. traffic continue to snarl as his driver maneuvered the big Suburban at a snail's pace across the Key Bridge over the Potomac. The city had dipped into night, and the bright lights of monuments, office complexes, and apartments showed through the cover of trees on both sides of the river.

He had hoped to leave the city earlier but had been caught up in several client calls that ran later than expected. His leased plane was waiting at *Ronald Reagan* to fly him home to Charleston for three days. He had several business meetings lined up, as well as Baz Al Zahrani's party the next night. His new girlfriend, Jenna, who had a shift tonight at the network and was unable to get away, would fly down commercial tomorrow. She had insisted he bring her down for Baz's party. It was certainly going to be a *"Who's Who"* affair and she did not want to miss it.

His cell chirped and he checked the screen. Recognizing the name on the Caller ID, he pressed the link to take the call. Brenda Dellahousaye was the widow of his old associate, Remy, who had been murdered this past year by one of his underlings, the gangster Xander Lacroix.

Remy Dellahousaye had taken over the vast family crime network from his deceased father, the patriarch, Asa. The father had been killed by the Charleston cop, Alex Frank, who couldn't seem to keep his nose out of trouble, Hayes mused. Lacroix had moved quickly to take out Remy and move into a leadership position in the syndicate. In the process, he had found himself serving a long prison sentence, again at the hands of Frank, who had more recently joined the FBI. Lacroix had managed, so far, to continue to run the many businesses of the crime organization from behind bars.

Brenda Dellahousaye and her twin daughters, Ida and Ophelia, had been left without a husband and father, but Lacroix had generously provided for their futures with sizable sums. Hayes knew that Brenda was far from satisfied with Lacroix's supposed generosity. She really cared little about her ex-husband's murder. They had been apart for years, and his many romantic indiscretions had soured their marriage years earlier. She did, however, care about the money.

Hayes said, "Brenda, how are you, my dear?"

"Senator, thanks for taking my call."

"Of course, how can I help you?"

"You know the matter we've discussed previously about our *friend* who is now fortunately behind bars."

Hayes knew where this was going. "Certainly."

"I am close to finalizing plans to deal with that whole situation. As you know, some of Remy's friends and past associates are interested in restoring our position with the business."

"Brenda, we really shouldn't..."

She cut him off, "Jordan, please, hear me out."

He waited for her to continue, concerned about what might come next on an unprotected line.

"I'm going to need some help. That idiot lawyer down here in Charleston was useless. You know, Holloway, who you set me up with."

"Brenda, I don't want to get into this on the phone," he said brusquely. "I'm on my way down to Charleston for a few days. We can meet."

"I assume you're going to Baz's party tomorrow night," she said.

"Right."

"I'll be there, too. We can talk."

"I look forward to it, dear," the ex-senator said.

Chapter Thirty-two

Hanna woke early as usual, the sounds of songbirds and morning traffic filtering through the windows across the front of her apartment. She reached beside her for Alex, then remembered he had called late to say he would stay at his own place since he was going to be down at the Bureau until well into the morning. She pushed the sheet back and swung her legs over to the bare wood floor, wiping the sleep from her eyes and brushing her tangled hair away from her face.

She had a mild headache from the wine the previous night. *Thank goodness, I switched to tea!* she thought as she stood to walk into the bathroom. The face staring back at her was tired and drawn. Her old faded gray t-shirt with the University of North Carolina logo was her usual choice in lieu of pajamas. She turned the cold water on full and splashed her face several times, then pulled the wetness through her hair several times to try to tame the mess.

She walked into the closet and reached for a pair of rumpled khaki shorts and pulled them on before going downstairs. In the kitchen, she pressed ON for the coffee machine. The clock on the stove read 8:15. She was, of course, already running late.

Turning on the small TV on the counter, she also threw a slice of wheat bread into the toaster and pulled butter out of the fridge. She remembered her call the previous night with

Christy Griffith. She had the name of a friend of the now-deceased Penny Hampton. The thought of the murdered girl sent another wave of guilt rushing through her.

Checking the schedule on her phone, she decided she would drive out to the office where Penny had worked and see if she could talk to the friend who also worked there. Any lead on the identity or backstory to the boyfriend and likely killer Alex and the Bureau team had captured yesterday would be of help, she thought.

An hour later, Hanna pulled up and parked in front of a small storefront in a strip shopping center. The name *Hanover Insurance* was on a sign above the office and stenciled on the glass door.

When she walked in, an older woman with almost white hair pulled up in a bun behind a counter greeted her. The rest of the small lobby area was vacant.

"Hi, my name is Hanna Walsh."

"Yes, miss."

"I would like to see Sophia."

"Sophia Guttierez?" the woman asked.

"Yes, can I speak with her please?"

"She doesn't work here anymore, Sweetie."

Hanna cringed at the woman's condescending tone and tried to hold back a snarky reply. "Do you know how I can reach her?"

The woman looked up and scrunched her wrinkled face. "I can't share that information with you."

"This is in regard to Penny Hampton's death," Hanna said.

"Yes, what a horrible thing."

In exasperation, Hanna pressed the truth some and said, "I'm an attorney representing the family and a friend of the family. It's important that I speak with Sophia today." She noticed a nameplate on the side of the counter... *Agnes Godfried.*

Agnes stared back with a frown, then said, "Did Sophia have anything to do with that?"

"No, no...," Hanna replied. "But she may have some useful information to help us build the case against the man in custody for her murder."

"Well, I suppose it wouldn't hurt. I believe I still have her cell." She turned to the keyboard at her desk and typed in some information, staring at the screen. She wrote out something on a message slip and slid it across the counter to Hanna.

"I told Penny she was looking for trouble when she started dating that Arab guy," Agnes said in disgust. "She was always talking about him. Probably a damn Al Qaeda spy, I told her!"

"Thank you, Agnes," Hanna said, looking at the number. "Do you recall anything else Penny may have told you about this man?"

"Nothing I didn't tell the FBI. Never spoke with the FBI before. Kinda gave me the chills!"

Hanna smiled, thanking her again before returning to her car. She started the engine to get the air conditioning running, then called the number she'd been given. After three rings, she heard, "Hello?"

"Sophia?"

"Yes, who is this?" came the impatient reply.

"My name is Hanna Walsh. I'm an attorney representing a friend of Penny Hampton. I think you know her... Christy Griffith."

A pause, then, "What does this have to do with me?"

"I'm working with the authorities to build a case against the man who's been arrested in Penny's murder."

"Excuse me!"

"I'm sorry, I assumed you had heard."

"Ohmigod! Penny's dead!"

"Yes, I'm sorry…"

"Was it Tariq?" the woman demanded.

Hanna hesitated, not sure how much information she should share. Alex would be uncomfortable she was pursuing any of this on her own. "Do you have some time this morning we could meet for coffee? I have a few questions."

"Tell me! Did Tariq kill her?"

"Yes, we think so. He is under arrest for the murder." Hanna replied reluctantly. "Can you please spare a few minutes?"

Sophia said, "I've been seeing his roommate. Penny and Tariq introduced me. I think I need to talk to the police."

"I'm working with the FBI," Hanna said, knowing she was stretching the truth but thinking that her next call would be to Alex to get him involved immediately.

Sophia Guttierez agreed to meet with Hanna and Alex at a breakfast restaurant near her downtown apartment. Hanna had called Alex to let him know she had been doing a little investigative work on her own. She could tell he was not very pleased about her efforts, but when she informed him of finding the Guttierez woman and that she was dating a friend or associate of the man under arrest for Penny Hampton's murder, she got his attention.

Hanna was waiting in a booth with three cups of coffee when Alex walked in. He spotted her in the back and made his way through the tables to join her.

"And why did you think it was a good idea going off and trying to find terrorists on your own?" he said without any other greeting.

Hanna knew this was coming and also knew his concern was legitimate. "I feel like I have an obligation to

Christy to help. I know I let her down by not getting you involved when I first spoke with her. For some reason, I just didn't feel a sense of urgency. Maybe I was too caught up in my own issues, but that's no excuse..."

"You need to stop beating yourself up about this," he said, sliding closer. "Now tell me again how you found this friend of Penny's."

"Christy gave me the name. She told me they were friends at work and that Penny often mentioned her."

"Why didn't the Bureau team speak with her when they went to Penny's office?"

"Because she doesn't work there anymore!"

"And she's been seeing an associate of the man we have in custody."

"Yes, and she's very concerned now that she's learned of Penny's fate. She wants to go to the police."

"We'll call in who we need to after I talk with her," Alex said.

Hanna looked up when a young woman walked into the restaurant matching the description Sophia had given her. She waved to get her attention.

Sophia Guttierez was tall and lean, dark complexioned with long flowing black hair. She was dressed casually in denim shorts and a sleeveless white blouse. Hanna watched as Alex stood to meet the woman and offer her a chair.

"I'm Special Agent Alex Frank with the FBI," he said softly, though there only two other customers in the restaurant far across the room. He showed her his credentials as she sat down.

As Hanna watched the woman sit down, she thought about the fact that Alex was not actually an active agent because of his suspension.

Alex continued, "Hanna has filled me in on your conversation. What's the name of the man you know who's connected to our suspect?"

His name is Hassan," she replied.

Hanna could see real concern, almost fear, in her face.

"A last name?" Alex asked.

"He would never tell me... just Hassan."

"And how does he know the man we have in custody?"

"They share an apartment with one other man."

"Have you been there?" Hanna asked.

"A couple of times," Sophia said and then recited the address as Alex took notes.

Alex reached for one of the coffees and asked, "Do you have any reason to believe these men may be planning some sort of attack?"

"An attack!" She sat for a moment, looking back. "There were a few things said and a few times Hassan behaved strangely, particularly the times we were together with Penny and Tariq." When she said the names, her eyes started to well up with tears.

"What was strange?" Alex asked.

"Well, they speak Arabic, so I never really know what all the chatter is about, but they were obviously stressed about something and were always yelling at each other. But again, I couldn't understand most of what they spoke about together."

"So, you were in the apartment?" Hanna asked. "Did you see anything suspicious or unusual?"

Sophia also grabbed one of the coffees and took a careful sip of the steaming liquid. She shook her head and said, "No, nothing I can recall, though they had three computer stations set up in different parts of the apartment and a lot of papers strewn about."

"Are you still seeing this Hassan?" Alex asked.

"No, it's been about a week. He hasn't tried to reach me or returned any calls." She took a longer drink, then set the cup down and held her face in her hands. "This is really freaking me out! Penny and I start seeing these two guys... kind of a lark. Now she's dead!"

Alex and Hanna both handed her their cards. Alex said, "You need to call me right away if you think of anything else or if this Hassan tries to contact you."

"Obviously," Hanna said, "you need to stay away."

"Don't worry!"

Sophia Guttierez had left a few minutes earlier. Alex was on the phone with Will Foster filling him on these new developments, including the address of two other men who were staying with Tariq Sendaya.

Chapter Thirty-Three

Baz Al Zahrani was near apoplectic with rage. "He still hasn't returned?" he yelled into the phone.

His man staying with the two remaining team members in the Charleston apartment had called with an update as Baz took his breakfast on the deck of his beach estate.

"And you still can't reach his phone?"

"No sir."

Baz sat for a moment, reflecting on the situation. "You should have called me earlier! You need to get them out of there now! Take everything with you. Nothing can be found there. Get them set up at the safe house."

"Of course."

"And have this man's family picked up and held in a secure place."

"I understand."

Baz ended the call, his hand shaking as he tried to lift a coffee cup to drink.

Special Agent Will Foster came back into the interrogation room after his call with Alex Frank. Tariq Sendaya was sitting with his face down on the hard steel table, apparently asleep, his hands still shackled.

"Wake him up!" he barked to his assistant, Jimmy.

Sendaya came back to wakefulness slowly, moaning at the discomfort of a long night locked to this table and sleeping upright in a chair.

"Tariq!" Foster yelled out. "Listen to me!"

The man turned and squinted.

"We've tracked down your friend, Hassan."

Foster watched as Sendaya was unable to hide his surprise. They had two teams interrogating him throughout the night, giving him little time to sleep. So far, no one had been able to get anything of substance from him.

"Where is my lawyer?" Sendaya protested.

Around midnight, Foster had made a call to D.C., and sent a request up the chain to get authorization to use *"Enhanced Interrogation"* methods. His request was denied. The political environment was too sensitive to return to techniques, some would call torture, that had been widely used earlier in the war on terror. He *had* been given approval to use a range of psychoactive drugs that would induce much more cooperative behavior from suspects. An expert was being flown in and should be arriving soon. He had also been given approval to delay the suspect's request for a lawyer.

In the meantime, they continued to press their captive. "We're sending a team to your apartment as we speak, Foster said. "They will all be arrested. This will go much easier on you if you cooperate now."

Tariq continued to shake his head slowly in defiance, then he closed his eyes and whispered, "They will kill my wife and my sons!"

Special Agent Sharron Fairfield led the six-person assault team as it approached the door to Tariq Sendaya's apartment. One agent took the opposite side of the door from her, weapon drawn. Two others were poised to use a heavy steel battering ram to breach the door. The others were stationed at exits to the building front and back.

Fairfield knelt and slipped a thin telescoping camera under the door. The picture coming back displayed on her cell phone. A sensitive microphone would also pick up any noise or voices inside.

She turned the lens across a full range of angles into the shabby apartment. There was no sign or sounds of occupants. She had a warrant to enter the property, but texted Foster first for final confirmation. His response came almost immediately. *Go!*

She nodded to the two men with the ram. They moved forward quickly, and with a powerful thrust, the door was smashed from its hinges and fell inward onto the floor.

Fairfield burst in first, followed by the rest of the team, all with weapons in firing position.

"FBI!" she yelled. "Everyone on the floor, now!"

The agents fanned out in all directions and in less than a minute returned to the hall entry to confirm the apartment had been abandoned. Fairfield reported back to Foster, who ordered them to tear the place apart for any evidence.

Hassan Al Farid thought he might wet himself. The man named Ahmad, who had come to the apartment looking for Tariq, was a frightening person. When he first arrived and found that their partner had not returned from the previous day, he had made it very clear he would not hesitate to put a bullet in both of their heads if they did not comply with every request.

They were riding now in a big SUV with the windows blacked out. He and his partner were in the back seat under the watchful eye of the man, while another drove. He had no idea where they were being taken. The assault was planned for the next morning, and even without Tariq, they would be able to carry out the mission. *They wouldn't kill us now when we are so close to fulfilling our holy Jihad.*

Thirty minutes later, outside the city, the driver pulled into an unmarked drive and down a narrow sand road, heavily wooded on both sides. Around a few turns, an old house came into view, roof sagging, paint peeling. There was one other vehicle, a late model van, parked outside.

The car came to a stop and the man in front commanded, "Out, now!"

Hassan turned when he heard another car coming up behind them. It was their rental car they had been using back in Charleston. The driver got out; another man Hassan did not recognize.

"Inside!" their captor ordered. "And take the boxes in the back with your equipment."

This was the first indication that perhaps they would be allowed to complete their work, and Hassan sighed in relief. *But, where is Tariq?*

Chapter Thirty-four

Detective Nate Beatty sat at his cluttered desk in the downtown Charleston Police precinct. He had been looking through the case files for the Phillip Holloway murder. It had been three days since the attorney and his lover had been found murdered, and Beatty was no closer to arresting a suspect.

The prime suspects, his wife Grace Holloway, the deceased woman's husband, Trevor Falk, and the Gangster Xander Lacroix all had a motive for the killing. Lacroix was in prison, but his men could have easily pulled off the hit if, somehow, Holloway had again managed to get on the wrong side of the mob he was doing legal work for.

Grace Holloway continued to confound him. She was the most obvious suspect. She had admitted to being in the house the night of the murders, supposedly just finding the bodies, then running in fear without calling 911. His follow-up discussions had yielded a bit more. She was desperate for money, had even asked Hanna Walsh for help in recovering money supposedly still squirreled away somewhere in the Caribbean. She knew about the attorney's gun, which had still not been discovered and may have likely been the murder weapon.

Trevor Falk, the husband of the now-deceased Jennifer Falk, didn't send off the same warning bells in Beatty's head.

He had a reasonable alibi for the night of the murders, and though he was certainly upset his wife was having an affair with her colleague from the law office, he seemed genuinely surprised when informed of that fact.

Lacroix was always an enigma. In the past, there were multiple instances of rivals or threats to his business who were disposed of, usually in extremely violent fashion, much like the murders of Holloway and Falk. He had avoided prosecution for years until the most recent case of the Remy Dellahousaye murders and his attempt to kill both Beatty's old colleague, Alex Frank, and his girlfriend, Hanna Walsh. The dead lawyer had repeatedly angered the Dellahousaye crime family even before Lacroix took over. There was even a surprisingly failed hit when the ruthless hitman known as Caine failed to complete his assigned kill on Holloway.

When Beatty confronted Lacroix about the murders, he didn't get a strong sense either way if the gangster was responsible. It also seemed unlikely a professional mob hit would have been so messy with an innocent person also killed and evidence like spent shell casings left behind.

Beatty looked over the contents of the files in front of him on his desk, including the gruesome photos taken the night of the murders. He shook his head, trying to think through all the scenarios and possible suspects. *And who else haven't we come up with yet with a reason to kill Phillip Holloway*, he thought.

He glanced at the physical evidence that had been taken that night. The cell phones of both victims had been seized. Passwords had been cracked and the forensics teams had pulled anything of interest. He reached for a document that listed all the appointments Holloway had on his calendar for the days following the murder. Beatty had looked at this before but hadn't seen anything that raised an eyebrow.

Glancing down the list again, he noticed an entry scheduled for tonight... *Party – Baz Al Zahrani – Isle of Palms – 7:00 pm.* Beatty, like most people, knew the high profile and wealthy Saudi, particularly since one of his palatial homes was here in the Charleston area.

It suddenly struck him as odd that Holloway would have an invitation to this gathering. What was his connection to Al Zahrani? Beatty had heard the rumors about the source of the Saudi's wealth, mostly legitimate businesses in a wide range of industries, but there were also occasional issues raised about more nefarious income streams, but nothing had ever been proven.

It wasn't a stretch to assume Holloway may have been involved in some of these pursuits. *He certainly had a track record*, Beatty thought.

The other file on his desk was the murder of Penny Hampton in her apartment downtown. The FBI had kept him informed about the arrest of the suspected killer, Tariq Sendaya, but continued to hold him as they were supposedly looking into some other affairs the guy may have been involved in.

He picked up his own phone and called Alex Frank.

"Hey Nate," came the reply.

"Alex, how you coming on the Hampton murder? You need to turn this guy over to us."

There was a slight pause on the other end, then Alex said, "Nate, we've got a situation coming together."

"A situation?"

"Let me check with Foster and we'll call you right back."

"Okay, but we need to get involved in this as soon as possible."

"I understand," he heard Alex say, and they ended the call.

Ten minutes later, Beatty's cell buzzed on his desk. Alex Frank was on the Caller ID. "Whatta ya got?"

"Nate, I've got Will Foster, Bureau chief down here on the line with me."

"Yes, how are you, Will?"

"Okay," he heard Foster reply. "Detective, we've been interrogating a suspect in the Penny Hampton murder..."

"And why are we just hearing about this now?" Beatty cut in.

"We have reason to believe this man is connected to a potential terrorist attack."

"Terrorist!" said Beatty, glancing over as another detective sitting nearby turned to look at him. "Here in Charleston?"

"We're still trying to sort this all out," Foster continued. "I've checked with DC, and we think it's time to call local and state authorities in on this. There are other possible cities targeted, we believe."

"What can I tell our Chief?" Beatty asked.

"I'm going to schedule a teleconference for later this morning," Foster said. "I'll get the invite to you to share with whoever your department thinks should be involved."

"Okay, fine. Now, what have you got on this guy on the Hampton murder?" Beatty asked.

Foster said, "Alex, will you brief Detective Beatty? I need to run and get back to this call we're setting up."

Alex said, "Nate, this looks pretty airtight. We've got surveillance footage of the perp at the woman's apartment on multiple occasions, including before and after the estimated time of death. He's married to a woman in New York but has been having an affair with the Hampton girl while he's down here in Charleston."

"And you all think he's tied into a terrorist attack? Beatty asked.

"We're trying to pin it down."

"Where and when?" Beatty asked, irritated they hadn't been called in earlier.

"Foster will brief you guys on everything we know later this morning. By the way, we've got a lead on a second guy dating a friend of Penny Hampton."

Beatty sighed and shook his head. "I need to inform the Chief," he said. "He'll probably have my ass for not knowing about this earlier since it's linked to an active murder investigation."

"Sorry, Nate. It's always *need to know* with the Feds."

"Sure, sure... I'll look for Foster's invite."

"Okay, man."

"Hey, one more thing. I'm working on the Holloway murder, and I'm looking at his calendar. He's invited to a gig at Bassam Al Zahrani's place out on the beach tonight. I'm trying to make the connection, but it seems our dead lawyer must have been doing some legal work for this wealthy Arab guy."

He waited for Alex to reply. Finally, "You feeling a little *twitchy* about this like I am?"

"Yeah," Beatty said. "Something doesn't smell right."

"We've got three murder victims now, a possible Arab terrorist as a suspect in one of the cases, and now an Arab oil tycoon invites our dead lawyer to a party."

"I wonder who else is coming to this party tonight?" Beatty asked.

"I'll fill Foster in. We may have some additional guests at this shindig tonight. I'll get back to you."

Chapter Thirty-five

Alex turned back to Hanna, still sitting beside him in the booth at the coffee shop. She had been listening intently to his guarded conversation with Nate Beatty. She had been giving him incredulous stares as he and Will Foster quietly informed Beatty of a possible terror attack here in their city. She hadn't been able to hear everything on the conference call, but she had apparently heard enough.

"An attack here in Charleston!" she said in a quiet voice, looking across the room of the coffee shop, a lone patron against the far wall and two workers behind the counter, hopefully out of earshot.

"Let's go outside," he said.

Out on the sidewalk, they began walking to their cars.

"What's going on?" Hanna asked.

They got to her Honda, and Alex leaned against the side, looking in both directions before beginning. "We haven't gotten much out of this guy yet. His two pals at the apartment have suddenly split, leaving the place entirely scrubbed."

"Somebody tipped them off?"

"Not sure, but they're gone."

"I didn't tell you this, but D.C. intelligence agencies are picking up chatter around the country that indicates something is coming down, maybe in multiple cities."

"Really!" Hanna replied. "And they think here in Charleston, too?"

"We're still trying to find out. Foster is stepping up the interrogation on the guy we picked up."

He watched as Hanna leaned against the car hood beside him. She said, "Should we be worried about Sophia and this other guy she's been seeing?"

Alex thought for a moment. *One girlfriend is already dead.* "I'll talk to Foster about it. We may have someone keep an eye on her, maybe Charleston PD now that we're getting them involved."

"Alex, I don't want any more blood on my hands!"

"Okay, I'll call Foster on my way back down to the office." He pulled out his phone and scrolled quickly down to check for messages. Turning back to Hanna, he said, "You ever hear of a rich Arab guy named Al Zahrani?"

"Who hasn't? He's in the media all the time."

"Well, he's got a big house out on the beach and throwing some kind of party that Phillip Holloway was invited to."

"Phillip?"

"Yeah, Nate found it in his calendar."

"And you think there's some connection?"

He thought again about the web of events and individuals that seemed to be crossing paths. "I need to get back and check in with Foster, but we may want to have someone check out this event tonight."

"How worried do I need to be about terrorists in my backyard?" Hanna asked.

He reached over and pulled her close. "You'll be my first call." He kissed her on the cheek and stepped away. "Obviously, you need to keep this between us until the Feds decide anything can be made public."

"Of course," she replied, reaching into her purse for her keys. "I've been trying to reach Jonathan, but he still won't pick up."

"I'm sure he'll let you know as soon as they get settled. I don't know what more we can do at this point."

"Don't you guys know how to trace cell phones?"

"Well... we do, but we would need a warrant to trace a U.S. citizen like that."

"Alex, please..."

He hesitated, but said, "I'll see what I can do. I've got Jonathan's number in my *Contacts*."

"Thank you!" She came over and hugged him, then turned to unlock her car. "Please have someone check on Sophia."

"I will."

Hanna drove through midday traffic on her way back to her office. The AC in her old Honda was running on fumes, and she had it set to *Max* to try to keep the temperature bearable in the heat of the day.

She tried to remain calm about her son's flight from rehab. On the one hand, she was reassured by the fact that Jonathan was an intelligent young man and would typically do the right thing. Unfortunately, an addiction to drugs didn't always bring about the most responsible actions. *Maybe he'll come to his senses.*

She thought again about Sophia Guttierez and her link to a man who may well be a terrorist planning an attack on the city. Her friend Penny had already been killed, probably because she had become aware of their plans.

The thought of Sophia suffering a similar fate was more than Hanna could stomach after her delay in getting people to reach out to Penny. She had Sophia's number in her phone *Recents* and pressed the call button.

"Hello?"

"Sophia, this is Hanna Walsh again."

"Yes?"

"I don't mean to scare you, but I'm concerned for you after what's happened to Penny."

"You think I'm not scared out of my mind?"

"I think you should stay away from your home and office until this gets resolved," Hanna said.

"I work from home. With my new job, I can work anywhere."

"Are you there now?"

"No, I'm just pulling in. Had to stop for a couple of errands," Penny replied.

"I really don't think you should be there alone. I've asked Alex to have someone watch your house, but they're all so busy..."

"I have a roommate," she replied.

"Still..." Hanna paused, her thoughts trying make sense of all that was going down. "Why don't you come to my office. I have a spare desk, and worst case, there's a sofa bed in my apartment there."

"I don't want to be a bother..."

"No, really! I insist," Hanna said.

She heard Sophia sigh deeply. "Well, okay. Thank you. I need to get a few things from inside before I come over."

Hanna gave her the address.

Another member of Baz Al Zahrani's vast network of assets sat in a car down the street from Sophia Guttierez's apartment building, shaded by a tall live oak. He perked up when he saw a car pull to a stop in front. The woman who got out matched the description he'd been given. He knew there was a roommate who would be away at work this time of day.

I'll give her a few minutes to get settled in, he thought. As he waited, he checked his phone and saw a new text message. *No loose ends.*

Understanding immediately the implied death warrant he had just been given to carry out, he pulled on a dark ball cap and sunglasses. He looked in all directions and used his car mirrors as well to make sure there were no threats or witnesses. From the glove box, he pulled out a Glock semi-automatic pistol. He ejected the clip and checked again to make sure the magazine was fully loaded, then slid it back into the gun. He reached back for the silencer and screwed that onto the barrel, then placed the weapon in a backpack on the seat beside him. He checked his cell one more time for the woman's apartment number.

As he started to get out, he saw her coming back to her car with a small bag. She got in and quickly sped away down the street past him. He waited a few moments, then pulled out and made a U-turn to follow her.

Chapter Thirty-six

Alex came off the elevator and walked across the hall to enter the offices of the FBI in downtown Charleston. The receptionist, a young woman named Barbara, greeted him with a nod and buzzed him through to the back offices.

Everyone knows I'm on suspension, Alex thought. *How long until someone reports or lets slip something about my continued work here to higher-ups?*

He made his way to the back of the building where the interrogation room holding Tariq Sendaya was. When he came up to the window in the wall masked by a mirror inside, he saw Will Foster and another man sitting across from the suspect. The second man was putting a syringe and other paraphernalia back into a black case on the table.

Sendaya looked exhausted, and his head began to bob forward as the drugs quickly took effect.

Foster began questioning him again, and for the first couple of minutes, Sendaya continued to resist and stonewall. Then, Foster asked slowly and deliberately, "Tell me the full names of your two associates."

The man hesitated, now weaving some in his chair. The man beside Foster rose and went around the table to steady him. "Who are they, Tariq?"

With a noticeable resigned tone, Sendaya replied in a low monotone, "Hassan Al Farid and Juto Farouk."

Foster looked at the D.C. interrogation expert holding the witness and nodded. "And where are you all from?"

"New York."

"Where were you born?"

"Hassan and I were born in Syria. Farouk in Yemen." The man's eyelids were half closed now.

"Why are you here in Charleston?"

Alex watched Sendaya jerk back, seeming to fight the drugs that had taken over his will to be silent.

"Why are you here?" Foster pressed.

"We have a mission."

"What is your mission?"

The man tensed again, trying to resist.

"Tariq!"

"We have a boat."

"What kind of boat?"

"A center cockpit runabout."

"What's on the boat?"

Again, Sendaya strained at the shackles holding him and his eyes closed shut, his face now etched with new determination.

"What's on the boat, Tariq?"

The answer came forced and almost a whisper. "Explosives."

Hanna's assistant, Molly, stuck her head through the door. "Hanna, there's a Miss Guttierez in the front to see you.

"Oh, thank God!"

"What?" Molly asked in surprise.

Hanna got up and dropped her pen on the desk, following Molly back out to the lobby. Sophia Guttierez was standing and looking at a painting of the skyline of Charleston on the wall done by one of Hanna's friends.

"Sophia!" Hanna said.

The woman turned and smiled. "You're sure this isn't a bother?"

"No, I'm just glad you're here and safe." Hanna took her by the arm. "Here, let me show you the office you can use."

When Hanna had her settled in the spare office across the hall from her, she said, "Let Molly know if you need anything. The kitchen is back down the hall, and there are drinks in the fridge and some snacks on the shelf. Please help yourself."

Sophia was spreading her work and laptop out on the desk. "Thank you! You're being much too kind."

It's the least I can do, Hanna thought before backing out and returning to her own office.

She was prepping for her next meeting when her cell rang, and she saw Alex was calling. "Hi, how's it going down there?"

Alex's tone was more serious than usual. "Our man is finally talking, with some pharmaceutical encouragement, but we still don't have it all nailed down. Something serious is coming down though. Still trying to find out when or where."

"Terrorists are planning an attack here in Charleston?" Hanna said again in disbelief.

"Appears so, and likely several other cities. We've got state and local cops involved now, and the resources committed to this are growing rapidly."

"I really can't believe this," Hanna replied.

"The reason I called," Alex continued, "Nate Beatty sent a squad car over to check on Sophia. There's no one there."

"Oh, I should have called you. She's here with me."

"What!"

"I just thought..."

"Hanna, this woman has been involved with people who are planning a deadly attack. They've already killed her friend who likely knew too much."

She could tell he was really angry. "I didn't think it was safe for her to be home alone."

Hanna looked to the door when she heard a commotion out front, first some loud conversation and then shouting.

"No, you can't go back there!" Molly yelled.

What the hell? Hanna got up and moved quickly to the door. She peered out just in time to see a man with a hat and sunglasses on and a backpack over his shoulder going into the office she had left Sophia. A bolt of fear swept through her.

She heard Alex's voice call for her on the phone back on her desk. *Hanna!* And again, more urgently, *Hanna!*

From Sophia's office, *No, please!*

Then Hanna jerked back in horror as she heard the sound of three soft wisps of air. She knew immediately they were silenced gunshots. Her feet felt like they were lead and she was unable to move.

From behind, Alex was still shouting out her name.

She turned and yelled, "Alex, we need help! Send help!"

Then the man came out of the office and saw Hanna standing six feet away. His face was masked with blue mirrored sunglasses, but in a split second, she could tell he was Middle Eastern. The panic racing through her was overwhelming and she couldn't bring herself to move, to run, anything to get away.

She watched as the assassin slowly raised his gun and then it was pointing directly at her face. The narrow black hole at the end of the silencer was like a snake ready to strike. In an instant, she knew she was going to die, and her last conscious thought was of her son, Jonathan.

The man seemed to smile just as Hanna saw his hand tighten on the gun's trigger.

Then Molly came racing back from the lobby, yelling something unintelligible.

Just as the gun jerked with another quiet pop, Hanna saw Molly run into the man, knocking him to the side.

A pain more severe than she had ever imagined ripped across the side of her forehead, and she fell to the floor.

On her side, Hanna could faintly see the man throw Molly to the ground, then turn the weapon on her. The gun bucked three more times before she lost consciousness, and everything faded to darkness.

Hanna! came another desperate cry from her phone.

Chapter Thirty-seven

Alex was running down the hall shouting into his phone to a 911 operator.

Foster came out of the interrogation room. "What's going on?" He followed him into his office as he was ending the call.

Alex looked over from his phone, a deep rushing panic searing through him. "It's Hanna," he managed. "She had the Guttierez woman come over to her office. They must have followed her!"

"Who followed her?" Foster asked.

"Whoever that asshole down the hall is working for!" he spat, tempted to run down and strangle the guy until they got everything they needed. "I have to get over there. I have to get to Hanna!"

"Let me send Jimmy with you in case you need backup."

"911 is sending cops and paramedics." He could feel himself starting to lose control. He took a deep breath, then another. "She was on the phone with me and then there was some kind of commotion or argument, and now she won't or can't come back to her phone. I gotta go!"

He grabbed his bag on the desk, where he carried his service weapon and two extra clips of ammo. "I need Jimmy, now!" he said as he headed for the door.

When Alex braked to a quick stop in front of the old house where Hanna had her offices and apartment, there were two Charleston PD patrol cars already parked nearby with lights flashing and an ambulance with the back doors open directly in front of the walk up to the house. As he got out, another ambulance pulled up and parked in the middle of the street. One of the cops came out to start redirecting traffic.

Jimmy came around the car and joined him, running up to the house. Another cop tried to stop them, but he flashed his FBI creds and raced past the man into the front lobby of the law offices. A third cop came up quickly trying to hold them both back.

"FBI!" Jimmy yelled, holding up his creds.

As the cop stepped back, Alex stopped in horror. In the doorway leading back to Hanna's offices, two legs in black leggings lay prone on the floor, motionless. One shoe had come off and then he saw blood splattered on the wall to the side.

He forced himself forward and got far enough to see it was Hanna's assistant, Molly, lying on the floor. She was on her back, her arms spread wide, the bullet wounds on her face and another leaking blood into the white blouse above her chest. From her vacant eyes and the severity of gunshot wounds, Alex was certain she was dead.

He pushed down the nauseous bile rising in his throat and hurried further back. In an office across from Hanna's, he was surprised to see Nate Beatty come out.

"She's gone, Alex."

He stopped and staggered back a step. "What do you mean gone?"

"The Guttierez woman. She took three rounds."

"Where's Hanna?" he pleaded.

"I don't know," Beatty said. "She wasn't here when I arrived. The second paramedic team said a woman was taken to the hospital with a gunshot wound to the head."

Alex felt his knees almost buckle. "Which hospital?"

A paramedic on the floor next to Molly yelled out, "University!"

Jimmy said, "Alex, I'll stay here. You go!"

He was on his way through the lobby when he heard Beatty yell out, "There's no sign of the shooter, but we're starting the search!"

Alex didn't stop to respond. He ran across the street, jumped into his car, and sped away.

The University Medical Center was less than a mile away. He kept trying to push aside images of Hanna on an ambulance gurney, blood leaking from her head. When he arrived, he quickly pulled in the driveway for *Emergency*, leaving his car running in front of the main entrance as he raced inside.

A woman at the admission desk called him over. "Can I help you?"

He held up his FBI badge for the second time that night. "Hanna Walsh! They just brought her in with a gunshot wound!"

The woman stood and said, "I'll let the doctors know you're here."

Alex wasn't going to stand and wait. He followed closely behind the woman and was by her before she could protest. A nurse saw him coming and rushed to intercept him.

"You can't be back here!" she said, holding her arms wide, as though she could corral him.

Holding his badge up, he said, "Where's Hanna Walsh, the gunshot victim?"

"Really sir," the nurse said, "you'll have to wait. They're working on her right now."

He pushed her aside and saw a flurry of medical staff assembled in and around a curtained area up to his left.

He moved more slowly now, a measured pace, unsure and terrified of what he was about to see.

A male nurse tried to hold him back, but he dragged him along to the opening in the curtain. He saw two men and a woman in green scrubs leaning in over Hanna. He knew it was her from her slacks and shoes he had seen earlier. He couldn't see her face, which was obscured by the medical staff. A monitor beside the bed squawked and flashed. A quick glance showed there was indeed a pulse, however weak. *Thank God!*

One of the doctors working on Hanna, a young woman, turned at the commotion and saw Alex. She stepped away and came over.

He held up his badge again, "I'm Special Agent..."

"I don't care who the hell you are!" the doc said. "You need to be out of here, now!"

Alex could now see a large white paper dressing over Hanna's face with a hole cut where they were tending to the wound. The paper was soaked in blood, and his panic went through the roof.

Almost in defeat, he said, "She's my fiancé..."

The doctor pushed him gently back out away from the medical team. Alex kept looking back, hoping to see some sign of life from Hanna's still body. One arm lay limp to the side of the bed and blood had dripped, leaving long trails down to her hand. He saw the engagement ring he had given her, and he closed his eyes and took in a deep breath.

He heard the doctor say, "We're not sure what we're dealing with yet. There's some damage to the skull at the side of her forehead, but we don't know yet about trauma to the brain."

He forced himself to look back at the doc. "She's going to be okay, though?"

"I can't say yet, sir. You need to let us do our jobs."

With that admonition, he began slowly backing out.

The doctor said, "Someone will come out as soon as we know something. Please wait outside."

He staggered back into the waiting area, several other people there staring at his wild and panicked expression. He managed to find a seat against the wall and tried to gather his thoughts.

After all they had been through together, he couldn't imagine losing her now. He had finally found a woman he loved and trusted and would do anything for, and now she was lying perhaps near death on the other side of that door. He couldn't hold back the tears that began welling up in his eyes.

He didn't notice the woman coming through the entry from outside until she sat down beside him. He looked up to see Sharron Fairfield from his office.

"Jimmy called us from Hanna's office," she said, reaching for his hand. "How is she doing?"

He just stared back at her, unable to respond.

"What's happened, Alex?"

Finally, he said, "I don't know…" He stopped and struggled to continue. "They don't know yet."

He felt her hand squeeze his more tightly. "I'm so sorry, Alex. Is there anything we can do, anyone we can call?"

He immediately thought of Hanna's son, Jonathan. He pulled his phone out and found the number. The call went quickly to Voicemail. "Jonathan, it's Alex. Your mother's been injured… badly. You need to call me." He left the number and ended the call.

Fairfield said, "Charleston PD is still looking for the shooter. Do you have any idea what happened?"

Trying to focus, he said, "Hanna had the Guttierez woman, the one who had been seeing the second terrorist suspect... she had her come to her office thinking she would be safer there. Someone must have followed her to Hanna's."

"Jimmy confirmed both the Guttierez woman and the office worker there are both dead."

Alex thought about how close Hanna had been to Molly, and his heart sank again as he thought about how much this would devastate her... if he ever has the chance to tell her.

"Crime scene techs were arriving when Jimmy called," she said.

He nodded, numb and confused, tears still dripping down his face.

"Alex, really, what can I do?" Fairfield pleaded softly. "Is there anyone else we need to call?"

He thought of Hanna's father in Atlanta, but then remembered he was away traveling with his wife, Martha, Hanna's stepmother. "You've met Hanna's father, Allen Moss," he said, breathing deeply to try to calm himself. I think he's traveling but could you get word to his office to call me?"

She nodded and stood to step away to make the call.

He let his head fall back against the wall and he closed his eyes tight, pushing even more tears down his face. He thought of the last time he had seen Hanna on the street outside the coffee shop where they had met Sophia Guttierez earlier in the day. He was certain he could still feel the light brush of her kiss on his cheek as she left him there.

Chapter Thirty-eight

Grace Holloway's first reaction was to turn around and run.

She had to park over a block away from Hanna's office and had just turned the corner onto her block. Ahead, the street was closed off with cops everywhere, two ambulances, and general chaos. *The last thing I need is more cops,* she thought as she kept walking, her curiosity getting the best of her.

As she got closer, she realized all of the commotion was in front of Hanna's old house. *What the...!*

She was only a few steps from the walk up to the house when a uniformed cop came up quickly to stop her. "You'll have to step back, ma'am."

Grace looked up at the house as a gurney was being taken out the front door by two paramedics with a black body bag zipped closed. She felt her chest grow tight and she gasped. "What's going on here?"

"Please, ma'am. You need to step back," the officer said again.

"My friend runs this place. What's happened to her?"

"I'm not at liberty to say..."

Then Grace saw a familiar face coming through the door, the detective, Nate Beatty. He saw her at the same time and came over quickly.

"What are you doing here?" he asked, waving the uniform away.

She was too stunned to reply at first.

"Miss Holloway, what in hell are you doing here?" Beatty pressed.

"What's happened to Hanna?"

"I asked you a question!"

"I was coming to see Hanna. We need to talk about something."

"And you just got here?" Beatty asked.

She struggled to answer, surprised by his question. "Well, yes... I just parked around the corner." She turned, pointing down the block.

Beatty called the uniform back over. "We're going to take Miss Holloway downtown for questioning."

"What are you talking about?" Grace said incredulously.

"Can I have your purse, please?" Beatty asked.

Grace was flabbergasted. "No! You have no right!"

Beatty held out his hand, "Your purse please, now!"

A deep hole in the pit of her stomach opened up as she realized what he was about to find. She slowly handed him the bag and watched as he opened it, looked inside, and then back at her with a narrowing gaze.

"What is this?" he asked, holding the bag open so she could see inside. Her husband's gun was on top of the other contents of the purse.

She tried to recover her composure, but her voice cracked when she said, "It's my gun..." She watched as Beatty pulled the bag up to his nose and took a deep sniff.

"This weapon has been fired!"

"Alex, it's Nate. How is she?"

His friend didn't respond at first and then, with a weak voice, said, "They just took her into surgery."

186

"What have they told you?"

He heard Alex take a deep breath.

"The round caught her on the side of head..." He stopped, again taking a deep breath. "There is damage to the skull, but they aren't sure about injury to the brain. I just don't know... they don't know yet."

"I'm sorry, man," Beatty said, his heart truly going out to his old colleague.

"Any leads on the shooter?" Alex asked.

"Well, you're not going to believe this," Beatty began. "We've got Grace Holloway in custody. I found her outside Hanna's office. She said she was coming to see her."

"What!"

"She had a .45 in her purse, recently fired."

"You've got to be kidding me!"

"There were no shell casings left at the scene, but we've got forensics looking for a match on rounds we've recovered from the..." He stopped, not wanting to say the word *bodies*.

"Nate, this makes no sense," Alex said. "Grace would have no reason to hurt Hanna, let alone the others."

"She said she came from a shooting range, practicing with the gun."

"Where did she get a gun?"

"We're still not clear on that," Beatty said. "I've got her down the hall. I wanted to check in with you before I get started with her."

"Thank you for calling," Alex said, resignation in his voice.

"I'll keep you posted, man. My prayers are with you and Hanna."

"Thank you..."

Beatty walked into the small interrogation room where they had been holding Grace Holloway for the past half hour.

She sat at the small table, her hands folded in front of her. Dark circles under her eyes stood out against the pale gauntness of her face. She was startled by his entrance as if she had been lost in thought about something.

She quickly gained focus and stood in defiance. "Detective, this is nonsense! What am I doing here?"

"Sit down, Grace!" he ordered, and she reluctantly complied. He sat across from her. "We have two dead bodies, and your old friend, Hanna Walsh, is currently in surgery with a gunshot wound to the head."

"Oh my..."

"And you show up with a loaded gun, recently fired."

"I told you, I was just down at the shooting range."

"Again, where did you get the gun?" Beatty asked.

"Who died at Hanna's office?"

"Tell me where you got the gun!"

Grace looked away for a moment, then back to Beatty. "It's my husband's. I got it from our safe at the house."

"What safe?"

"It's hidden in Phillip's den."

"Why haven't we heard about this before?"

"I don't know..."

"Why did you get the gun?"

Grace leaned in. "You still haven't found Phillip's killer! What if he's looking for me! I need to protect myself!"

"Do you know something about your husband's killer you're not telling us about?" he pressed.

"No! That's your job!"

"Grace, please..."

"Why haven't you found this guy!" she shouted back. "And now Hanna!"

Beatty shook his head in frustration, rubbing his hands back through his short-cropped hair. "Grace, we have a ballistics team checking your gun against the rounds fired at the scene. We're also checking with the shooting range you claimed to be at. I'm going to hold you here until we learn more. You were given your Miranda rights back at the crime scene. You might want to call your lawyer."

Chapter Thirty-nine

Baz Al Zahrani walked barefoot in the sand, his white pant legs rolled up. Low waves swept in, washing over his feet. The late morning sun was high and hot, with few clouds to break the glare. The beach ahead was nearly deserted. The air smelled of salt and fish and beach fires from the previous night.

Two men with concealed weapons walked twenty yards behind. He pulled his sat phone from his back pocket when it buzzed. It was his man at the safe house.

"What's happening?" Baz asked.

"Our men are secure here," came the reply. "Still no sign of the third."

"We have to assume he's in custody."

"Perhaps he ran, knowing this was a suicide mission."

Baz thought for a moment. *It was possible.* "We have to assume he's in custody and talking. He knows we will take this out on his wife and children. I really don't think he's tried to get away."

"The packages are complete here, ready to go for morning."

Baz knew he was referring to the explosives assembled by a separate team at the safe house here and nine others around the country.

"You'll supervise the transfer to the boat," Baz said. It wasn't a question.

"Of course."

"How are our two drivers faring?"

"They will be fine. I've made it very clear they have no other options."

"What of the other matter?" Baz asked, referring to the elimination of another threat at the office of the lawyer.

"The girlfriend has been dealt with. There was some collateral damage, but our man is away safely."

"Good," Baz replied. "I want a status report from all the other sites within the hour."

"Yes, sir."

Baz put the phone back in his pocket and stopped to look out over the ocean. A light southwest wind pushed out from shore. The water was a deep blue with low swells reaching out to a gray haze on the far horizon. Otherwise, the skies were clear and would be again in the morning for the attack.

Three long shipping freighters coasted out far to the east on their way into Charleston Harbor. Baz smiled as he watched them slip slowly along. *What a shame this beautiful beach and those for miles in both directions will soon be an environmental disaster*, he thought.

Glenn Pyke could not keep the sweat from pouring out on his forehead. He dabbed at it repeatedly with a handkerchief he kept pulling for the breast pocket of his sport coat. It was a rare occasion for him to dress in anything other than shorts and sandals, but his meeting with the newspaper editor required a more professional look.

His lawyer had briefed him repeatedly on how to handle this interview. He had rehearsed his responses several times on the flight up from New Orleans as well as overnight at the hotel here in Manhattan.

Pyke's stomach was doing flip turns and he hadn't been able to touch the room service breakfast he had ordered. He looked up in surprise when the conference room door opened, and the editor and a reporter came in. It was the same person from the first interview.

For the next twenty minutes, they both grilled him about financial improprieties at *Green*. His practiced responses seemed to be working, and his confidence was growing. Then came the next question.

The editor said, "We have a person from your organization who has come forward."

Pyke felt the churn in his gut again.

"They are willing to testify to significant fraud and embezzlement, at your direction, I might add."

"You're bluffing!" Pyke shouted, his composure suddenly gone.

The editor shared the name of the informer, and Pyke blanched. It was the assistant to his Chief Financial Officer. She would know everything. The CFO was deeply involved in all the financial manipulations.

"We're done here!" Pyke said, standing and reaching for his leather bag.

"Mr. Pyke," the editor continued, "we're running with the story this afternoon. I imagine the Justice Department will be the next call you receive."

Pyke's airplane was at 2,000 feet and climbing out of *LaGuardia Airport*. He had just come out of the elegantly appointed bathroom at the front of the plane, where he had vomited repeatedly.

He sat down to collect himself and, when he felt sufficiently recovered, pressed a number on his cell. His CFO answered on the first ring.

"How bad is it?" the man asked.

"It couldn't be worse!" Pyke said, his anger rising. "That little blonde you brought in and have been banging, by the way, and yes, I know all about that."

"Glenn..."

"Shut-up! Your young protégé has turned on us. She's going to testify. She's already talked to the paper. The story is going to run this afternoon."

"Oh shit!" came the panicked reply. "What are we going to do?"

"*WE* are going to execute Plan B and get the hell out of the country. I'm on my way back to New Orleans to pick up a few things and then taking off. You are going with me."

"I have a wife and kids!"

"You'll send for them when this blows over."

"And when is that going to be?"

"I have no friggin' idea!"

Chapter Forty

Alex looked at his phone as it buzzed in his hand. The Emergency waiting room was empty for the first time since he'd arrived.

"Jonathan, I don't know where in hell you are, but you need to get back here, now!

"What's going on?" came the reply.

Alex gathered himself and tried to contain his anger with the boy for running away and not only endangering his own life but scaring the hell out of Hanna. "Your mother has been injured in a shooting incident."

"What! Is she... is she okay?"

"I don't know. I honestly don't know. She's in surgery. You need to get back here, now!"

The boy didn't answer at first, then said, "We're back in Chapel Hill."

"Why in hell..."

"We needed to get away... we need some time."

"You need to get back here," Alex insisted.

"Of course, I'll leave right away. You really don't know anything?" Jonathan pleaded.

"I'll call you back as soon as the doctors have anything to share."

"Thank you, Alex. I'm sorry," the boy said sadly.

"Just say a prayer for your mother!"

Agent Fairfield had brought him a sandwich and coffee from the hospital cafeteria and then left to go back to the office. There was still no update on Hanna's shooter other than Beatty's call about Grace Holloway.

He still wouldn't bring himself to believe Grace had been involved in this. The Guttierez woman must have been the target. The terror cell they were trying to track down was the only logical explanation for what was, otherwise, a senseless shooting.

Alex had dealt with his own near-death experiences on three occasions from gunshot wounds, one back in the war and two more recently on duty. He knew how traumatic the experience was, even in recovery. *Hanna is going to recover!*

He was going crazy waiting with no word from the doctors. He reached for his phone for a moment of distraction. He pressed the contact for Will Foster, not expecting him to pick-up, but he answered right away.

"How's she doing?" Foster asked.

"I still don't know."

"How long has she been in surgery? Sharron filled me in."

"Over an hour, I guess," Alex replied, looking at the clock on the wall. "How are you coming with Sendaya?"

"The drugs started wearing off and he clammed up. The doc is working on him again and I'm about to go back in. We tried to get to his family in New York, but they're nowhere to be found."

"Oh great," Alex said, "these guys have already got them."

"Looks that way."

"Let me know..." Alex began.

"You just stay put and be there for Hanna."

"Right."

195

"Hey, before I go back in, I've been thinking about this Al Zahrani guy. Had some folks up in Washington dig a little deeper. CIA finally shared that he had a brother back in sand land who got taken out by a Hellfire last year."

"Al Qaeda or ISIS?" Alex asked.

"The former. You think this Baz fellow might harbor a few bad feelings?"

"Nice of CIA to get off their ass and share," Alex said in disgust.

"I've got Fairfield going out to this gig he's throwing this afternoon. She'll tighten the screws and see what this guy has to say."

Alex wanted to get back into the search, but knew his place was here. He needed to be here for Hanna.

The not so *honorable* ex-Senator Jordan Hayes waited in the backseat of the limousine with his driver, standing by to pick-up his girlfriend who was coming in commercial for Al Zahrani's party. They were pulled up to the curb at *Arrivals* at the Charleston airport. A security cop came up and knocked on the driver's window, asking them to move the car. The driver flashed the credentials of the United States Senate and the cop nodded and walked away.

Another perk, Hayes thought, smiling as he watched the exit door up ahead. He had just gotten off the phone with his friend, the editor of the New York paper. They were bringing the hammer down on Glenn Pyke and his *Green* organization in this afternoon's issue.

Good, Hayes thought. I'll have some positive news to share with Baz tonight.

The two big glass doors slid aside, and Jenna Hawthorne came out, turning heads from all directions with her fabulous and famous face and curves.

The driver got out and took her garment bag, taking it around to put it in the trunk. Hayes pushed open the door and she slid in beside him, leaning in to give him a wet kiss on the cheek.

"Hey, honey," she cooed. "Sorry I couldn't join you earlier on the jet. These commercial flights are a bitch! Everyone wants an autograph and a picture."

He felt her hand slip between his thighs as the car started away. He regretted they hadn't had that private time together on the plane. *It was always fun!*

"Let's get to my place downtown," he said. "You can get cleaned up and changed."

"Do I look like I need to get cleaned up?" She smiled back.

"You know what I mean."

"Pop, it's Alex."

"Hey, son, what's up?" answered Skipper Frank, standing on the deck of the *Maggie Mae* back in port and docked in front of his house.

"Hanna's been hurt."

"Excuse me! What do you mean, hurt?"

"We think a shooter came into her offices down here in Charleston to take out someone she was helping," Alex said. "Unfortunately, Hanna got in the way."

"Did you say *shooter*?"

"Yeah, she's been shot, pop."

"Oh, son. I'm so sorry," the Skipper said, walking back into the pilothouse of the old boat and sitting in his captain's chair. "How's she doin?"

"I still don't know," Alex said. "She's in surgery. Looks pretty bad."

"God, I don't know what to say."

"I just wanted you to know," Alex continued. "I'll call back when I learn anything more."

"Okay son. God, I'm sorry!"

His son ended the call, and Skipper looked out the windows down the river toward the ocean. *Alex and Hanna have had to deal with so much... and now this*, he thought.

He felt the boat list a bit as someone came onboard. He looked back and saw his ex-daughter-in-law stepping through the walkway. As usual, Adrienne was barely dressed in short denim shorts, a sleeveless white t-shirt cut low in front, her feet bare. Her long auburn hair was piled in wandering curls on top of her head.

She spotted him in the pilothouse and came in. Her heavy perfume cut through the smells of fish and shrimp and diesel oil.

"Hey, old man!" she said with a big smile.

"I'm not your *old man*."

"Sure... hey, are you going out today?"

"Yeah, in a while."

"Scotty would like to go."

He had taken her son on one other occasion. The boy didn't really want to go the first time. His mother just wanted him out of her hair for some time to herself. *Probably has a new guy she's shacking up with*, he thought.

"Leaving around three," Skipper said, looking at his old Timex. "Tell him not to be late and to be ready to work. This ain't no joy ride!"

"Thanks, old man!" she said, laughing and turning to leave.

"I ain't your old man, dammit!" he growled. "Hey wait..."

Adrienne stopped and turned back in the doorway.

Alex called, and Hanna's been hurt bad."

"What happened?"

"Crazy gunman came into her office. She's still in surgery. Thought you should know."

"How's Alex doing?"

"Not great."

"Sure. Hey, I'm sorry."

"Yeah, just thought you should know."

Chapter Forty-one

Alex looked up at the wall clock again and realized he'd been in the waiting room for nearly two hours. He was exhausted not only from the stress of all that was coming down, but also from being up half the night with Foster interrogating Sendaya. He pressed his palms to his forehead and squeezed his eyes tight, trying to fight off the fatigue.

He couldn't bring himself to believe there was even the slightest chance Hanna wasn't going to come out of this just fine. He could not imagine losing her like this. Yet, he was also aware there was only so much doctors could do if an injury took a dangerous turn, particularly a brain injury.

He also kept coming back to who was ultimately responsible for the carnage over the past few days. There was a cell of terrorists who had already killed on multiple occasions, had left Hanna near death, and now may be planning a massive attack on U.S. cities. There was a rage burning deep within him that only intensified when he saw Hanna lying on the hospital gurney earlier.

His law enforcement work continued to put her in jeopardy, though he remembered the initial connection to Penny Hampton, Sophia Guttierez, and their terrorist boyfriends had come through a past friend of Hanna. Still, now he was on suspension and perhaps out of a job soon. *Maybe it's for the best.*

He shook his head vigorously to try to think positively, to will Hanna to survive if that's what it took. They would sort the rest out later.

He didn't hear anyone approach and was startled by a woman's voice.

"Mr. Frank, excuse me."

He looked up and saw one of the doctors he had confronted outside Hanna's room earlier. He stood up quickly, his breath coming in shallow gasps. He quickly scanned her face for any sign of hope.

"We believe we have her stabilized."

He heard the words but wasn't entirely sure how to react. "Stabilized?" he repeated.

"The wound has been thoroughly examined and treated. Preliminary x-rays and a CT scan show a severe skull fracture but no penetration of bone or bullet fragments in the brain cavity."

He was beginning to feel the fog lift around his head. "She's going to be okay, then?"

"She most likely has a severe concussion which if not carefully monitored can still cause some serious issues," the doctor continued. "She's under heavy sedation, so we really won't know definitively until morning."

"She's not conscious?" he asked, his confidence waning again.

"No, and we want her to have uninterrupted rest tonight or as long as possible."

"So, I can't see her?"

"She won't know you're there, and we want to minimize the risks of disturbing her."

He nodded slowly, taking it all in. He bowed his head and took a deep breath. "Thank you, doctor. I appreciate all you've done."

"Of course."

He handed her one of his cards. "Will you make sure everyone here tonight knows how to get in touch with me?"

She nodded.

Another thought struck him, and images of a killer coming back to finish a job while he lay injured flashed through his mind. "How is your security at night?"

"Security?"

"Hanna was almost killed by an assassin today. If he finds out one of the three victims survived and could likely identify him, he may have reason to return to finish his work.

The doctor grimaced. "I would have to say that we're not really prepared to fend off assassins."

"I wouldn't think so. I'm going to speak with one of my contacts down at the Charleston PD to request an officer on duty here overnight, he said.

The thought of the need for security for Hanna brought back the chill of fear he'd been feeling all afternoon. Without thinking, he reached out to the doctor with open arms, and she returned his hug. "Thank you, doctor."

She stood back and smiled, then turned and walked back through the door.

Alex stood staring. Beyond, Hanna Walsh lay unconscious, a serious head wound that could have easily killed her and an uncertain prognosis that could still have many dangers. He thought again of the men responsible and knew deep in his heart he would do whatever it took to find them and kill them all.

Alex's call to the Charleston PD proved effective and they assigned two officers to take shifts until morning to guard Hanna's room. He would be there first thing to relieve them.

He walked into the FBI offices downtown and back to the interrogation room. He looked through the observation window. Tariq Sendaya had his head down on the table, apparently sleeping. No one else was in the room. He fought the urge to go inside and deal with the man personally. *Someone needs to beat the truth out of this sonofabitch.*

A voice from behind caught him by surprise. "How's she doing?"

Alex turned to see Will Foster coming up. His face was tired and haggard. He'd obviously had little time for sleep. "The doc says they have her stabilized, whatever the hell that means."

"That's good, right?"

Alex nodded. "The bullet caused a serious skull fracture on the side of her forehead, but there were no bone or bullet fragments in the brain. She's got a bad concussion and will probably have a hell of a headache when she comes to."

"I don't quite know how to say this," Foster said, "but I can't figure why the shooter didn't stay to make sure she was gone. He clearly didn't hesitate with the other two women... three rounds each."

Alex had been having the same thoughts. "Thank God he didn't. The only thing that makes sense is either he thought his shot was fatal, or he was interrupted by something or someone and left quickly."

"Well, whichever, she's a lucky girl."

"Yeah," Alex responded, thinking how close Hanna had come to dying with the others. It sent a chill through him, and he flinched.

"You okay?" Foster asked.

"I'll be alright." He looked back into the interrogation room. "What's the latest with this asshole?"

"The doc is having trouble getting the drugs to work again. The guy has totally clammed up. He's got another dose working now and we're about to go back in. D.C. still won't let me use any hard stuff, though I've got a guy coming down from Langley who specializes in that. The longer we go without getting a line on these guys, the more dangerous the situation becomes. We may have to go there."

Alex said, "Anything more on this Al Zahrani guy?"

"We just got a full brief on the guy. Big money. Seems all legit, though there are possible links to bad guys... drugs, weapons, the usual."

"And his dead brother's Al Qaeda connection," Alex added.

"Right, but no direct ties to any terror groups that we can find yet. With all that money though, it's not a stretch to think he's funneling cash to them and who knows what else."

"You said Sharron's going out to this event he's hosting this afternoon?" Alex asked.

"Yeah, it's at 5 o'clock. She'll be headed out soon."

"I'd like to go with her."

Foster hesitated. "I don't think that's a good idea."

"Why is that?"

"We're pushing this already, Alex. You're supposed to be on the sidelines. I need all hands on deck right now, but I need to keep you in the background."

Alex turned back to look at their captive, a man who planned to inflict serious damage and death on the city, whose associates had already killed several innocent people and nearly killed Hanna. His rage burned even deeper as he felt helpless to find them, to stop them.

"I need to go find the doc," Foster said. "I want to get back to work on this guy." He left and headed down the hall.

Alex didn't respond. He looked back at Tariq Sendaya. The image of Hanna lying in the hospital... so much blood. The rage that was consuming him suddenly boiled over. He walked quickly around to the door to the interrogation room and walked in, closing it behind him. He flinched at the smell. The man hadn't showered in days and the stink of fear was all over him.

Alex's face felt hot, and his hands tingled as he grabbed the man by the hair and jerked him up. "Wake up, you sonofabitch!"

Sendaya moaned, the drugs dulling his senses.

Alex slapped him hard across the cheek with his other hand. "I said wake up!"

Sendaya's eyes met Alex's. They were bloodshot and clouded.

Alex hit him again, this time harder. "Where are the others!"

Another moan, but no attempt to pull away or protest.

A third slap sent the man hard back against the chair as Alex let go of his hair. His temper burned full out of control. "Where are they?" he shouted, leaning in inches from his face. He was about to throw a punch into Sendaya's nose when Foster burst through the door and wrapped his arms around Alex, pulling him away.

"Enough!" Foster screamed. "Have you lost your mind?"

Alex struggled to get loose to go back after Sendaya. "Let go!"

Foster threw him up against the wall and held him there with one hand, the other pointing a finger at his face. "This is totally out of line!"

Alex was about to swing at Foster when some sense of reason seemed to come back to him. He let his arms fall to his side and tried to catch his breath.

"You may have ruined all the progress we've made with this guy!" Foster fumed. He pushed away from Alex, seeing he was regaining his composure. "You need to go home!"

Alex looked down at Sendaya, now hunched over the table, moaning something unintelligible. *I may have killed this guy,* he thought, struggling to gain control.

"Alex, do you hear me?" he heard Foster say.

He looked up at him, still breathing heavily. "I'm sorry...."

"I want you out of here! Go home!"

"I'm sorry," he said again. "I need to help you find these guys."

"Not in this condition," Foster scolded. "Go take care of Hanna. She needs you now."

A sad resignation came over him and he pushed past Foster and out of the room.

Chapter Forty-two

Hanna's first conscious thought was someone had taken a large railroad spike and driven it deep into the side of her head. Her eyes were crusted shut and her body felt pressed down into the bed. She was lying on her back. She managed to open a slit in her eyes. The room was dark.

Where the hell am I?

She lifted her right hand to try to clear her eyes and felt it held by some wire or tube. She moaned as a wave of pain pulsed in her head. As her vision focused, she saw the outline of a window to her left with light around closed blinds. There was a door open to a hallway beyond. Looking over, she saw there were multiple leads from her body going up to a monitor hanging beside the bed with readouts for various vital functions she didn't care to decipher.

A hospital. What am I doing here?

She lifted her other hand to her head and felt bandages wrapped tight almost down to her eyes. When her hand grazed over the left side of her forehead, the pain flared, and she moaned louder.

Hanna lay back, trying to convince the pain to subside.

An image flashed and she saw Molly on the floor, a man standing over her, a gun.

No....!!!

It all started coming back to her. *Sophia... Molly... the man with the gun. The gun was pointing at me... the barrel of the gun aimed directly at my face... the pain across my forehead as I fell... the man pointing the gun at Molly... pulling the trigger.*

Oh God!

She felt tears forming in her eyes and an overwhelming sense of sadness, then fear. *Who was this man? Why had he come? Sophia! Are they both dead?*

She turned and saw a red button hanging from a cord on the side of the headboard. She reached for it, pushing through the pain, and squeezed it for help. A nurse came in moments later.

"You're awake!" the woman said.

"Where am I?"

"University Hospital."

"What happened?"

"You were brought in earlier today with a gunshot wound to the head."

Hanna closed her eyes, and all the images came back.

"How is Molly?" she asked.

"If you mean the other two women, I'm sorry, they didn't survive."

Hanna felt her heart lurch. She touched the dressing on her head again. "This pain is unbearable. Do you have something I can take?"

"I'll check with the doctor and be right back."

"Wait, how bad is this?" Hanna asked.

"You were very lucky, Hanna."

"Lucky!"

"A few millimeters further in and you may not have made it," the nurse said, looking at the monitor and holding Hanna's wrist to check her pulse. "Your fiancé was here earlier. We thought you'd be out all night, so we convinced him to leave a while ago."

"Alex has been here?"

"Yes, he made quite a scene down in *Emergency* trying to find you."

"I need to call him," Hanna said. "Where's my phone?"

The nurse went over to the closet and looked through her personal things. "You must not have had it with you when they brought you in. You can use the phone there on the nightstand. Would you like me to dial?"

"Yes, please," Hanna said, thinking Alex must be terribly worried. She gave the nurse the number and watched her make the call. *And what about Jonathan? Where is he?*

The nurse handed her the phone. Hanna watched her leave and closed her eyes again, trying to block out the horror of the scenes back at her office. She had asked Sophia to come so she would be safe. *And now she's gone! Someone must have followed her.*

She heard the call click through.

"Hello?"

"It's me."

"Hanna!"

"I just woke up."

"Oh, thank God! Alex said. "They told me you would be out, maybe all night... that I shouldn't disturb you. How are you feeling?"

"My head feels like I got kicked by a horse. A nurse just went to find a doctor to get me something for the pain."

"I was just on my way back to my place. I'm not far. I'll be right over."

"What happened?" she asked, the frightening images flashing in her mind.

"Someone from this terror cell must have followed Sophia Guttierez back to your office. They were probably waiting for her at her apartment."

"And Molly's gone?" She was barely able to say the words.

"I'm sorry."

"Oh, Alex, what have I done?"

"This isn't your fault! You were trying to help. These guys would have found her anyway."

"Has anyone talked to Molly's family?"

"Yes, the police are reaching out."

She had known Molly for years and counted her as one of her closest friends, almost family. *This can't be happening!*

"We need to find Jonathan!" she said, suddenly remembering the rest of her family.

"I spoke with him."

"You found him!"

"I left a message on his cell you'd been hurt. He called right back."

"Where is he?"

"They went back up to Chapel Hill. He's on his way back."

"Back to school!"

"Yeah, I know. We're also trying to get a message to your dad."

"Thank you... I don't want him to worry."

"Let's just worry about you for now. Try to get some rest. I'll be there soon."

When Alex walked into Hanna's room, it was darkened from the closed blinds, but he could see she was asleep again. The nurse told him on the way in they had given her something for the pain that included a sedative. He pulled a chair quietly up to the side of the bed, trying not to wake her.

Her head was heavily wrapped in white dressings. A small circle of bloodstain stood out on the left side of her forehead. The sight of the blood got his anger flaring again. *We will get these guys, Hanna!*

The monitor at the other side of the bed sent an eerie glow over the dark room. Occasionally it would buzz or beep softly. Her pulse seemed steady, and he tried to let the relief that she had survived this deadly attack soften the anger that was overwhelming him.

He got up and walked quietly out into the hall and down to the nurse's station. Hanna's nurse was sitting behind the counter. "How long do you think she'll be out?" he asked.

The woman looked up with a thin smile. "Hard to say, but it could be several hours."

"Okay... good," he responded, thinking again about the men who had brought this violence and death to their city. "I'm going to run out. Here's my number," he said, handing her a card. "Please call me right away when she wakes up."

"We will."

"Tell her I'm trying to find the people who did this."

The nurse nodded as he turned to leave.

Chapter Forty-three

Alex sat in his car in the parking lot at the hospital. He had just *Googled* the address for the Saudi Al Zahrani's house out on Isle of Palms.

Will Foster had been very clear he was to stay on the sidelines, and after his outburst with the suspect down at the FBI office, he was clearly out of the investigation... *at least officially*, he thought.

He checked GPS on his phone and saw it was about 20 miles out to the beach house. He started the car and pulled out.

The security gate on the drive out to Isle of Palms was the typical grand structure, heavily landscaped and manned by a uniformed security guard. Alex pulled up and rolled down his window as the guard came out.

"Yes sir, how can I help you?" the man asked.

"I'm going up to Mr. Al Zahrani's house," Alex said, knowing it wouldn't be that easy.

"It's a private party, sir. What is your name?"

"I'm not on the guest list." He pulled out his FBI creds wallet and showed it to the guard. The man looked closely at the I.D., then peered back with a puzzled expression.

"I already let one of your people through. Mr. Al Zahrani's security man approved it."

"Yes, Ms. Fairfield, right?"

The guard nodded.

"I'm joining her," Alex said, studying the guard's face.

"A moment please," the man said, starting back into the office.

"Wait!" Alex said, and the guard turned back. "This is official business. It will compromise our investigation if they know I'm coming."

"Investigation?"

"I need to join Agent Fairfield," Alex said firmly. "This is a matter of national security."

The guard hesitated, thinking through how he should handle a second FBI agent trying to gain access.

"Time is essential here... Officer Crandall," Alex stressed, reading the guard's nameplate.

The guard seemed to appreciate the recognition as a fellow "officer of the law," though certainly much further down the line in terms of law enforcement.

"Very well, Agent Frank," the guard relented. "Do you know how to get down there?"

"I have GPS," Alex replied, holding up his phone.

"The guard nodded. "Just go to the second stop sign and turn left. You'll see all the cars.

"Thank you, Crandall."

"Certainly, sir. Good luck with your investigation." He went back inside, and Alex saw the gate go up in front of his car.

Senator Hayes had his arm around the waist of Jenna Hawthorne, making sure everyone at the party knew the beautiful and famous news anchor was there with him. They were talking with another couple. The man was a retired Hall of Fame pitcher for some major league baseball team Hayes couldn't remember. He had become even more famous lately as the celebrity pitchman for commercials selling reverse mortgages to senior citizens. The crowd for Baz's party continued to grow around the deck of the fabulous pool looking out over the ocean.

He looked back up to the house and saw Brenda Dellahousaye come out on the verandah. He excused himself and walked over to meet her coming down the steps.

He opened his arms to greet her. "Ah, the lovely Mrs. D," he purred into her ear as they hugged and gave each other kisses on the cheek.

"Hello, Senator," she replied, stepping back. "Do you have a minute?"

"Certainly." He reached for her arm and led her away across the lawn where they could speak freely."

"I mentioned we are ready to move forward," she began. "Three of Remy's former and most loyal soldiers are prepared to move against Lacroix on my final go ahead."

"I'm pleased to hear that, Brenda," Hayes replied. "It's only right that the Dellahousaye's carry on with managing the *business*. Is there anything I can do to assist?"

"There are certain legal issues that remain cumbersome."

"Legal issues?" Hayes asked, amused that a woman attempting to take back a crime network was concerned about legalities.

"The lawyer, Holloway, that you put me on to was useless."

"And now he's dead."

"Not only was he useless, but also a bit too greedy," Brenda continued.

"I have another name for you."

"Please, we need to move quickly. I'm afraid Lacroix is getting suspicious."

He gave her the name and number of another lawyer from the contacts in his phone. When she was done tapping in the information on her own phone, Hayes said, "I'll call him tonight and give him a brief overview before you call, okay?"

"Thank you, Jordan." She leaned in and kissed him on the cheek.

Alex parked at the end of a long line of cars along the lushly landscaped road leading past the drive to Al Zahrani's house. He got out and went around to the trunk, which was popping open from his key fob. He reached in for his shoulder holster, putting it on and moving his weapon from his belt. In the back seat, he grabbed a blue blazer and put it on to cover the holster.

As he approached the driveway, Alex saw two men posted, both of Arab descent, wearing black coats that were most likely also obscuring weapons. They moved to block his path and he held up his credentials. "I'm here to join Agent Fairfield," he said, matter-of-factly.

The two men conferred quickly in an Arabic dialect Alex certainly didn't understand. "Do you have a gun, sir?" the man on the left asked.

Alex pulled back his coat.

"I'm afraid we cannot allow that," the other man said.

Alex thought for a moment and then decided not to protest. "I'll be right back."

He pretended to put the gun in the trunk but instead slid it into the waistband on the back of his pants. He returned to the guards, holding his coat open again, showing the empty holster. Neither man spoke as he passed.

Serious dudes!

Ahead, he could see lights through the heavy cover of tall live oak and other flowering trees. He also heard music, and it grew louder as he approached the house, which now came into view. There were even more cars parked along a large circular drive along the grand entrance to the house and in a parking area in front of a four-car garage to the left. All of the vehicles were expensive sports or luxury cars or big SUVs.

Another guard stood at the open double doors to the house. Alex saw the radio earpiece and assumed the man had been alerted to his approach. Indeed, the guard waved him through with a stone-faced nod.

Inside, Alex was struck by the opulence of the huge gathering room leading off to other elegantly appointed areas and to a vast wall of windows across the ocean side of the house. The music was louder now, a classical piece he recognized, but had no idea of composer or whatever.

There were several groups of people standing about in conversation with drinks in hand, all dressed very fashionably, the men in suits or sport coats, the women in dresses, both long and short. He didn't recognize anyone and started toward the doors out to the big pool and beach beyond.

The early evening sun was still high, and the ocean water was a deep blue out beyond a row of low dunes. As he walked out, Alex saw easily a hundred people milling about in small groups around a long pool with bright blue water that curved in several directions and framed by an infinity edge across the line of dunes. Dozens of palm trees and other ornamentals were clustered about, creating a lush tropical ambiance.

He had found a picture of Al Zahrani online and scanned the crowd to find the man. He was walking down the smooth granite patio, continuing to look for his man, when he saw one familiar face. The defrocked Senator Jordan Hayes stood across the pool, a beautiful young woman on his arm that Alex recognized from a TV news show, and several other people laughing at something Hayes had just said. He also knew Hayes from his association with the Dellahousaye family and previous run-ins.

He started in that direction when he was touched on the shoulder from behind.

"What in hell are you doing here?"

He turned to see the familiar face of Sharron Fairfield.

"Hello," Alex said, stopping to explain.

Fairfield continued, "Will said you were to stay away."

He didn't answer.

"Alex, you need to get out of here. I'm taking care of this."

"Have you talked to Al Zahrani?"

"No, he hasn't come out yet. Alex, really, you need to leave."

"Let's say I'm here... unofficially." He turned and started to walk around the pool.

"Alex!"

He had Hayes in his sights and the two men made eye contact. Alex watched as the man's expression turned suddenly serious. He said a few words to the group he was with and stepped away, coming around the pool to confront him.

Fairfield came up alongside him. "Don't do this..."

Hayes walked up and smiled. "Who called in the cavalry?" he said in his deep, distinguished voice.

"Senator," Alex acknowledged. Fairfield stood beside him now and didn't speak.

"Special Agents Frank and Fairfield, the dynamic duo. To what does Mr. Al Zahrani deserve the honor of your presence?" Hayes held a cut crystal glass of bourbon on ice with a napkin catching the condensation.

Fairfield said, "Senator, sorry to interrupt..."

Alex jumped in, "And how do you know this guy? You seem to run in all the right circles," he said, with no attempt to hide the sarcasm.

Hayes didn't seem fazed by the affront. "Baz and I go way back. He's a dear friend."

"Of course, he is," Alex said.

Fairfield pulled at Alex's arm, but he didn't budge.

"I thought after the Dellahousaye affair, you'd be a bit more careful about the circles you run in," Alex said.

Hayes continued to remain calm and even smiled. "How are the Dellahousayes?" he asked. "Martha and the twins?"

"I wouldn't know," Alex responded.

"Alex, I think..." Fairfield began, turning to start walking away.

Alex cut her off. "I understand your friend, Mr. Al Zahrani, had a brother who had a Hellfire missile dropped on his head. Al Qaeda, I hear."

Hayes stared back hard now, the smile gone. "I wouldn't know about that. How unfortunate."

"Unfortunate? For the Al Qaeda asshole!" Alex said, trying hard to push the man's buttons.

"For Baz," Hayes replied. "To lose a family member like that."

"So, where is our host tonight?" Alex asked, turning to look around the crowd.

Hayes said, "Well, actually, he's coming over right now."

Alex turned in the direction of the man's gaze and saw an immaculately dressed middle-aged man of Arab descent walking through the crowd, occasionally stopping for a quick *hello* with some of the guests. He spotted the Senator and kept on toward them.

Alex watched the smile return to the Senator's face as he welcomed their host. "Ah Baz, so nice to see you!" He reached out his hand and the two men shook and gave each other an embrace. "Let me introduce you to two of my past acquaintances, Alex Frank and Sharron Fairfield from the FBI."

Alex watched the man's left brow lift in apparent surprise though he was sure security had briefed Al Zahrani on their arrival. "The FBI! To what do I owe this pleasure?" He didn't offer a hand in greeting.

"Mr. Al Zahrani..." Fairfield began.

"Baz, please." the man said.

Alex jumped in. "We heard about your brother's run-in with our anti-terror forces last year."

"Alex!" Fairfield whispered, pulling at his arm again.

Baz didn't flinch but stared back with dark penetrating eyes. "My brother lost his way, I'm afraid."

"Seems some of his friends may have found their way here to Charleston," Alex pressed.

"How do you mean?"

Hayes tried to cut Alex off. "Baz, I really have some people you have to say hello to."

"We have one in custody," Alex continued.

"I'm really not sure what you're suggesting, Agent Frank," Baz said, a small crack in his composure evident in his expression.

"We've uncovered a cell, perhaps several across the country, who are planning a serious attack on U.S. soil," Alex said. "I would think you'd be interested in helping us."

The tension in the air continued to rise as Al Zahrani stared back, a slight twitch starting in his left eye.

"Frank!" Hayes said, "I think that's really enough. You have no right..."

Several people conversing in a group nearby looked over in surprise as Haye's admonition drifted out over the crowd.

Alex ignored him. "We have a man, Tariq Sendaya, in custody, a Syrian."

"Syria is a very large country, Agent Frank," Baz replied.

"He's been very cooperative," Alex continued. "We should have his two associates picked up any time now," he said, hoping the lie would trigger some response.

"Well, I hope your investigation continues to be fruitful," Baz said. "I really must attend to my other guests."

Alex glared back at the man, then said, "These men have already killed at least three innocent people here in Charleston. I would think you'd be more interested in working with us." He chose not to mention the near-fatal attack on Hanna.

"I'm afraid I wouldn't be of much assistance."

"Apparently not!"

Baz let the accusation slide. "I understand your concern, and good luck with your efforts to head off this incident." He walked away before Alex could respond again, followed closely by two security men. A third stepped between Alex and Fairfield and the Senator.

"I must ask you to leave now," the big man said in a low, threatening tone. "This is an invitation only affair."

Alex looked back, not making any effort to leave.

Hayes said, "Always a pleasure, Frank," then stepped away.

The looming security man continued to stare down Alex and Fairfield, who said, "I think we have what we came for, Alex."

He watched Hayes return to his girlfriend, then Al Zahrani mingling with his other guests. *This guy is dirty!* he thought, fuming he was this close to a man who may likely be plotting to kill even more Americans.

"I will see you out," the security man said.

Alex felt Fairfield's hand on his arm, guiding him away.

Chapter Forty-four

Alex heard Will Foster yelling on the other end of the call. He had never seen the man so angry.

"I don't know what you were thinking!" Foster fumed.

Alex didn't respond.

"I want you down here, now! I want your creds and service weapon on my desk! I should have done it earlier. Alex... do you hear me?"

"Loud and clear." He was still on a knife's edge of anger following his encounter with the wealthy Saudi. "Will, this guy has to be brought in."

"You have nothing to go on! Just get your ass back here!"

"Will, there's no question in my mind, this guy is involved. He may even be pulling all the strings."

"Alex, I just had a call from the Director's office. Some very powerful people in Washington have already been informed of your little cowboy stunt and are not very happy the FBI is targeting this guy. He apparently has some very influential friends in D.C."

"Dammit, Will, I know this guy is dirty!" He looked in his rearview and the lights from Fairfield's car were still close behind as daylight was beginning to fade. "Will!"

"Just get back down here," Foster said. "Sendaya just broke."

Alex and Fairfield walked back into the Bureau office and found Foster in his office on the phone. The lights of the Charleston skyline shone back beyond the windows behind him. He gave Alex a malevolent glare.

"Yes sir, I understand." He put the phone down and stood, holding out his hand. "I want your creds and your gun... now!"

"Will...."

"Now!" Foster demanded. "That was my boss. My ass is on the line because of your little escapade. I should have known better than to keep you involved. I understand completely now why you're on suspension. You have no filter. You don't know to keep within the guardrails. I thought you would have learned a lesson after the Lacroix disaster."

Fairfield cleared her throat, standing to the side.

Alex said, "Will, I really don't give a shit about your boss or my suspension! We've got a bunch of assholes, including this guy out at the beach, who are about to bring down a major shit show on America, and we need to go outside the damn guardrails!"

Foster hesitated.

"What did you get from Sendaya?" Alex asked.

"You're out of this, now. I want you to go home or wherever, just out of my sight!"

"Will, you need all the help you can get..."

"I said, you're out!"

Alex placed his creds wallet and gun on the desk and stepped back, shaking his head. "How many more people have to die before we bring the hammer down here, Will?"

"We'll take it from here," Foster said, pointing to his door.

Alex parked his car in a dark section of street, one block down from the FBI office parking garage. He looked at the time on his phone, just a little past eleven. He thought of Hanna, lying in terrible pain just a few blocks away at the hospital, the men responsible about to launch a major attack. There was no way he was going to stay out of the fight.

He popped his trunk and got out to go around to the back of his car. His personal 9mm semiautomatic was in a locked steel box in the spare tire compartment. He placed the weapon in his belt holster and a second clip of ammo in his pocket. He returned to his seat and called the nurse's station at the hospital.

"This is Alex Frank. I'm checking on Hanna Walsh. Is she still sleeping?"

"Hello, Mr. Frank. Yes, she's still out," said the nurse. "The doctor gave her some strong stuff for the pain."

"You have my number when she wakes up?"

"Yes sir."

"Thank you."

He placed the phone on the seat beside him.

The first of three black SUVs pulled out of the garage and turned left, headed away from Alex toward the expressway. He was sure Foster was in the lead vehicle. They were obviously following up on whatever they had learned from the captured terrorist. He gave them another block's head start and then pulled out to follow.

On the highway, he stayed about a quarter mile back from the convoy. They were headed east out of the city toward the ocean. *Where in hell are they going?* he mused, trying to think through the intel Tariq Sendaya must have provided… hopefully, the location of the other two terrorists.

And what am I going to do when we get there? he thought, knowing Will Foster wouldn't let him anywhere near the takedown.

About ten miles out, all three vehicles exited onto a secondary highway Alex was not familiar with. He followed, again far enough back not to raise suspicion.

When they all turned again a few minutes later, Alex stopped just back from the intersection and waited. The name on the street sign was unfamiliar. The road appeared to be gravel. After he felt he had given them enough of a gap, he turned onto the road with his headlights off. The taillights from the FBI convoy were probably a half-mile ahead.

He kept on driving slowly, the lights from occasional streetlights up in the heavy tree cover and from the few houses along the road sufficient to help him see. The convoy ahead turned to the right, and again, he pulled over to give them time.

One minute later, he pulled to a stop on the side of the road just before the driveway the SUVs had turned down. He got out and walked far enough that he could see down the narrow trail. There was no sign of the vehicles or their lights. He decided to proceed on foot but first drove forward several hundred yards and pulled the car off into the woods where Foster and his crew wouldn't see it if they came out first.

He walked back to the narrow drive and started walking slowly, keeping to the right and low, not wanting his silhouette visible to the FBI team ahead. The night sky above, through the break in the heavy tree cover, was filled with stars, and the air smelled of wood fires nearby. The screech of tree frogs helped to cover the sound of his approach.

The trail turned several times and then he stopped suddenly when he could see the looming shadows of the SUVs parked ahead and the low murmur of voices. As quietly as he could, Alex stepped into the heavy cover of trees and palmetto scrub, trying to put the thought of angry snakes out of his mind. He kept moving forward carefully, aware of every footfall.

Behind the cover of a wide trunk of a live oak tree, he could see eight people assembled in the thin light from the night sky. Several wore the clear outline of tactical gear and helmets, assault rifles pointed to the ground. He guessed they were from the Counter Terror force out of Atlanta.

Then, the group broke apart and two men went left into the woods and two to the right. He could see Foster now at the center of the remaining force, continuing to whisper orders, then leading the remaining team members forward.

Alex continued to follow as closely as he could. He watched as Foster and the assault team crouched low, and he did the same behind them in the woods. Ahead, he could see the dark outline of a low house. There were no lights on and no sign of people or other vehicles.

Foster sent two more team members forward in the dark gloom toward the house. A creeping mist drifted in just off the ground.

Suddenly, the scene exploded in a flash of light and thundering sound as two flash grenades went off inside the house, two windows briefly outlined from behind.

The assault team raced toward the house and then inside, a collection of voices yelling, *FBI! FBI!*

Alex expected to hear the sound of gunfire cut the night, but there was only the shouting of the men clearing the few small rooms. In a few moments, he saw lights come on inside and then on the front porch. Then Foster came out with a cell phone to his ear.

At once, Alex realized the terror cell had gone. *Had they been tipped off? Had his little conversation with Al Zahrani led to this?* He felt a sick rumble in his gut as he realized he may have helped these guys get away.

Foster directed men out into the woods to search for whatever or whoever they could find. Alex sunk back further into the woods.

Within twenty minutes, Foster left with more than half the team in two of the vehicles. In another half hour, the remaining men loaded into the last SUV and drove away.

Alex's legs and back were on fire from crouching for so long in the heavy cover. He stood slowly, listening for any threats, stretching to get the circulation back in his body. Only the sound of the frogs and the recent arrival of a Whippoorwill split the night air.

He was certain the FBI and Counter Terror crew had swept the place thoroughly, but he still wanted a look. He started toward the house, less concerned now about the noise of his approach with the area abandoned.

Then, he stopped short and ducked behind a tree when he saw the form of a man moving inside the house. *Foster left someone here?* was his first thought. *No, not without a vehicle. One of the terrorists must have been hiding nearby.*

He pulled his 9mm and moved forward again toward the house, this time concealing his approach. With lights on now he could see the house was in terrible disrepair, the roof sagging, faded white paint peeling. As he got near, he could hear the man speaking inside, probably on his phone to his handlers, Alex thought.

He crept up and knelt by the side of the house, an open window above his head. The man inside was speaking excitedly in an Arab dialect and Alex had no idea what he was saying. The voice moved away from the window, then outside, and Alex pushed himself against the side of the old house when he saw the man walking away down the two-track drive, still talking into the phone.

He must have a vehicle hidden nearby, Alex thought as he rose to follow, weighing his options. *If I take this guy down, we'll have to go through the long slow interrogation process to find out where his buddies are.*

There's no time! I need to follow him to the rest of the cell!

As he came around the corner of the house, he flinched when he saw the form of another man rush at him from the right on the porch. Then he saw the gun.

As he raised his own weapon in defense, he felt a crushing and painful blow across the back of his head. His knees buckled, and as he began falling helplessly to the ground, his last conscious thought was Hanna and how he had let her down.

Then all went dark and silent.

Chapter Forty-five

Hanna groaned and tried to roll over as her brain began to come out of the fog of the sedatives and painkillers. As she gained focus and clarity, she saw she was still connected to numerous wires and tubes that hindered her from moving. She sank back into the pillows behind her. A dull ache still throbbed in her forehead. Her mouth was as dry as fire ash.

She looked to the side and saw a cup of water with a straw. It was warm but a welcome relief. There was a clock on the wall. It was just past midnight. She suddenly felt ravenously hungry and pressed the button for the nurse.

A young man dressed in blue scrubs came in after a few moments. "How are you doing?" he asked as he came around the bed and stared at the monitor.

"Like I've been run over by a train," she replied.

"Good, you're improving!" the man said, as he turned and smiled down at her. "What can I get you?"

"A cheeseburger and a coke!"

"Not sure what the kitchen has at this hour, but I'll get you something. Be back in a minute."

Hanna watched him walk through the door and then groaned again as she listened to the cop outside speaking with someone.

Grace Holloway came into the doorway then stepped aside to let the nurse out. She walked in and over to the bed. "Oh, honey! I'm sorry, but you look terrible!"

Hanna could hardly control her anger. "I'm not your *honey,* and what the hell are you doing here?" The ache in her head seemed to flare, and she placed a hand to her forehead.

Grace said, "I've been trying to find you. I went by your office and the police were there. They said someone had been shot."

Hanna immediately thought of Molly and her horrific demise.

"The cops thought I was involved. They even took me downtown! I had one of Phillip's guns in my purse. They finally let me go when the ballistics report showed it wasn't Phillip's gun." Grace continued until Hanna cut in.

"I really don't need this right now," she pleaded.

Grace said, "You and Alex wouldn't pick up, so I finally got in touch with Jonathan. He was in his car on the way back from North Carolina. He said you'd been hurt."

"Grace..."

"Please tell me what's happened."

Hanna closed her eyes and breathed in deeply, the pain only flaring more. Looking back at her former friend, she said, "I can't get into the details, but there was an attack at our office, a gunman. Molly is dead, Grace, and another woman I was trying to help."

"Oh, my Lord!"

"Please, I need to get some rest," Hanna pleaded.

"Hanna, I'm so sorry."

"Please, Grace..."

"But you're okay?"

"Do I look okay?"

Grace turned and reached for a chair, pulling it over beside the bed and sitting close.

"I really need you to leave!" Hanna said, reaching for the call button to get some help.

"I just need a minute."

Hanna ignored her and pushed the red button for the nurse.

"I need to share something with you."

"This is definitely not the time..."

"I found something..."

"Grace!"

"In Phillip's office. He has a safe. There was a file with documents about an account in the Caymans that I'm guessing Phillip and or your husband opened."

The nurse came back in. "Still working on your supper."

Hanna said, "Can you please get this woman out of here!"

Grace turned to the man. "I just need a minute."

He came over and stood by the chair, looking down. "You heard her. She needs to get some rest."

Grace was about to protest again, but the officer watching Hanna's room came in.

"I'm going to have to ask you to leave, ma'am. Now!" the cop said.

Grace pushed the chair back and stood. "I'll come and see you in the morning."

"Don't bother!" Hanna said, reaching for her water again.

Hanna looked down at the tray of food and her appetite quickly waned; a cold piece of something that looked like chicken, soggy vegetables, a fruit cup. *I wanted a damn cheeseburger!*

At least the coffee was hot, and she took a sip from the steaming cup. She was also still *steaming* from Grace Holloway's latest intrusion. *The woman won't give up!*

She pushed the cart aside with the food.

The fact that her husband may have stashed some more illegally gained money somewhere offshore was the last thing she cared about. She made a mental note to call Will Foster at the FBI in the morning to have him go after Grace and the money, though she quickly realized Foster and Alex were deeply involved in tracking down the terror cell that had taken Molly's and the other's lives, and who knows what else they had planned.

Thinking of Alex, she reached for her phone beside the bed. She knew it was late, but Alex would want her to call.

After numerous rings, she got his voicemail. She listened to his greeting, then said, "It's me. Just wanted you to know I'm a little better. They told me you stopped by. I wanted to know how you're coming in tracking these guys down. Call, it doesn't matter how late."

Chapter Forty-six

Baz Alzahrani listened intently as his man updated him on the attempted takedown of the operation out at the safe house. He stood at the window in his office looking out over the dark waters of the Atlantic, lights from a few boats sparkling out on the horizon.

He had been frantic for the last several hours after the two FBI agents were asked to leave. They were obviously getting too close, he had feared, and he had the Charleston cell pulled to a backup location. Apparently, it was just in time as he listened and learned more about the FBI's full tactical assault that had fortunately failed.

His man continued, "The three men you ordered left behind to observe were preparing to depart after the FBI vehicles left when they discovered another man."

"What!" Baz yelled out. "I thought you said they all left the site."

"He came up to the house soon after they departed. He must have seen some of our team in the house as they were preparing to leave."

"What happened?"

"We captured the individual, sir."

"Who is he?"

"He was armed but held no official credentials. His driver's license has the name of Alex Frank from Charleston."

"Frank! He's FBI, too!"

"We found his vehicle hidden down the road from the safe house."

"What have you done with him?" Baz asked, walking away from the window, now trying to sort out this new complication.

"We have him secured, waiting on your orders, sir."

"You didn't kill him!"

"If that's what you like, sir."

Baz thought for a moment. *One more dead American was certainly worth the effort, but a federal agent. What are the implications and risks? What are the opportunities? He may have some value.*

"Where are you holding him?" Baz asked.

"At the launch site, sir."

"Down at the waterfront?"

"Yes."

"Is he aware of what the team there is about to do later this morning?"

"No sir!"

Baz paused again to think this through. He went over and sat behind his desk. *Yes, he may be of some value.*

"I'm sending Ahmad down to question the man," Baz finally responded. "We need to find out how much they know about our operation. Keep Frank secluded."

"Yes sir!"

Baz ended the call and then placed another to his chief security man, who was in his office within minutes. He briefed Ahmad on the new situation.

"I want you down there now," Baz demanded. "Get what you can from Frank, then dispose of him."

"Yes, sir," the big security man said. "Is everything else in order for the attack today?"

Baz stood and looked at the status reports spread out across his desk. "Yes, the other teams have finalized all preparations and are poised to attack on schedule."

"Excellent sir!"

Alex came to, the side of his face lying on a hard concrete floor. He blinked several times, trying to clear his mind and vision. A shock of pain from the back of his head caused him to groan. He tried to sit up but quickly realized his hands were bound behind him with the sharp edges of plastic zip ties cutting into his wrists. Both arms ached from the uncomfortable position.

Where am I?

He was able to lift up and lean back again, the wall behind him, his feet bound in front of him. The room was dark as pitch, with only a thin line of light beneath a door off to his right. The air smelled of diesel fuel and rotting garbage.

He struggled to free the restraints on his wrists, but it was useless and only intensified the pain. As his thoughts continued to clear, he remembered the old house in the woods, the FBI tactical assault, the men who had stayed behind. Another flash of pain from his head almost made him pass out. As he struggled to stay conscious, he remembered he was going to follow the man he had seen back to wherever the cell had moved. That was the last he could remember.

He thought of Al Zahrani. The bastard had tipped off the terrorist cell that the FBI was closing in. Alex realized again it was his fault that his encounter with the Saudi had prevented Foster and his team from taking them down.

Fortunately, no one was hurt! he thought, though it did little to ease the guilt that was haunting him. *What are these guys up to? Who and where is the target?*

The door opened and a blinding flash of light filled the room. Alex shut his eyes and squirmed again, trying to free his restraints. He heard footsteps coming toward him and squinted into the light to see three men approaching, silhouetted from the glaring light behind them.

As his eyes quickly adjusted, he saw they were all Middle Eastern, all dressed in black shorts and black long-sleeved t-shirts. One man's face was familiar. The big man leading the group toward him had been with Al Zahrani's security team out at the beach, verifying his assumption of the man's involvement in whatever this terrorist attack was going to be.

A sudden fear came over him as he realized the danger of his situation. *Why didn't they just kill me earlier? Because they want information!*

He tried to remain calm as he anticipated what was to come.

"Get him up!" shouted the man in front. 'Get him on that chair!"

Alex looked over and watched as one of the other men grabbed an old metal chair against the wall and slid it over to the middle of the room.

Oh shit! Alex thought, knowing this was going to hurt.

Two men grabbed him under each arm and dragged him over to the chair. They threw him down hard and the chair almost toppled over. Pain shot through his body and the back of his head felt like he'd been hit by a bat.

Alex looked up as the big man came over and stood in front of him.

"Special Agent Alex Frank," the man said in a heavy Arabic accent. "Nice to see you again."

"I wish I could say the same," Alex replied, staring up.

"As I'm sure you can imagine, there are two ways this can go, Agent Frank."

Alex didn't respond, feeling a cold chill wash over his body.

"My name is Ahmad. We have a few questions for you... and we *will* get the answers.

Alex had a sudden and sobering realization that regardless of how much he was forced to reveal about the FBI's readiness to thwart this attack, he would not survive to experience the ultimate outcome. There was no way they could let him live when he now had incontrovertible evidence that Baz Al Zahrani was involved with, if not leading this terrorist plot.

He had endured a lot of pain in his life, his injuries in Iraq, gunshot wounds in the line of duty. He had not been exposed to torture, and now at the hands of a man who likely had considerable experience, knowing the environment in his home country. He tried to push down the fear that was simmering and about to erupt in full-fledged panic.

Chapter Forty-seven

Glenn Pyke walked out the door of his office building, pulling a suitcase on wheels with important files and personal items he wanted to take with him on his escape to Nicaragua. His plane was waiting at the commercial hanger. His CFO was waiting for him there, *or at least he better be!* Pyke fumed.

The sounds of downtown New Orleans at night were lost on him, the distant echoes of jazz music at a nearby club, the cable car bell, horns honking, people yelling. He was thinking of nothing more than getting away.

The story in the paper was posted online at 4 p.m. It was more devastating than he could have ever imagined. The whistleblower had laid open all their schemes and scams, even details of several environmental "accidents" he had orchestrated. His office phone and cell phone had been ringing virtually nonstop since he'd returned to the office to pack and get away. He didn't take a single call. *All that is over!*

Everything he had worked for was coming apart at the seams. *At least there is still the money!* he thought as he walked down to his car parked along the curb.

With his last look online of bank statements and other assets, his rough count was nearing $20 million. It seemed a staggering sum, and he had been tempted on many occasions to just walk away, disappear, change his identity and live out a more than comfortable life. *Now I'm running!*

He popped open the back hatch of the big Tesla SUV and lifted the suitcase in along with his leather bag on his shoulder. As he pulled the hatch closed, he felt a hand on his shoulder, then something hard pressing into his lower back.

He turned his head and saw two men, both Middle Eastern. The closest pressed the gun more firmly into his ribs and said, "We saw the piece in the paper this afternoon, Mr. Pyke. We thought you might be thinking of making yourself scarce."

"Who are you?" Pyke demanded, trying to mask the cold fear he was really feeling.

"You're coming with us," the other man said as a car pulled alongside, and the back door was pushed open. He was thrown inside, followed by the man with the gun. He watched as the other took his keys and recovered the luggage in the back of the Tesla, putting it in the trunk of the car and then getting into the front seat with the driver.

The man turned and looked back at Pyke with narrow black eyes. "Our common friend wishes for no loose ends."

Pyke panicked and tried the door handle with no success as the car pulled out into traffic.

"Please don't make me shoot you here, Mr. Pyke," the man beside him said. "It would make such a mess in my car!"

At that moment, Pyke knew he was a dead man. *No loose ends!*

Chapter Forty-eight

Will Foster and Sharron Fairfield sat in a long conference room in the FBI's office downtown, the skyline of Charleston lit up through the windows along one wall. It was just past 4 a.m., and Foster stood at a whiteboard with a scribbled array of notes and arrows connecting various parts of the messaging.

Both knew there was enough intel to predict a major terror attack at multiple sites across the country. They didn't know where or when, and the frustration of the situation had been building throughout the night.

They had one suspect in custody, and he had revealed enough to lead them to a house in rural Charleston, where apparently the terror cell members had been preparing explosives for whatever the attack was to be. Somehow, they had been tipped off, and the place was abandoned when Foster and the assault team arrived.

The captured terrorist, Tariq Sendaya, had been little help since. The drugs used to get him talking had apparently drained all he was able or willing to reveal.

National intel sources were still picking up chatter online and through phone intercepts, and there appeared to be a high probability of other attacks in New York, Boston, Miami and New Orleans. Since all were major seaports, other cities with large commercial ports had also been put on alert.

Foster and Fairfield had just gotten off a Zoom conference call with their counterparts in these cities and the FBI counterterror team in Washington. Military and Coast Guard assets were being mobilized, but it was highly unfocused with little knowledge of the specifics of the intentions of the terrorists.

Foster took a sip from the cup of coffee in front of him, then spit it back. "God, that's awful!"

Fairfield leaned forward across the table, her hands folded in contemplation. "So, what have we got to go on at this point?"

"We're not going to get anything more from Sendaya," Foster said.

"Nobody on the call had anything solid," Fairfield replied. She squeezed her eyes shut in contemplation and rubbed at her face, exhausted. She looked back at her partner. "You know, Alex is convinced Al Zahrani is mixed up in this."

Foster stared back for a moment and then looked back to the whiteboard. There was a notation about the wealthy Saudi and his brother's connection to Al Qaeda cells in Syria. He had been killed the year before by a U. S. drone attack. Foster had shared this several times with the central planning team but had been cautioned about pursuing it any further. They had already received a "stand down" order after Frank and Fairfield had crashed the Saudi's party out at the beach. Apparently, he had some very highly placed friends who had intervened on his behalf.

"What if Alex is right?" Fairfield posed.

Foster looked back, thinking through what he had learned about the interaction with Al Zahrani out on Isle of Palms. "See if you can get Alex on the phone."

Fairfield reached for her cell and placed the call. She put it on speaker mode. They both heard multiple rings before his voicemail message came on.

Foster responded, "Alex, it's Will. We need to speak with you. Call me right away."

"Maybe he's with Hanna down at the hospital," Fairfield said. "I know it's late, but…"

"Call her!"

She looked up the number and again placed the call on speaker, and set the phone down on the table. Hanna picked up on the second ring.

"Hello?"

"Hanna, this is Will Foster and Sharron Fairfield. Sorry to call so late. How are you feeling?"

"Well, not great, actually, but I'll survive."

"We were very sorry to hear about your friend and associate," Fairfield said.

"Thank you. I still can't believe what's happened."

Foster said, "We've been in continuous contact with the Charleston PD, and they still don't have any leads on the gunman."

"They have a man here keeping an eye on me," Hanna said.

"Probably a good idea," Foster replied. "Hanna, we're trying to reach Alex. Is he there with you?"

"No," came the puzzled response. "I assumed he was working with you trying to find these guys. I tried to call him earlier, but he didn't pick up."

"We just tried, too," Foster said. "If you hear from him or he comes in, please have him call us right away."

"I will."

"Get some rest," Fairfield said. "Sorry to call so late."

"Not a problem," Hanna said. "When you get in touch with Alex, tell him I've been trying to reach him."

"Will do," Foster said, ending the call. He looked across at Sharron Fairfield, her face as tired and drawn as he was sure his looked. "Strange that Alex isn't picking up. Does he have a landline at home?"

Fairfield checked her *Contacts*, found the number, and dialed. *No answer.*

"Something doesn't smell right here," Foster said.

"Should we try to track his cell on GPS?"

"Yes," Foster said, "and let's send someone over to his apartment just to be sure." He left the room to get someone on it.

Fairfield pulled up the GPS tracking app on a laptop on the table beside her and typed in the required information on Alex's cell. With a few more clicks, she picked up the signal. A small green dot was blinking on a map of Charleston. She zoomed in on the map to check the location. It was a road on the way back to downtown from the terror safe house they had raided. The phone with Alex, presumably still with it, was still miles from the city. She pulled in closer and got the detailed satellite image of the location. It appeared to be a farm field with no houses within at least a quarter-mile. *What the hell?*

Foster came back into the conference room.

Fairfield said, "Take a look at this," pointing to the laptop screen.

Foster came around. "Alex's phone?"

"Right... and it's out on some rural road in the middle of nowhere, but on the way back from the house we raided."

"What? How did he...?"

"He must have followed us out there."

"Why am I not surprised," Foster said. "Call the Sheriff's Department and see if they've got anyone nearby who can check out that location."

Fairfield placed the call.

Chapter Forty-nine

Alex was beyond feeling the pain of the next blow.

His head snapped back and then fell to the side, blood from his nose and mouth dripping heavily on his clothes and down on the floor.

The beatings had been coming for what seemed like hours. The big Saudi named Ahmad had come back in countless times through the night. Early on, when Alex was still somewhat lucid, he had continued to refuse to answer any questions.

Now, his body and brain were so battered and his mind so dulled that he had no idea of what he might have revealed more recently. He was somewhat reassured by the fact that he had very little to share because he simply didn't know much. Nor did the FBI, unfortunately.

He felt his hair grabbed and his head jerked up. He looked up through blurred vision, one eye nearly swollen closed, at the big man dressed in black in front of him. He also saw light reflect off the blade of a large knife in the man's right hand.

"Agent Frank," Ahmad said in a low, menacing voice. "You are trying my patience. I'm afraid we will need to take this a bit further." He dropped his hold on Alex's hair and moved aside as another man pulled a small table over. Ahmad stepped behind Alex, and he expected to feel the sharp edge of the knife across his throat. He tried to prepare himself for this final pain when the deadly slash of the blade was delivered. He was beyond fear, only a sad sense of finality. Again, he thought of Hanna, the last images of her badly wounded in a hospital bed. His temper sparked as he steeled himself for his final breaths.

Instead, he felt his arms jerked back painfully behind him, and the zip tie binding his wrists was cut by the knife. His arms fell limp to his sides, the pain radiating up through his shoulders. He moaned and leaned forward, his face hitting the table.

He heard Ahmad come around and pull a chair up to sit across from him. "Tie his hands again!" he ordered. A man came over and lifted both of Alex's arms up on the table, then bound his wrists again in front of him.

"Make him watch!" Ahmad demanded.

Alex's head was jerked up by the hair again and he saw the Saudi sitting across from him, the knife pointing up in his right fist. He felt blood dripping off his chin onto the table. He watched as the man grabbed his wrists and pulled them toward him.

"Agent Frank," Ahmad said slowly, leaning in, "I will ask you again and then again until there are no fingers left on either of your hands."

Alex jolted back in fear and struggled to pull away. He was constrained by a man behind him, and Ahmad had a firm grip on his hands.

"How much has our man, Tariq, revealed, and what are your friends at the FBI planning?"

Alex looked back at the Saudi and didn't respond. Then, in a final show of defiance, he gathered all the blood left in his mouth and spit in the face of the man named Ahmad.

He watched in horror as the man's expression flared in fury and then the big knife came down hard, slicing through the top of his left hand, pinning it to the table. The pain was beyond excruciating. He felt his sense of recognition and reason fading, and he fell forward on the table, his last conscious thought of Hanna.

Sharron Fairfield saw the call back from the County Sheriff's Department. "This is Agent Fairfield." She placed the call on speaker and her phone down on the conference table between her and Will Foster.

"Ms. Fairfield, this is Sheriff Pepper Stokes."

"Sheriff, how are you?"

"Good, good. Nice to speak with you. Anything more on this terror alert? Our department got the call last night."

"Sheriff Stokes, this is Will Foster. Nothing more yet."

"One of our men picked up Alex Frank's phone. When he got close on GPS, he called the number. It lit up in a ditch about five miles from Dugganville, out in the middle of nowhere. What the hell's going on. Where's Alex?"

"We don't know," Foster said, trying to think through what they had just learned. "We need to get that phone down here to Charleston."

"I'll have my deputy head your way right now."

"Thank you."

"Is Alex okay?" they heard the sheriff ask.

Neither responded, looking back at each other.

"Will?"

"Sheriff, we just don't know at this point. We had a tip on a location these bad guys might have been using. They were gone when we got there. Alex may have followed us there. Where the phone was found is on the way back to the city from that location."

"Followed you? Why'd he have to follow you?"

"He's been suspended from duty."

There was no response from the old sheriff.

"Thank you for your assistance, Sheriff," Foster said. He ended the call and looked across at Fairfield. "I think Alex is in some serious shit here."

Fairfield nodded. "You think they picked him up?"

"It's possible. He follows us, sticks around after we leave. Some of the bad guys come back or were hiding nearby and take Alex."

"Let's hope not!" Fairfield said.

Foster stood, the anger on his face burning red. "I'm taking another shot at our man, Tariq." He looked at the clock on the wall as he walked out. It was nearly 5 a.m.

The terrorist suspect, Tariq Sendaya, lay sleeping with his head on the table in the interrogation room when Foster came in. Fairfield followed and closed the door behind him. He didn't wake up until Foster picked his head up by the hair and slammed his face down on the table.

Sendaya screamed out in a low exhausted moan.

Fairfield yelled, "Will!"

Foster jerked Sendaya up and slapped him hard across the face, and then again.

Sendaya looked back with terrified eyes.

Foster reached for the man's right hand and pulled the thumb back near the point of breaking.

Sendaya screamed out in pain.

"I need a location and I need it now!" Foster barked, increasing the pressure on the thumb.

Sendaya screamed again, his eyes rolling back in terror and exhaustion.

Foster delivered the next blow with his left fist, knocking the man backwards against the chair, not relinquishing his hold on the thumb."

"No, please...!" Sendaya pleaded. "No more!" he cried out in resignation.

"Where are they!" Foster yelled as the man's thumb broke and his screams echoed through the room. Foster grabbed another finger.

"No! No!" Sendaya screamed. "The waterfront... they're at the waterfront."

"Where?" Foster yelled back.

Fairfield was dialing her phone to start assembling the assault team as Sendaya gave Will Foster the address of a warehouse on the waterfront in Charleston Harbor.

"Why are they at the waterfront?" Foster shouted, going to work on Sendaya's index finger.

"The ships!" Sendaya screamed. "The oil ships!"

"When, dammit!" Foster roared as the finger snapped.

Sendaya howled, "This morning! This morning! Please... no more!"

Chapter Fifty

Hanna was beside herself with worry. She'd been up most of the night trying to reach Alex on his cell at his home number, calling the FBI and the Charleston PD. She couldn't reach Will Foster or Nate Beatty. No one else would take her call.

Alex seemed to have simply vanished.

With a rush of adrenaline, she managed to sit up and slide her legs to the floor. As she tried to stand, a wave of dizziness overwhelmed her, and she sat back on the hospital bed. She took a few moments to catch her breath and gather herself, then tried again to stand. This time, she hovered unsteadily and placed her hand on the bed.

She removed the blood pressure sleeve on one of her fingers. There was an I.V. tube leading from the back of her hand to a bag of some clear liquid hanging on a rack next to the bed that pulled back at her. She peeled off the tape and gauze holding it in place, then, with a quick pull, slid the needle from beneath her skin. Blood began dripping and she placed the bandage back to stem the flow.

She had no idea where to go to keep looking for Alex, but she knew she needed to try. As she took a first step toward the bathroom, she almost fell back onto the bed again. The pain from the wound on her forehead flared and she stopped to wait for it to pass.

She was wearing a blue hospital gown, open in the back, sock slippers on her feet. When she staggered out of the bathroom, she was startled by two familiar faces. Skipper Frank and his wife, Ella, stood in the doorway, a look of surprise on both of their faces.

Skipper said, "Thought you'd checked out when we saw the empty bed."

"What are you two doing here?" Hanna asked.

"Wish we'd been able to get here sooner, Sweetie," Ella said. "Couldn't drag the old damn fool here out of *Gilly's*!"

"We needed to come to town this morning for an early meeting with our damned accountant," Skipper said. "The sonofabitch drives me crazy with all this finance bullshit for my shrimp business! Thought we'd come by. How you doin' Hanna?"

She made her way back to the bed, trying to cover her bare backside, and sat down. "I've been better, honestly. Have you heard from Alex?" she asked.

"Not for a day or so," Skipper said.

"I've been trying to reach him all night!"

"When's the last time you heard from him?" Ella asked.

"He came by early last night, but I was out of it on these pain meds. I've tried to reach him everywhere! I swear something's happened!"

"Now, slow down, woman," Skipper said. "You sure he's not just sleepin' off a late night?"

"Can you take me home to get some clothes?" Hanna pleaded. "We need to find Alex!"

"Not sure they want you checkin' outta here yet, girl," Ella said.

"Ella, please!"

The nurse on duty and the cop watching her room had tried to keep her from leaving, but Skipper Frank helped to escort her out in a wheelchair he found down the hall. Her house was only a few blocks away. Ella assisted her up the stairs and into some fresh clothes.

Skipper was waiting for them in the small kitchen, a fresh pot of coffee steaming on the counter. He poured them all a cup. Hanna sat at the table and took a sip, her head on fire, her body aching all over, exhaustion in every motion and thought.

Skipper Frank said, "Just got off the phone with Pepper Stokes down at the Sheriff's Department. Didn't know who else to call."

"Has he heard anything from Alex?" Hanna asked, looking up expectantly.

"FBI called him last night. Seems Alex and an FBI assault team went after a bunch of goddamn terrorists somewhere out near Dugganville. When Alex wouldn't return any calls, they put a GPS trace on his phone. Called Pepper to get a man out to pick it up."

"Wait a minute!" Hanna demanded. "Alex wasn't with his cell phone?"

Skipper shook his head. "Deputy found the damn thing in a ditch between Dugganville and Charleston. No sign of Alex."

Hanna felt her senses go into full panic mode. "Do they know where he is?"

Ella stepped in. "What in hell's going on?"

"Pepper didn't know much and wouldn't share, but when I pressed the old bastard, he told me there was a major terror threat down at the waterfront. Feds have mobilized all law enforcement in the region... land, sea, and air."

"Where on the waterfront?" Hanna asked, opening a laptop on the table and punching keystrokes in to get to a Maps app of Charleston.

"Pepper said he's got all units in the county checking everywhere, all along the coast. I should get back and take the *Maggie Mae* out there and find these sonsabitches!"

"But he has no idea where Alex is?"

"No, but he said most of the effort is headed downtown here, near Union Pier Terminal."

Hanna stood up, wincing at the pain. "You need to take me down there!"

"If they got these terrorist assholes penned up down there on the waterfront, ain't no way we're getting close."

'I don't care! Just get me down there! It's not far."

Chapter Fifty-one

Alex woke with a start. A pain beyond anything he could have ever imagined shot up from his left hand through his arm. His face was lying to the side on a table. As his one eye that wasn't swollen shut from the beatings began to focus, he tried to comprehend what he was seeing... and then it began coming back... Ahmad... the knife.

He sat up and even the slightest move sent searing jolts of pain up through his arm. He looked down, unbelieving, at the big knife piercing the top of his left hand, both hands bound together with a white plastic tie. He couldn't move. There was nothing he could do to free himself that didn't cause excruciating pain. He felt weak and nauseous, near passing out again.

The room was empty. They had all left.

He could hear yelling beyond the door. Men running and shouting.

Then gunfire erupted, multiple rounds from many weapons. He flinched back and the pain flared again. The gunfire and chaos beyond the door intensified.

In desperation, he leaned forward, got the hilt of the knife in his teeth, steeled himself for the pain and then pulled as hard as he could. As the knife came free, he let it fall to the table and screamed out into the abandoned room. He watched as blood gushed from the wound.

Somehow, he found the strength to get to his feet. The old metal chair fell backward and clattered to the cement floor. The gun battle outside continued to intensify.

He stood unsteadily, then almost fell over before staggering over to a wall to catch himself. He managed to get back over to the table and took the hilt of the knife in his mouth, and after several tries, was able to get it into position to snap the plastic tie binding his wrists. To staunch the blood flowing from his left hand, he placed it under his opposite armpit and squeezed it as tight as he could.

The gunfire had subsided to sporadic bursts. Then, he heard shouts of *"FBI! Down on the floor! Down on the floor!"*

He started toward the door, then stumbled and fell to one knee, catching himself on the table and moaning as the pain was nearly unbearable. He reached the door and listened again. The gunfire had ended. Multiple voices were shouting in a cacophony he couldn't make out.

Slowly he pulled back the door and peered out. He could see a large room that looked like a warehouse, high windows along one side letting light filter in. Men and women were rushing in all directions, some in tactical assault gear, some with FBI stenciled in large letters on the backs of their jackets.

Then, to the side, he heard a familiar voice. "Alex? What the hell!"

He turned and saw Sharron Fairfield coming toward him in one of the blue FBI jackets and an FBI ball cap pulled tight over her blonde hair. Her service weapon was drawn in her right hand, pointing down.

He slumped to his right knee again, losing his balance and feeling an overwhelming sense of relief and exhaustion come over him. He felt Fairfield's hand on his back as she knelt beside him.

"Alex? Let me get you some help!"

He heard the sound of Will Foster's voice and looked up. "Alex! Holy shit!"

Alex felt he was close to passing out again, and he fell over on the floor. Foster tried unsuccessfully to try to catch him, then leaned in close.

"We'll get someone over here. Just lay still," Foster said.

"Did you get them?" Alex asked weakly.

Foster was shouting out an order to someone running by and didn't respond.

"Will," Alex demanded, "did you get these assholes!"

Foster turned back. "We've got several men here in custody. No sign of boats though."

"Boats?" Alex asked.

"Sendaya finally was *persuaded* to talk. That's how we found this place... and you. What the hell happened?"

Alex tried to sit up and Foster helped him lean back against a cement wall. "I followed you out to the old house, then stuck around to check it out. A few of these guys came back. One caught me from behind. Next thing I know, some big Arab named Ahmad is using my face for a punching bag."

"I think Ahmad is dead," Foster said, looking over at the prone figure of a man lying nearby. "He's Al Zahrani's head of security, right?"

Alex nodded.

Foster noticed the bleeding hand. "What happened?"

"Our friend over there decided to stick me to the table."

A paramedic rushed up and knelt beside them. Foster said, "Get something on that hand to stop the bleeding."

"What about the boats?" Alex asked as he watched the woman pull bandages out of her bag and inspect his wound.

"Air and Sea are all over out there. The target is one or more oil freighters."

"What?" Alex said, trying to think through the intent. "Oil spill? A giant oil spill?"

"That's what we think... here and likely a dozen other ports around the country."

Alex thought quickly through the scenario of a massive oil spill and the environmental and economic carnage that would be caused throughout Charleston waterways and out along the Atlantic coast. He looked up and saw Foster talking on his radio.

"Alex, I need to go," Foster said. "There's a helicopter waiting."

"Go! Go get these bastards!"

"They'll take care of you here. I'll catch up with you later."

Foster rushed off. Alex looked at the face of the woman tending to his damaged hand.

She said, "You had a helluva night."

"Not one of my favorites," he replied, then leaned his head back against the wall and closed his good eye, trying to let the relief in his rescue dull the pain.

Hanna stood with Skipper and Ella Frank behind temporary barricades that were being put up as they rushed to the warehouse that seemed to be the center of the chaotic scene of police cars, fire trucks, ambulances, all with lights flashing, people running in all directions.

As they had approached the area a few blocks back, Hanna was horrified to hear the first sounds of gunfire. They were stopped quite far back from the waterfront but parked and started moving toward the sounds of the battle or whatever was coming down.

Several times she had to stop and lean against a wall or parked car to gather herself. Her head wound was throbbing and her legs weak.

Three Charleston PD uniformed cops were assembling to keep onlookers away. Hanna pushed toward one of them through the crowd. "I need to find someone! I think I know someone in there!"

"Sorry, ma'am," came the officer's reply. "You'll have to stay back."

"I need to find Alex Frank!" she persisted. "He worked at the Department. Do you know Alex Frank?"

"No, ma'am, sorry. You'll have to wait here."

Just then, the roar of a helicopter drowned out their voices and Hanna saw a black aircraft with FBI markings lift off from behind several fire trucks to her left. She saw Will Foster in the open door on the side and then the helicopter banked hard to the left and sped away.

"Do you think he's in there, honey?" Ella asked, looking toward the big open door on the old warehouse building.

"I don't know," Hanna replied, trying to hold her panic in check. "I don't know."

Skipper said, "Hope they got those sonsabitches!"

Hanna looked over when she saw two paramedics pushing a gurney through the crowd toward one of the ambulances. A bloodied man lay prone on the gurney.

"No!" she yelled out and rushed past the cop before he could stop her.

"Wait!" she heard from behind.

Adrenaline propelled her forward, despite her own weakened body.

"Alex!" she yelled out as she approached.

One of the paramedics, a woman, held up a hand for her to stay back.

As Hanna got close, she revolted back in horror as she saw Alex's battered face and bloody clothes. One of his hands was heavily bandaged. She pushed forward, ignoring the paramedics. "Alex?" she said again, tentatively.

He looked over and she could see one of his eyes was totally swollen shut, the other a thin slit. His face was bruised and swollen, his nose seeming to have been pushed to the side.

She heard his weak voice, "Hanna?" and felt a rush of relief that he was still alive.

She reached the gurney and walked alongside, ignoring the paramedic's protests. "Oh, Alex..., what's happened?"

"I'll be alright," he said weakly, and she saw a hint of a smile across his swollen lips.

"You don't look alright!" she said. "Alex..."

Skipper Frank's voice bellowed out behind her. "What the hell!"

Two cops tried to push between them and Alex's gurney. Hanna felt herself being pulled back by one of her arms.

"Ma'am, you need to get back," one of the cops warned.

She watched as the paramedics lifted the gurney into the ambulance, one jumping out to drive, the other shutting the doors as the vehicle raced away, siren blaring.

Hanna caught a last glimpse of Alex looking back at her, a thumb raised upright to reassure her he would be okay.

Chapter Fifty-two

Will Foster felt the wind rush through the open door of the helicopter, the roar of blades overhead deafening. The scene of downtown Charleston Harbor spread out below. The pilot had them racing out toward the mouth of the harbor and the sparkling blue of the Atlantic Ocean beyond. To the right, he could see Fort Sumter, Sullivan's Island off to his left.

Ahead, the sky was full of aircraft, two other helicopters and two Air Force fighter jets crisscrossing the harbor from north and south. Out ahead, he saw several large commercial freighters coming and going from the harbor mouth. Smaller boats dotted the surface, moving in all directions, their wakes leaving a telltale trace of their courses.

One boat caught his eye, a large center cockpit motorboat with a light blue hull and three outboard engines across the back moving at high speed toward one of the big freighters. Even from a distance, Foster could see a blue tarp covering a large pile of something filling the front of the boat.

He yelled into his radio over the roar of the helicopter's rotors. "The blue center cockpit! I'm going down to take a look!" He radioed to the pilot up in front to move in as close as possible. Within moments they were directly overhead, keeping pace with the boat.

Foster could see two men up close now, both dressed in black, including black ball caps. They had beards and dark skin. He asked the pilot to put his radio on the loudspeaker.

"This is the FBI! Stop now and prepare to be boarded!" He saw two Coast Guard assault boats approaching from both sides.

The two men ignored the order and instead increased their speed.

"Pull up, now!" Foster yelled into the radio, but again, the two men ignored him. He tried to get a better look at the cargo hidden beneath the tarp across the front deck of the boat. He had to assume it was the explosives Sendaya had told them about.

He looked up and they were rapidly approaching the tall hull along the side of the big oil tanker. He ordered the helicopter up and away.

He watched as an Army Apache attack helicopter raced in from his right toward
the boat, which was now less than a few hundred yards from the tanker. "Take it out!" Foster yelled into the radio.

The flare of one, then a second Hellfire missile shot out from the Apache, their tracer smoke trail leaving a path across the sky. The two Coast Guard boats approaching both opened fire on the cockpit of the terrorist's boat with 50 caliber machine guns mounted on their foredecks.

Both missiles found their target and Foster watched a massive explosion engulf the boat in flames and smoke that climbed high above the surface of the harbor. Parts from the boat flew out from the blast, flaming and falling into the water. Anyone onboard had likely been incinerated by the initial blast. The helicopter he was riding in flared to the left to avoid the plume of smoke and fire.

As they veered, Foster saw the big tanker continuing on into the harbor, the flaming wreckage of the attack boat drifting by to its side.

Sharron Fairfield was standing outside the big warehouse talking to the police chief and two other members of the FBI anti-terror unit. Four men lay dead inside, all of Middle Eastern descent. The smell of cordite still lay heavy on the air following the recent gun battle.

It appeared no law enforcement personnel had been wounded, let alone killed, she had just been informed. She led the group over to one of the dead bodies. "This man is named Ahmad. He worked for Bassam Al Zahrani. He was head of security." The corpse lay there with multiple gunshot wounds to the head and chest.

"Al Zahrani!" the chief said in surprise.

Baz stood on the beach in front of his house, looking out over the sun coming up to the east and sparkling back across the blue Atlantic. He had his secure satellite phone to his ear, taking updates from the attack cells across the U.S.

His last call had been from his man, Ahmad, in downtown Charleston. The call had been interrupted by the sounds of gunfire. He had heard Ahmad drop the phone as the gunfire intensified. Ahmad was yelling and apparently returning fire as law enforcement teams moved in. He had reassured his boss the attack boat had been able to get away. He had not come back to the phone as the gunfire began to subside. Baz had ended the call, a sick feeling in his gut about the success of the mission.

He started walking down the beach to the south, the mouth of Charleston Harbor several miles down. He stopped in surprise as the flare of a huge explosion rose above the far tree line, a massive cloud of smoke and flames rising up. Then the concussion and sound of the explosion reached him. A great sense of satisfaction rushed over him as he imagined the enormous hole blown into the side of the big oil tanker, the rush of crude oil pouring out into the harbor.

As he watched the inferno of the distant blast, he pressed the number for his cell leader in San Francisco. *No answer!*

Similarly, no answer from Houston or New Orleans.

What is happening?

Chapter Fifty-three

Hanna was frantic as Skipper Frank's old truck raced toward the hospital she had just left a short while ago. They hadn't been able to catch-up with the ambulance but assumed they would be bringing Alex here to the closest facility.

As Skipper turned quickly into the drive to the Emergency Room entrance, Hanna saw an ambulance parked, back doors open, lights still flashing. *It must be the same one!* she thought.

Skipper screeched to a halt behind the ambulance and jumped out with surprising agility for the crotchety old shrimper. He ran around the front of the truck to help Hanna down from the high seat. Ella followed them through the doors.

Inside, Hanna stopped to catch her breath, holding on to a chair in the center of the waiting room. As she struggled to gain her balance, she watched as Skipper hurried over to the nurse's desk along the back wall.

"I need to see my son, Alex Frank! They just brought him in."

"I'm sorry, sir..." the woman began.

"No, you didn't hear me!" Skipper cut in. "I need to see him now!" Without waiting for an answer, he started off to the double doors to the back.

"Sir, wait!" the nurse yelled, standing to go after the old man.

Hanna had to sit, and Ella came over and sat beside her as they watched Skipper hurry through the doors and disappear, the nurse rushing close behind. Then, they heard shouting and a commotion in the back. The doors burst open again and Skipper was pushed back out, escorted by a uniformed police officer. The cop held on to him until they were standing in front of Hanna and Ella.

"I'm not going to ask you again!" the cop said. "You sit your ass down here, or I'm going to have you taken downtown."

The nurse came up beside the cop. "Mr. Frank, I just spoke with the doctor. She'll be out as soon as she can with an update. They're taking your son into surgery for his hand."

"What the hell happened to his hand?" Skipper roared.

"We were told it's a knife wound, sir," the nurse offered.

"A knife wound!" Hanna cried out, attempting to stand, but falling back into the chair. "What happened to his face?" she pleaded.

"Please," the nurse said. "A doctor will be out as soon as they have anything to share."

Hanna felt the cell phone in her jeans pocket buzzing and she reached for it as the nurse and cop left them there. Skipper was still fuming, but Ella got him to sit down beside her. She looked at the call screen. *It was her son!*

"Jonathan!"

"Mom, I'm back in town. Where are you? Are you okay?"

"Oh, Jonathan, thank God you're back! I've been so worried."

"Please," Jonathan begged, "I told you not to worry! Alex said you'd been hurt."

"I'll be okay."

"What happened?"

"I'll tell you the whole sad affair, but it's Alex..." she paused, the images of his battered face and body flooding her mind. "We're down at the hospital again. Alex has been terribly injured in a terror attack down at the waterfront."

"I've been hearing about something on the radio driving in from the airport."

"We're at the Emergency Room at University Hospital. Please come over as soon as you can."

"I'm on my way!"

Hanna looked up when a young female doctor came through the doors, scanning the room. They made eye contact and she started over.

"Are you the family of Special Agent Frank?" the woman asked.

"I'm his father!" Skipper said, standing quickly.

"He's my fiancé," Hanna said, struggling as she attempted to stand.

The doctor had a stern look as she said, "Agent Frank suffered a serious beating with significant cuts and bruising around the face. We'll have to do x-rays after surgery on his hand. It appears he may also have several broken ribs."

"What about his hand? What happened?" Skipper asked.

"There was a significant knife wound that completely penetrated his left hand. There appears to be considerable bone and tendon damage," the doctor shared. "The surgeon is working on it right now."

"Is there anything life threatening?" Hanna asked, afraid of what answer she might get.

"I don't think so. We'll be back as soon as we know anything more."

Michael Lindley

"Thank you, doctor," Ella said as the doctor walked back to the exam rooms.

Jonathan said, "I can't believe this happened here in Charleston."

Hanna sat down beside her son, trying to convince herself Alex was in good hands and would be okay. "You sure you're alright?" she asked Jonathan.

"I'm doing okay... I'm sorry we ran off. I just couldn't get my head around the thought of another round of rehab. I feel like I can beat this."

"It's not you," Hanna said. "It's the meds. You need professional help to get past this.'

Jonathan nodded with a sober gaze. "Let me talk to Elizabeth. She stayed back in Chapel Hill with friends."

Hanna reached for his hand and rubbed it affectionately. "I'm so glad you're back."

"So, tell me what happened to your head," Jonathan asked.

Hanna hesitated, not wanting to get into all the detail of the gunman's attack at her office. Shaking her head, trying to push back the images, she said, "I was working with a friend of a client who was trying to hide from this terrorist cell. They followed her to my office." Again, she hesitated, then, "They shot and killed her... and Molly, too."

"Oh no..." Jonathan said, closing his eyes. He had been close to Molly for many years.

"I managed not to duck," she said, trying her best to lighten the mood.

"You could have been killed!" Ella said.

"I was very lucky."

Skipper said, "Alex and the Feds need to catch all these damn sonsabitches!"

Alex! she thought. *What he must have gone through!*

265

Chapter Fifty-four

Senator Jordan Hayes watched the newsfeed on the television on the wall of his Charleston office. He was having a hard time comprehending what he was seeing. A terror attack had been thwarted in Charleston harbor. A helicopter news crew had captured video of the burning wreckage of what was left of a big motorboat surrounded by fire crews trying to put out the blaze.

The video shifted to shots of a large oil tanker coming into the harbor. He turned up the sound.

"... *an FBI spokesperson was quoted as saying a major terror cell had been discovered in Charleston and several other cities around the country. Updates are just starting to come in on similar attempts to detonate explosives in the hulls of large oil tankers, apparently to create significant oil spills and environmental catastrophes.*"

Hayes switched channels to another major news network.

The same video clips were running. The news anchor was saying, "... *sources say there are unconfirmed reports of the involvement of the environmental activist group, Green.*"

"What!" Hayes said out loud, turning up the volume.

The reporter continued, "*Green founder Glenn Pyke cannot be located for comment.*"

"*Green!*" Hayes repeated to himself. "What the hell is Pyke doing getting involved in something like this. He's lost his mind!"

Hayes continued to watch the news report, but he was thinking about his client, Baz Al Zahrani, and his request to bring more media attention to the exploits and financial shenanigans of Glenn Pyke and his organization.

And now Pyke's trying to create major oil spills all over the country? he thought, trying to understand the motivation. *What the hell does he expect to accomplish?*

Baz walked down the steps of his beach house and into the open door of his Maybach limousine. His jet was waiting at a private terminal at Charleston Airport to fly him home to Saudi Arabia.

His original plan was to remain here in the states following the aftermath of the terror attacks as if nothing had changed in his routine and schedule. Updates coming in the past half hour from his contacts at the other attack sites were not good and his own situation and involvement was likely highly compromised. Of the ten planned attacks, only one had successfully reached its target.

An oil freighter just entering San Francisco Bay had been hit by one of Al Zahrani's boats there. The explosives were successfully detonated and caused major damage to the hull in the most vulnerable location to allow a massive release of oil into the bay.

All attempted attacks had been linked to Pyke's Green organization as Baz had planned to deflect attention from the Middle Eastern factions who were the usual suspects, as well as himself.

Fortunately for Pyke, Baz mused as he got into the limo, *he won't be around to face the criminal investigation that was sure to follow.*

He tried to remain calm as this massive failure of an assault that had been meticulously planned for months had now been mostly averted by law enforcement in all but one city. His mind was racing on the implications and risks.

Like Pyke, the surviving members of the terror cell team involved but not actually on the boats would all be dealt with by the end of the day. *There will be few if any traces leading back to me,* he thought.

His sudden and unplanned departure would likely raise suspicions if anything did get linked to his involvement. The risks were simply too great to remain here in the States.

His thoughts turned to his close associate and friend, the big security man, Ahmad, who now lay dead or seriously wounded following the FBI assault on their Charleston location. *For his own sake, he's better off dead!*

Chapter Fifty-five

Will Foster jumped from the helicopter as it touched down back at the warehouse. He saw Sharron Fairchild talking with two other law enforcement officers. The place was crawling with investigators processing the scene for any further clues related to one of the largest terror cell attacks in the nation's history.

On his way back across the harbor after the successful takedown of the terror boat here in Charleston Harbor, he had been receiving updates from around the country from other targeted cities. It seemed only San Francisco had been unable to prevent the attack. It was still too early out there to determine the extent of the damage and impact from the rapidly spreading oil spill.

As he walked up to Fairfield, he saw forensics technicians processing the prone bodies of four terrorists. He was still amazed none of their assault team had been wounded or killed. The terrorists had been heavily armed and put up a vigorous fight.

"Will!" Fairfield yelled out. "One of the dead guys over there is a man named Ahmad. He's the head of security for Bassam Al Zahrani. Alex and I saw him at the party last night."

Foster nodded to the two other men, then turned to his partner. "Al Zahrani? You're sure?"

"Absolutely!" We've got two teams on their way to his house out on the beach and to his private terminal at the airport, just in case he decides to skip town."

"Okay, good," Foster replied. "Let me know as soon as you hear back from either of them. What do you all make of this *Green* connection? From what I'm hearing, there's more evidence being uncovered of their involvement."

Fairfield shook her head. "Makes no sense to me, unless this Pyke fellow is trying to demonize the oil industry even more than he's already tried."

"And why would there be a connection to Al Zahrani?" Foster posed. "I've spoken with our New Orleans office on the way back in. No sign of Pyke. They're still trying to track him down."

Baz watched the television monitor in the back of the seat in front of him in the big limo as they raced to the airport. His fury continued to burn at the ultimate collapse of his plan. *Only one in ten missions successfully executed!*

The evidence left behind at each of the staging sites will clearly implicate Glenn Pyke and his organization, Baz thought, *but how will this all continue to play out?*

The fact his head of security was captured or killed at the Charleston site was a continuing worry. *How do I explain that?*

He thought through several scenarios. He could always claim the man had acted on his own, that Admad was actually the head of the terror cell working with Glenn Pyke and *Green*, and *I had no knowledge of either of their plans.*

If this gets too hot, U.S. authorities will never be able to extradite me from Saudi Arabia, he thought. *Surely, the King will discreetly back me and my family.*

The long car turned in through a tall metal fence gate at the private terminal. His driver maneuvered the car around the building and out to his plane, already running with the steps down and door open for his arrival. As he got out of the vehicle, he saw two dark SUVs racing toward them from the side of the terminal.

How have they connected me to this so quickly! he thought in panic as he sprinted to his plane. He ran up the stairs and shouted to the attendant to close the doors immediately and to the pilot for an immediate departure. *They must have Ahmad!*

He sat down in one of the plush leather seats, trying to catch his breath. Peering through one of the windows, he saw the two law enforcement vehicles quickly approaching.

"Go! Go!" he yelled out to the two pilots up in front.

He heard the sounds of the jet engine revving up as the big plane began to accelerate and quickly move out into the taxi lanes to the runway. One of the SUVs pulled alongside the plane, lights on top now flashing. The driver's window was down, and he was signaling to the pilots to stop the plane.

"Do not stop!" he yelled to the two men upfront.

"Sir!" one of the pilots yelled back. "There are three planes ahead of us for departure!"

"Go around them, you idiot!"

Baz felt the plane lurch as it was steered onto the grass. He watched as they raced past the two other waiting planes then spun quickly at the start of the runway. The plane didn't slow down and was just beginning to accelerate for takeoff when a thundering collision caused the plane to veer hard to the right, throwing Baz from his seat, landing painfully across the aisle and into the side of the plane.

One of the SUVs must have rammed us!

Baz managed to stand. The plane had come to a stop and tilted hard to one side. He heard the engine winding down. The flight attendant rushed over to help him up.

"Are you okay, sir?" the man asked, blood dripping from a cut on the side of his face.

Am I okay? Surely not, he thought. *All I've worked for... no revenge for my brother. All is lost!*

Senator Jordan Hayes was also on his way to the airport. As the news of the terror attacks continued to come out in the news, his panic finally took over and he knew he needed to get out of Charleston as quickly as possible and back to Washington.

Though he still wasn't entirely sure, the recent events surrounding Al Zahrani and Pyke's *Green* organization could not have been coincidental. His own involvement with both men these past few days would certainly come to light.

I need to get back to D.C. to bunker down, prepare my response, assemble my defense.

His news anchor girlfriend sat in the backseat beside him, talking animatedly into her phone as she worked with her crew back in Washington to help cover the story of the terror attacks. She had also insisted they get back as soon as possible.

He'd been through many scandals and seemingly impossible scenarios before and always survived, one way or another.

As his car pulled into the same commercial terminal that Al Zahrani kept his plane, Hayes felt his heart lurch when they came around the building. Out at the far end of the runway, he could see Al Zahrani's plane pushed to the side onto the grass, a big black SUV impaled into the front. Other police vehicles with lights blazing were racing towards the scene.

Immediately, he knew he needed to get away. He could not be seen here with Al Zahrani. "Get me back to the office!" he screamed to the driver.

Jenna Hawthorne put her phone down. "Jordan, we need to get back! I need to get back to work!"

Hayes looked back from the chaotic scene out on the runway to the face of his beautiful young girlfriend and felt his heart sinking. *All is lost!*

Chapter Fifty-six

Hanna leaned in and kissed the battered face of Alex Frank. He lay still on the bed in the hospital room, both eyes shut, one terribly swollen. She cringed as she looked over the damage to his face, the large bandages on his wounded hand, more bandages wrapped tight around his middle for his damaged ribs. His bare upper body and arms were covered with welts and bruises.

She tried to hold back tears as she kissed him again.

He began to stir and slowly come back to consciousness.

"Alex..."

He groaned and tried to move and then moaned more loudly in pain.

"Alex, I'm here." She reached for his hand, and she felt him squeeze back weakly.

His one good eye opened and caught her gaze. "Hanna..." He tried to sit up but groaned again and rested back on the pillow.

From behind, Hanna heard Skipper Frank say, "Son, they got the bastards."

"What?" Alex whispered with labored breath.

"Will Foster called me to check on you," Hanna said. "They took down the terror cell here in Charleston. They stopped the attack."

She watched Alex try to process what she'd just told him. Finally, he just nodded his head slowly and a thin smile stretched his battered lips.

Alex listened to Hanna and his father continue on about the failed terror attack. His mind was elsewhere, the memories of his night bound and tortured by the big Arab, Ahmad, a terrifying reality he couldn't block out. *And then the knife!*

He tried to shake away the images in his mind and looked back at Hanna. Her face was pale and tired, bandages wrapped tightly around the top of her head to protect the gunshot wound that had almost taken her life.

"You should be resting," he said weakly.

"I'll be alright," he heard her reply, and he watched as she gently leaned down and rested her left cheek on his chest and gave him a light hug.

"Hanna, I'm so sorry I got you in the middle of all this," he said, the guilt suddenly overwhelming him.

"I got myself into all of this," she said, pushing up to stand beside him.

He looked around Hanna and saw his father and his wife, Ella, standing with Jonathan. *The boy made it back... good!*

He lifted his left hand and inspected the huge bandage that enveloped it. The image of the knife stuck in the table came back to him and he felt a nauseous surge in his throat. He pushed away the thought and lowered his hand gently to the bed.

"They got these guys?" he asked.

"Will said they took down the entire cell."

He felt some sense of satisfaction and relief in knowing he had endured the night of torture and pain without revealing anything that would have compromised the takedown.

He felt Hanna's warm hand on his chest and looked up as she leaned in again and kissed him ever so lightly on the lips, barely touching him.

She whispered, "I love you, Alex Frank."

Chapter Fifty-seven

Skipper Frank listened to the sounds of the small BlueGrass band playing in the corner of his backyard, filled with friends and family to celebrate the first anniversary of his marriage to Ella. *And what a year it's been!* he thought.

The night sky was filled with stars he could see through the canopy of live oaks, a thin moon just visible above the roofline of the house. He felt a pull on his arm and turned to see his wife. Ella, come into his arms and gave his big body a tight squeeze.

"I love you, you big jerk!" she gushed, her voice slurred from too many beers.

He put his chin down in her red hair, pinned up in flowing swirls with a big flower tucked on one side.

"Happy anniversary, woman!" he said, pulling her even closer.

She stepped back and joined him in looking across the crowd assembled, all the familiar faces laughing and joining in the celebration.

He saw their good friend, Gilly, who ran the bar they practically lived in. Sheriff Pepper Stokes had come, accompanied by some new girlfriend Skipper had never met. All of his pals from the bar and shrimp business were milling about with wives and boyfriends and girlfriends. Hanna's son and girlfriend were dancing with several other couples to the music of the band, a local group who had been friends of his here in Dugganville for years.

Then, he spotted Hanna standing with his own son, off to the side, deep in conversation. Alex had a crutch under his right arm to steady himself. It had only been two days since he'd been taken to the hospital after the terrorist attack, but he and Hanna had insisted they both come tonight. Hanna was also a bit unsteady, still dealing with the aftermath of her own injuries.

He scowled when he saw his former daughter-in-law, Adrienne, walking toward Alex and Hanna. She had organized this celebration for them, and he had thanked her several times, but deep down, he suspected this was all just another excuse to get Alex back to Dugganville and her another shot at redemption.

Crazy bitch! He thought.

He pulled Ella close again, took another sip from his cold bottle of beer and said, "What the hell we gonna do with your crazy daughter?"

Alex saw Adrienne approaching and his defenses went up. "Hanna, let me handle this." He could see Hanna bristle beside him as his ex-wife approached.

"Alex, Hanna!" Adrienne gushed as she came up. She was dressed in a bright red short dress revealing lots of leg and skin. Her long auburn hair was done up like she was a bridesmaid in a wedding.

She came right up and kissed him on the cheek. He flinched as the pain in his ribs flared. He watched as Adrienne then turned and did the same to Hanna, who stepped back with a frown on her face.

"Thank you both for coming," Adrienne said. "After all you've been through this week, I didn't expect you'd be able to make it."

"Wouldn't have missed it," Alex said, the note of sarcasm clear in his response.

"God, I'm sorry, but you look terrible, Alex."

"Thank you, I feel terrible."

"It must have been horrible," Adrienne pressed.

Hanna jumped in. "Enough, already!"

"Oh, I'm sorry, Hanna, I shouldn't..."

"No, you shouldn't!" Hanna said accusingly, staring the woman down.

Alex knew he had to break this up. "Adrienne, thank you for organizing this for Pop and Ella. Very thoughtful of you." He saw Hanna seething beside him.

"It's the least I could do," Adrienne cooed. "They seem so happy together... I mean, when they're not trying to kill each other!" She managed a silly laugh.

Alex just stared back, and he saw that Hanna's expression had not changed, despite the joke.

Adrienne said, "I'd ask you to dance, hon, but not sure that's such a good idea tonight..."

Hanna had clearly had enough. "Adrienne! We need to go sit down."

"Of course, Sweetie."

"I'm not your *sweetie!*"

Adrienne started to protest, but Alex stepped gingerly between the two women and started to lead Hanna away. "Adrienne, again, thank you."

As he walked away slowly, the crutch under his arm helping to keep him from toppling over, he heard Adrienne yell out.

"Get a little rest! We'll have that dance later!"

Alex felt Hanna try to pull away to go back after his ex. He held her arm tightly and said, "Not now. Let's not spoil a perfect night for Skipper and Ella."

"Who's spoiling a perfect night?" Hanna protested.

"Let's just get through this without a major scene."

"Alex!"

"I'm sorry, I know it's all about Adrienne."

"You're damn right!"

They both managed up the two steps onto the back deck. Skipper and Ella were standing there, smiling as they came up.

Alex said, "You mind if we pull up a chair? It's been a helluva week!"

Skipper immediately scurried about to pull over four chairs for them all to sit. He went over and came back with four more beers dripping ice from the cooler, handing them out.

Alex took the beer and lifted it up, "Happy anniversary, you two!"

They all clinked bottles then drank.

Ella said, "We're so happy you could come out. Wasn't sure they'd even let you out of the hospital."

Hanna said, "I'm so happy for both of you," and clinked both their bottles again.

Skipper turned to Alex. "What're you hearing from the Feds about the investigation?"

"Can we not get into business tonight," Ella pleaded, taking another long pull from her beer.

"It's okay, Ella," Alex said. "Pop, you know Will Foster down at the FBI."

"Sure."

"I spoke with him again before we drove out for the party. They've got this rich Saudi, Al Zahrani, in custody. I knew he was dirty. I was out at his house the night before the attacks."

"What's all this nonsense about this *Green* asshole?" Skipper asked.

"Glenn Pyke," Alex confirmed.

"Right."

"Seems Pyke and this Arab fellow were working together. More evidence is showing up about Pyke's involvement. Unfortunately, he was found dead in a ditch outside New Orleans this morning with a big dent in the back of his head and the gators chewing off major chunks of him."

"Oh, my Lord!" Ella said.

"Serves him damn right!" Skipper declared.

Hanna said, "Will has been able to link the man who came to my office and killed..." she had to stop to gather herself. "He was one of the men they took down at the warehouse. They matched a weapon found on him there with the one used at my office."

"I'm sorry about your friends," Skipper said.

Alex watched as Hanna shook her head and stared away. She said, "Not sure I'll ever forgive myself."

Alex reached for her hand and squeezed it tight.

Alex was talking to an old friend from Dugganville sitting next to them now on the back deck, and Hanna watched both Elizabeth and Jonathan out dancing next to Skipper and Ella Frank to the sound of the BlueGrass music. It was as if none of them had a care in the world and it gave Hanna some satisfaction and peace there was at least an ounce of reason and normalcy returning to their lives.

She was still trying to process all the trauma and chaos that had descended on them this past week. Her head was feeling better, but the doctors had warned her concussion could cause issues for several weeks and that she needed to be very careful. The gunshot wound would heal over time and leave a nasty scar on her forehead, but that was the least of her worries.

She had met with the parents of her good friend, Molly, earlier in the day to console them on the death of their daughter. She would be attending the funeral in the morning back in Charleston. It literally broke her heart to think she had caused the situation that led to the young girl's death, let alone the other woman, Sophia Guttierez."

She stood slowly to go over to a cooler that had bottles of water. She was in no mood or condition to drink tonight. She twisted the cap off and took a sip, looking out over the crowd. Her spirits sank even further, and her temper flared when she saw an unexpected familiar face working her way through the crowd.

She made eye contact with Grace Holloway and left Alex there on the deck to go intercept the woman.

"Grace, really!"

"Your office said you were up here."

"This is not the time!"

"I needed to see you before I leave town in the morning."

Hanna felt relief in hearing the woman would be leaving Charleston. *None too soon!* she thought.

"Our *friend*, Detective Beatty, down at Charleston PD called me back in this afternoon."

"What have you done now?" Hanna said, her patience fading quickly.

"No, not me. It was about Phillip."

"What about Phillip?"

"He was doing some work for this rich Saudi guy they've got under arrest for the terror attacks."

"What!" Hanna said, her mind racing.

"Beatty and the Feds are still pulling it all together, but they've found clear evidence this Al Zahrani guy had Phillip killed that night. Apparently, he posed some threat."

"And the woman Phillip was with that night?"

"That tramp, you mean!" Grace replied, her face flaring in anger. "Unfortunately for her, in the wrong place at the wrong time."

"Phillip working with terrorists!" Hanna repeated, still unbelieving.

"Anything for a buck for my dear departed husband," Grace said. "It sounds like was representing this Arab guy in some of his business interests and maybe got a little close to other things the man was involved in."

"Oh, Phillip..." Hanna said, thinking back on how many times he would put himself at risk with the decisions and connections he made. *Always out there on the edge!*

"And speaking of bucks," Grace continued, "I'm headed down to the Caymans in the morning with my new lawyer. I've got Phillip's records indicating some serious cash stashed away down there. The grieving widow, me, has every right to the money, right!"

"I wouldn't know about that, Grace," Hanna replied, not surprised in the least the woman was still scheming to recover lost money, but grateful she would be gone, at least for a while.

"We still need to get together on Ben's accounts," Grace continued, "but that will have to wait."

"Yes, indeed, it will," Hanna said firmly.

Hanna tried to step out of the way of Grace's sudden approach and hug but didn't move quick enough.

"I love you, dear," Grace whispered. "I'm so sorry... about everything."

Grace stepped back and Hanna saw the real look of regret in her former friend's eyes.

Alex walked slowly with the aid of the crutch and Hanna's helping arm to walk out to the end of the pier where his father's shrimp boat, the *Maggie Mae*, was tied up. The dark river current drifted by beneath them, lit from the light at the end of the pier. The old boat smelled of stale shrimp and diesel oil, but the night air was crisp, cooling from the day's heat, bright stars arrayed above.

There was a wooden bench at the end of the pier and they both sat looking down the river at the lights of his old hometown, Dugganville, shining through the trees.

"Quite a week," he heard Hanna say.

He didn't answer, trying to let the peace of the evening calm the frightening thoughts and images that he hadn't been able to escape.

"Alex?" she asked, pushing over closer to him and putting her arm gently around his shoulders.

"I'll be okay," he finally said, though his face and body felt like a freight train had used him for tracks.

"We'll get through this," he heard Hanna say in the dim light.

"I know."

"We should be happy we're even here tonight."

He thought about how right she was, how close both of them had come to painful deaths. "I need to tell you something." He turned to face her, and she stared back. "I'm officially out at the Bureau."

"What!"

"I spoke with Will Foster earlier this afternoon. My crazy attempt to go after Al Zahrani and then following Foster and his team out to the terrorist's safe house, it was the final straw for the higher-ups in Washington."

"But you were right!" Hanna protested.

"Doesn't matter. I ignored direct orders several times."

"I'm so sorry..."

"No, really, I think it's for the best."

"Why? How can you say that?"

"I need to be here," he began. "I need to be here with you."

He watched her looking back, her beautiful face marred by the ugly bandages wrapped tight and the bruising from the bullet wound across the side of her face.

Hanna pulled him close, and he felt himself flinch from the pain in his sore ribs. She sat back. "I'm sorry..."

"Nothing to be sorry for," he replied and leaned over to kiss her gently on the cheek. "We've got a wedding to plan, remember?" he said.

"Yes, we do!"

"As soon as possible," Alex said.

"Absolutely!" Hanna replied. "But what are you going to do... about work, I mean?"

"Haven't even thought about it yet. Charleston PD might take me back. Pepper might take me on here at the Sheriff's Department. Maybe I'll put my own shingle out... *Alex Frank, Private Investigator.*"

"I like the sounds of that."

Footsteps behind them caused both of them to turn. Alex cringed when he saw his ex-wife coming down the dock, a bit unsteady from the night's drinking. Her feet were bare now, the tall heels evidently left somewhere up at the party.

"Thought I'd find you two down here," Adrienne said, coming up behind the bench and holding on to steady herself.

Alex stood and saw Hanna do the same.

"Adrienne, please, we need some time..."

"Band is about to pack up. We haven't had that dance."

Alex was about to respond when he watched Hanna walk quickly around the bench and stand face-to-face with his ex. He was going to move to separate them when Hanna spoke.

"There's only one woman dancing with my man tonight!"

And before Alex could get between them, Hanna grabbed Adrienne by both arms and shoved her back into the night, her legs flying up as she fell out into the river. He heard the big splash and rushed to the edge of the pier. Adrienne must have gone deep because it took her some time to struggle back to the surface of the murky water.

She came up coughing and thrashing, her long hair down over her face.

He couldn't help himself and started laughing, and it hurt to laugh, but he couldn't stop. He felt Hanna come up beside him as he looked down at the frantic scene below.

"How about that dance?" he heard Hanna say, as she pulled him away back down the dock toward the house.

As they walked away, he was thinking about gators and snakes and other bad critters lingering nearby in the river, then thought, *they can have her!*

Chapter Fifty-eight

Hanna felt the cool breeze off the Atlantic on her cheeks, the soft curls of her brown hair falling around her face and the thin white veil that matched the knee-length dress she had found for her wedding day. Her bare feet nestled into the sand as she stood with her son, Jonathan, about to walk down the short aisle lined with chairs on both sides with the few family members and friends they had invited. Her family's old beach house stood as a glorious backdrop for the ceremony.

It had been two weeks since the bandages had come off her forehead, but an ugly scar and bruising still remained, hidden some by the veil. She felt much better, and all thoughts of those few horrific days were pushed aside, at least for now. At the end of the aisle stood the man she was going to marry and their friend, Judge Diane Kraft, who would be presiding over the ceremony.

Alex smiled back at her with a face that had also healed some but still bore the marks of that terrible night on the waterfront of Charleston. Again, she pushed the thoughts aside as the music from a small quartet of violins sitting off to the side began playing the *Wedding March*.

Hanna looked up and smiled at her tall son, Jonathan. She felt him squeeze her arm and he smiled back. He had been given permission after numerous requests to leave the rehab facility for this special day with his mother. She looked back down the aisle and saw his girlfriend Elizabeth's beaming and beautiful face, her blond hair blowing in the ocean breeze.

The sight of the two of them together and happy and safe made this day even more satisfying, she thought.

Jonathan said, "Ready?"

She nodded and he began walking with her through the soft sand. She smiled and nodded to friends along the way. She saw Alex's old partner, Lonnie Smith's wife, Ginny. His colleague from Charleston PD, Nate Beatty, was there with his wife. The old sheriff from Dugganville, Pepper Stokes, sat beside another woman, different from the one he'd been with at the anniversary party a few weeks earlier. *He's such a rascal*, she thought as she passed.

At the front, her father Allen Moss was there with his always gushing second wife, Martha. Hanna smiled back at both of them, as her father stood to kiss her and give her a warm embrace. She turned across the aisle and Skipper Frank was almost unrecognizable in a white shirt and tie and a blue blazer freshly pressed. His thin hair was combed wet straight back. It occurred to her she'd never seen him without an old dirty ball cap on. Ella sat beside him, her red hair beautifully styled and face aglow. She wore a simple light blue dress and matching sun hat.

She looked up and Alex was suddenly there, standing before her, holding out his hands to take hers. His wonderful smile shone through the awful bruising that remained on his face, his nose surgically repaired and still covered with a small line of tape to hold it in place. He was dressed in a smart tan suit with a white cotton shirt open at the neck, his feet also bare in the sand. A bright red rose had been pinned to his lapel.

Hanna felt the reassuring grip of Alex's hands in hers as they stood facing each other.

"We made it," Alex said softly between them.

"Wasn't sure for a while there," Hanna replied softly.

They both looked up at Judge Kraft as she began, "Welcome everyone to this wonderful occasion on this beautiful day on Pawleys Island…"

"… you may kiss the bride," Alex heard the judge say as he stared into the glorious face of the woman he had come to love more than any other. He pulled Hanna close, and their kiss was deep and lingering.

He heard the crowd behind them cheering and clapping, and he pulled back to look into Hanna's eyes, the tiny wrinkles at the corners, the deep hazel color with gold flecks.

"I love you, Hanna Walsh Frank," he said above the raucous noise behind them.

Her smile was so warm and loving, he had to kiss her again.

THE END

NOTE FROM AUTHOR MICHAEL LINDLEY

I hope you're enjoying the stories of Hanna Walsh and Alex Frank in the Low Country of South Carolina. Thank you for your time with my stories!

Next up in the series is **THE FIRE TOWER.**

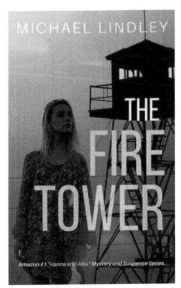

As Hanna and Alex begin to settle into their new life together on Pawley's Island, a mysterious death and the return of a ruthless rival send them off on a perilous journey to bring him to justice again and find out how Ally Combes died at
THE FIRE TOWER.

*****

"Wish there were more in this series." (There are!)
"Hard to put down!"
"Engaging story with twists and turns."
"As always, there was never a dull moment in this book!"

Get all of Michael's books at ***https://michael-lindley-novels.myshopify.com/***

Follow Michael Lindley on Facebook and Instagram at Michael Lindley Novels. If you would like to join his mailing list to receive his *"Behind the Scenes"* updates and news of new releases and special offers, send an email to *michael@michaellindleynovels.com* and you'll also receive a FREE eBook copy of the *"Hanna and Alex"* intro novella, **BEGIN AT THE END.**

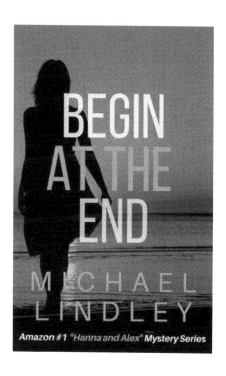

Made in the USA
Middletown, DE
25 July 2024

57995997R00166